James Patterson

James Patterson first took the bestseller lists by storm with his phenomenally successful international No 1 bestseller 'Along Came a Spider' in 1993. It introduced homicide detective Alex Cross, his highly popular hero who has also appeared in *Kiss the Girls*, *Jack & Jill*, *Cat & Mouse*, *Pop Goes the Weasel*, *Roses are Red*, *Violets are Blue*, *Four Blind Mice* and *The Big Bad Wolf*. James Patterson lives in Palm Beach County, Florida, with his wife and their young son.

Visit www.AuthorTracker.co.uk
for exclusive updates on James Patterson.

AVAILABLE
FROM HARPERCOLLINS

JAMES PATTERSON

HIDE AND SEEK

HarperCollins*Publishers*

HarperCollins*Publishers*
77–85 Fulham Palace Road,
Hammersmith, London W6 8JB

www.harpercollins.co.uk

First published in Great Britain by
Hodder and Stoughton in 1986
1

ISBN 978 0 00 783499 0

Set in Berkeley

Printed and bound in Great Britain by
Clays Ltd, St Ives plc

For Carole Anne, Isabelle Anne, and Mary Ellen:
the mothers of invention

HIDE AND SEEK

I

I LAY WITHOUT MOVING in the low, narrow crawl space under the front porch of our home near West Point. My face was pressed tightly against the brutally cold, frozen ground littered with dry leaves and scratchy brambles. I knew I was going to die soon, and so was my baby girl. The words from a song, Crosby, Stills, and Nash — *"Our house is a very, very, very fine house"* — played in my mind.

"Don't cry . . . oh please don't cry," I whispered into my baby's ear.

There was *no way out* — no escape from here, at least not carrying the baby. I was smart, and I'd thought of every possible escape route. *None of them would work.*

Phillip was going to kill us when he found our hiding place. I couldn't let him. I just didn't know how I could stop it. I kept my hand lightly over Jennie's mouth. "You musn't make a sound, sweetheart. I love you. You musn't make a sound."

I could hear Phillip raging above us inside the house. *Our house.* He was rampaging from floor to floor, ransacking rooms, overturning furniture. Angry. Relentless. Absolutely crazy.

Worse than he'd ever been. It was cocaine this time, but really it was life that Phillip couldn't handle very well.

"Come out, come out, wherever you are, Maggie . . . come out, Maggie and Jennie . . . *it's only Daddy.* Daddy's going to find you anyway," Phillip screamed over and over until he was hoarse. "Come out, come out, Maggie . . . game's over.

"Maggie, *I command you* to come out wherever the hell you're hiding, you disobedient little bitch."

I lay shivering under the old sagging porch. My teeth were chattering again. *This couldn't be happening. It was unthinkable.* I gently held my little girl, who had wet her pants. "You musn't cry, Jennie. Please don't cry. Don't cry. You're such a good little girl. I love you so much."

Jennie nodded, and stared into my eyes. I wished that this were a nightmare. That it would go away. But it wasn't a bad dream. This was as real as my mother's fatal heart attack when I was thirteen years old and the only one home. This was even worse.

I could hear my husband, *my husband,* stomping up and down the stairs of the house. He was still screaming . . . hadn't stopped screaming for over an hour. Pounding his fist against the walls. *Captain Phillip Bradford. Math instructor at the Academy. Officer and gentleman.* That was what everyone believed, what they wanted to believe, what I had believed myself.

The hour stretched to two hours.

Then to three hours in the pitch-black, freezing-cold crawl space — in this living hell.

Mercifully, Jennie had finally fallen asleep. I held her to my chest, tried to keep her warm. I wanted to sleep myself, give up the fight, but I knew I musn't do that. It was very early in the morning. One of Phillip's witching hours — maybe three A.M.? Maybe four?

I heard the front door slam like a clap of thunder in the night. Loud footsteps exploded on the porch just over my head.

Jennie woke up. *"Shhh,"* I whispered. *"Shhh."*

"Maggie! I know you're here. *I know it!* I'm not a stupid man. There's nowhere to run to."

"Daddy . . . Daddy!" Jennie cried out, the way she had so many times in the safety of her crib.

A flashlight suddenly shone under the porch. Bright, terrifying light blinded me. A thousand sharp splinters in my eyes.

"Peekaboo! There you are! There's Jennie and Maggie. There's my two girls," Phillip shouted in triumph. His voice was so hoarse and raw, it was nearly unrecognizable. I could almost make myself believe that this insane man *wasn't* my husband. How could he be?

Two deafening shots came from his gun. He fired right at us. He meant to kill either Jennie or me, maybe both of us.

I had a surprise for Phillip, just this one time.

Peekaboo yourself!

I fired back.

II

SOMETIMES, I feel as though I'm wearing a horrifying scarlet letter — only the letter is *M*, for *Murderess*. I know this feeling will never completely go away and it seems so unfair. It *is* unfair. It's inhuman and indecent.

The memories are jagged and chaotic, but at the end so vivid and horrifying that they are etched into my brain. They will be with me forever.

I'll tell you all of it, sparing no one, especially myself. I know that you want to hear. I know this is a "big news story." I know what it is to be "news." *Do you have any idea?* Can you imagine yourself as a piece of news, as cold black type that everybody reads, and makes judgments about?

Area newspapers from Newburgh, Cornwall, Middletown called the first shooting the worst "family tragedy" in the history of West Point. To me, at the time, it seemed as though it had happened to someone else. Not to Jennie and me, or even to Phillip, as much as he may have deserved it.

Yet a dozen years later, after time and my own denial had clouded the events still further and made even my emotions hazy, a *second killing* has forced me to remember West Point in all of its horrible vividness.

I obsessively confront the questions that pound in my brain: Am I a murderer?

Did I kill not one, but two of my husbands?

I don't know anymore. *I don't know!* As crazy as that sounds, I honestly don't.

It gets terribly cold here — sometimes it seems as cold as it was that Christmas Eve when Phillip died. All I can do is sit in this prison cell, in torment, and wait for the trial to begin.

I decided to write it all down. I'm writing it for myself — but I'm also writing it for you. I'll tell you everything.

When you've read it, *you* decide. That's how our system works, right? A jury of my peers.

And, oh yes, I trust you. I'm a trusting person. That's probably why I'm here, in all of this terrible trouble.

BOOK ONE

STAR-CROSSED

1

***

Early winter, 1984

More snow. Another Christmas season. Almost a year after Phillip's death — or as some would have it, *his murder*.

I sat back in the yellow cab as it bounced and plowed through the slush-filled New York streets. I was trying to put my mind in a calm place, but it wouldn't be still for me. I had promised myself I wouldn't be afraid — but I was *very* afraid.

Outside the streaked, wet taxi window, even the Salvation Army Santa Clauses looked miserable. Nobody sane or sensible was out walking today; those who were would not take their hands from their pockets to make a donation. The traffic cops looked like abandoned snowmen. The pigeons had disappeared from every windowsill and rooftop.

I glanced at my own reflection in the cab's window. Very long, blond hair, mostly with a mind of its own, but my best physical attribute, I thought. Freckles that no amount of makeup would ever cover. Nose a little out of proportion. Brown eyes that had, I knew, regained at least some of their half-forgotten sparkle. A small mouth, thickish lips — made, as Phillip joked in the happy days, for fellatio.

The thought of him made me shudder. The idea of sex still makes me afraid, and much worse.

It had been a year since the terrible shooting at West Point. My recovery was slow, both physically and mentally, and it wasn't complete. My leg still hurt, and my brain didn't function with the clarity I'd once taken pride in. I found myself frightened by small noises. I saw threats in nighttime streets when none existed. Previously in pretty good control of my feelings, I had lost that control. I would cry for no reason, grow angry at a neighbor's kindness, be suspicious of friends and afraid of strangers. There were times when I hated myself!

There had been an investigation, of course, but no trial. If Jennie hadn't been so badly beaten, if it had been only me with bloodied hair and a damaged leg, I might have been sent to prison that first time. But the fact that my three-year-old was injured too made our claim of self-defense more convincing.

No prosecutor wanted to take on the case, and the military academy was only too happy to have it hushed up.

Officers, it was a well-known fact, *did not attack their wives and daughters. Wives and daughters really didn't exist at the Point. We were decorative.*

So I took flight, and traveled to New York City, where I rented a two-bedroom apartment. It was a second-floor walk-up in a dreary brownstone on West Seventy-fifth Street. I located a day school for Jennie. Our lives began to move at a slower pace.

But I hadn't found what I wanted most: an end to the pain, a beginning to a new life.

I was twenty-five years old. I wore the letter M. I had taken someone's life, even if it had been in self-defense.

No guts, no glory, I urged myself on. I was definitely moving on sheer guts that day. I was chasing a dream I'd held on to and cherished for more than a dozen years.

Perhaps today that new life would start. But was I doing the right thing? Was I ready for this? Or was I about to make a horribly embarrassing mistake?

I tightly held a briefcase in my lap, filled with songs I had written during the past year. Songs — the music and the words — were my way of exposing my pain and expressing my hopes for the future.

Actually, I'd been writing songs since I was ten or eleven. Mostly in my head, but sometimes on paper. The songs were the one thing that everybody seemed to like about me, the one thing I did well.

Were they any good? I thought maybe they were, but Jennie and a squirrel named Smooch were the only ones who had heard them, and, eager for praise as I was, I knew enough not to trust the opinion of a four-year-old, or a squirrel.

Soon, though, there would be another listener. I was on my way to audition the songs for Barry Kahn, *the* Barry Kahn, the singer-composer who had electrified America a decade ago and now was one of the most important record producers in the world.

Barry Kahn wanted to hear my songs.

Or so he said.

2

I WAS PETRIFIED.

And then it got much worse.

"You're late," he said. Those were his very first words to me. "I work on a very tight schedule."

"It was the snow," I said. "It took forever to find a cab, and then it kept skidding. I guess I was nervous and asked the driver to go faster, only he went slower, and —"

Jesus, I thought. *You sound like a dumb parakeet. Pull yourself together, Polly. Right now!*

He was unmoved. Seemed like a real bastard. "You should have left earlier. My days are full. I plan ahead. So should you. Would you like coffee?"

The question, the sudden politeness, took me by surprise. "Yes, please."

He rang for his secretary. "Cream and sugar?" I nodded. His secretary appeared. "Coffee for Ms. Bradford, Lynn. The works. Danish?" I shook my head. "Nothing for me," he instructed, his voice filled with the huskiness that made his singing so distinctive.

He dismissed Lynn with a wave, then sat at his desk with his eyes closed, as though he had all eternity. I wondered: *Who the hell is this guy?*

He was in his early forties, I guessed, with a receding hairline and brown hair, a long nose, thin mouth, and a slight perpetual stubble on his chin. A homely face (the fans who think he's "sexy" are attracted by his soul, not his looks), but its lines suggested struggle and its repose peace. At our first meeting he was dressed casually, in gray flannel slacks and a blue shirt, open at the neck, obviously expensive but worn with lack of care. Barry Kahn *looked* rather sweet and harmless.

Single, I deduced, and living alone. I wasn't interested in him that way, but I noticed anyway. I'm good with details. I always notice things, especially about people.

Lynn returned with coffee in a china cup, and I took it from her, splashing it on my wrist. Not very relaxed. Indeed, kind of an ass. That's how I felt at the time anyway.

Petrified! As in wood — that never, ever moves.

Barry stood to offer assistance, but I waved him away. "I'm fine." I'm in control. I'm cool. Pay no attention to the scarlet *M.*

Barry sat back down. "You're quite a letter writer," he said. I *guess* it was a compliment.

In the hospital, as my recuperation progressed and I began composing song after song, I had planned to write only one letter to him, telling him that I admired him and hoped I could audition for him someday. But the one letter gave rise to another, and by April, I was writing him nearly every week, letters from deep inside my heart, to a person I had never met. *Hooo boy!*

Weird, I know, but that's what I'd done. I sure couldn't take the letters back now.

He didn't answer any of them, and I wasn't even sure he read them. I only knew they were never sent back unopened. But I continued to write the letters. Actually, the letters kept me going. Talking to somebody, even if the person didn't talk back.

In a way, I think writing the letters helped me recover. I

15

gradually got stronger, began to believe that one day I would be all right again. I knew Jennie would be okay, or at least as okay as you can be if, at age three, you've witnessed horrible mayhem in your own house.

My sisters traveled from upstate New York, and took turns watching her. The hospital let Jennie visit as often as they could bring her. She was fascinated by my wheelchair and the electric bed. And she could thrill me whenever she hugged me and pleaded, "Sing me a song, Mommy. No. Make up a new song, and sing it."

I sang to Jennie often. I sang for both of us. I wrote a new song a day.

Then, an amazing thing happened. A miracle. A letter arrived for me at West Point Hospital.

Dear Maggie, the letter said.
Okay, okay, you win. I've no idea why I'm answering you, but I guess I'm an easy mark even though I don't like to think so and if you tell anybody else, that'll be it for us forever.

In fact, your letters moved me. I get lots of mail, most of which my secretary throws away without showing it to me. And the letters she does give me I throw away.

But you — you're different. You remind me that there are real people out there, not just sycophants wanting to get into my studio. I feel I've actually come to know you a little bit, and that says a whole lot about what you've written so far.

I was impressed with some of the lyrics you sent me. Amateur stuff — you need a songwriting education — but powerful all the same because they say something. None of this means that (a) the education will do you any good; or (b) you can write music for a living, but okay, okay. I'll give you the half hour of my time you asked for "to find out once and for all if I've got a talent for songwriting or not."

16

When you get out of the hospital, call Lynn Needham, my secretary, to set up an appointment. But in the meantime, please don't write me any more letters. You've taken up enough of my time already. Don't write to me — write more songs!

3

HE SIGNED THE LETTER "Barry," and now here I was and he was looking at me, and I felt hopelessly out of place, one of those "sycophants" he had grumbled about. I definitely hadn't overdressed — that wasn't my style. I had on a white peasant's blouse, pink camisole, a long black skirt, flat shoes.

But at least I was here. I was going for it.

I was trying so hard not to have any negative thoughts . . . but things like this, really good things, never happen to people like me. They just *don't*.

"Do you sing your songs, or do you just write them?" he asked.

"I sing them too, at least I hope you'll call it singing." *Stop apologizing, Maggie. You don't have to apologize for anything.*

"Ever performed professionally?"

"I did some backup singing in clubs around West Point, Newburgh. But my husband didn't like it when I did."

"He didn't like much, did he?"

"He thought I was exposing myself. Couldn't stand other men looking at me." *So I shot him — three times.*

"But you'd be willing to try it now? Sing in public? You could do that?"

My heart raced at the thought. "Yes, I could." It seemed the right thing to say.

"Good answer." He gestured toward a beautiful, shining black Steinway at the far end of his office. "But your first test's in private. Did you bring anything?"

I picked up my briefcase. "Lots. Do you want to hear ballads? Blues?"

He winced. "No, Maggie. Just one. This is an audition, not a gig."

One song? I thought. My heart sank.

I had no idea which song to pick. *One* song? I had brought at least two dozen, and now I stood rattled and confused, as though I were standing naked in front of him.

Put it in gear. He's human. He just doesn't act like it. You've sung these songs a thousand times before.

"Go on," he said, looking at his watch. "*Please,* Maggie."

I sucked in a deep breath and sat down at the piano. I'm fairly tall, self-conscious about it, so I prefer to sit. From the seat I could see the silent chaos of Broadway through his window.

Petrified wood.

Okay, I thought. *You're here. You're actually auditioning for Barry Kahn. Now, knock his socks off. You . . . can . . . do . . . it.*

"This is a song called 'Woman in the Moon.' It's about a . . . a woman who works nights cleaning buildings in a small town. How she always sees the moon from a certain window while she works. What she dreams about all night in the offices she cleans."

I looked over at Barry Kahn. *Jesus, I was in his office. I was the Woman in the Moon.* He was sitting back, feet on the bottom drawer of his desk, fingers steepled together, eyes closed. He didn't say a word.

Musically, "Woman in the Moon" was like Barry's own "Light of Our Times." I began to play, to sing in a soft, uncertain voice that suddenly seemed dreary and ordinary to me. As I sang, I sensed I was losing him.

I finished. Silence. I finally dared to look at him. He hadn't changed position, hadn't moved. Finally he said, "Thank you."

I waited. Nothing more came from Barry Kahn.

I put the music back in the briefcase. "Any criticism?" I asked, dreading his answer, but wanting to hear something more than "thank you."

He shrugged. "How can I criticize my own child? It's my music," he said, "not yours. My voice, imitated by yours. I'm not interested."

I could feel a deep blush redden my face. I felt so humiliated, but also angry. "I thought maybe you'd be pleased. I wrote it in honor of you." I wanted to run out of the room, but I forced myself to stay.

"Fine. Okay, I'm honored. But I thought you were here to play *your* songs. If I want echoes, I'll sing in a subway tunnel. Are all your songs like mine?"

No, goddamn you. They're not like anybody else's songs! "You mean do I have something more original?"

"Originality's what I'm looking for. Originality's a start."

I began leafing through my sheet music. My fingers felt numb and unsure. A full marching band was stomping around inside my head. "Would you listen to one more?"

He stood up. He was shaking his head, trying to stop me from going on. "Really, Maggie. I don't think —"

"I do have one. Many. My own, not yours." I had promised myself I wouldn't be embarrassed.

He sighed, having already given up on me. "Since you're here . . . *one* more song. One song, Maggie."

I plucked out "Cornflower Blue." It was a little like an old Carole King hit. Maybe not original enough. *Too precious. Too clever. More bullshit.* The noise inside my brain had become a loud roar like the sound of an approaching subway train. I felt as though I were about to be run over.

I stuffed "Cornflower" back in the briefcase and chose another song — "Loss of Grace." Yes. This was a better choice. I had written it recently, since I had come to New York.

One song.

I could feel Barry Kahn's eyes on me, feel his growing impatience. The room felt hot. I didn't look at him. Just at the music for "Loss of Grace."

The song was about my marriage to Phillip. It was deeply personal. The initial ecstasy, the love I'd felt, or thought that I did. Then the mounting terror. The horror of that first fall from grace . . . and never being able to stop falling.

One song.

I turned to the piano, took one deep breath, and began to play.

I sang very softly at first, then with mounting passion as the song gripped me and I remembered exactly what had inspired it. *Phillip, Jennie, myself, our house near West Point.*

I could sense something new in the room as I sang, a kinship and understanding I had longed for in my letters, a bond between me and the man sitting silently at the other side of the room.

I finished, and waited for what seemed like forever for him to say something. Finally, I turned around. His eyes were closed. He looked as though he had a headache. Barry Kahn opened his eyes.

"You shouldn't rhyme 'time' with 'mine,' " he said. "It's a false rhyme, and while you might get away with it in a country song it's distracting when you're trying something serious."

I began to cry. I couldn't help it. It was the last thing in the universe I wanted to do. I was furious at myself.

"Hey," he said, but I had already jammed the song into my briefcase and was heading for the door. I almost started to run. *I wouldn't run though.*

"Hey," he repeated. "Stop crying. Hold on a minute."

I turned to him. "I'm sorry I took up so much of your

precious, valuable time. But if all you can talk about is one lousy rhyme, when I've just sung my heart out, then there's no way we can work together. And don't worry. I won't bother you again."

I rushed out the door, past an astonished Lynn Needham, and took the fancy Deco elevator to the lobby. *Screw him. Screw Barry Kahn.*

I was tough enough to deal with this — I had to be. I had a little girl to take care of, not to mention myself to look out for. That was why I had written to half a dozen music companies besides Barry Kahn's from West Point Hospital. Tomorrow I would see one of the others. And then another. And another after that if I needed to.

Somebody was going to like my music, my songs. They were too good, too *true*, for somebody not to listen, and to feel something.

It's your loss, Barry Kahn, Mr. Big Shot. Mr. My-Time-Is-So-Precious!

You missed out on Maggie Bradford!

4

DID YOU EVER want to say, even to shout out loud, *Hey, I'm smart. I'm an okay person. I have some talent.*

I shouted those very words in Times Square. No problem. Nobody even noticed. I fit right in with the rest of the loony-birds there.

I wandered for a couple of hours, oblivious to the falling snow, then went to pick up Jennie at her school on West Seventy-third. I felt like absolute crap and hoped I didn't look it. *Sheesh, what a day.*

"Let's celebrate," I said. "Tomorrow starts the Christmas holiday. Give your favorite mom a big hug, and we'll go to some fancy New York restaurant. Just the two of us. Where do you want to eat? Lutèce? Windows On The World? Rumpelmayer's?"

Jennie carefully thought the offer over, wrinkling her forehead and pulling on her chin, as she always does when she has to make an important decision. "How 'bout McDonald's. Then we can go see a flick."

"Quarter Pounders it is!" I laughed, and took her small hand. "My sweet bunny rabbit, you're what's important. And you like my songs."

"I *love* your songs, Mommy."

The two of us began to babble at each other — just like always. We were "best friends," "girlfriends," "the original motormouths," "soul sisters," "the odd couple." We would "never be alone, because we would always have each other."

"How was your day, Sweetie? Boy, you've got to be tough to make it in New York. Fortunately, we're tough."

"School was fun. I made another new friend named Julie Goodyear. She's *real* funny. Mrs. Crolius said I'm *smart*."

"You are smart. You're also pretty, and you're a very nice person. You're awfully *short* though."

"I'm going to be bigger than you, don't you think so?"

"Yes, I think so. I think you'll be around seven foot or so." On and on and on like that.

The motormouths.

Best friends.

We were both doing pretty well actually; getting used to New York — kind of; getting over Phillip as well as we could.

To hell with Barry Kahn.

You blew it, Mr. Big Shot!

It was as dark as Phillip's heart by the time Jennie and I got home. All my feelings of defiance had evaporated, and I looked at the front of our run-down brownstone with complete dismay.

Shit, shit, shit. I guess we'll have to live here a while longer. Like maybe the rest of our lives.

I opened the front door, and it yawned as it always did. Typical New York reaction.

Damn, damn, damn! The lights had gone out in the hall and on the first-floor landing.

All I could see was a pattern of light edging its way through the first-floor window from the lamppost in front of the house.

"Spooky," Jennie whispered. "Scary and spooky."

"No," I said. "This isn't spooky. This is fun in the Big Apple." I took her hand and we started up the "fun" stairs.

I stopped moving. My body tensed, and I tucked Jennie behind me to protect her.

Somebody was sitting in the shadows on the landing. The person was silent, unmoving. It was somebody tall and well built.

This wasn't good. This *was* scary and spooky.

I moved toward the figure cautiously. "Hello. Who is it? Hello up there," I called out, thinking of the horror stories I had heard about New York — and about the horrors I had recently endured in West Point.

The person seemed to be wearing something on his head. A strange top hat? *Something* weird as hell.

Phillip! I thought the unthinkable. I knew better, but the flashback came anyway.

Phillip loved to frighten me, jumping out from behind a bush, from behind a closet door, knowing he could scare me and thinking it funny when he did. Once, on Halloween, he wore an Indian headdress and came at me with a tomahawk. It was the worst of the scares. At the end, of course, it was I who had jumped out at him, had leaped at him with the gun in my hand, firing . . . firing . . .

But Phillip was dead, I told myself, and there were no such things as ghosts, not even in New York.

I inched closer. Still, the figure did not move. I neared the landing. "Hello!" I called again. "This *isn't* funny. Please talk to me. Just say hi."

The sound of our stealthy footsteps on the stairs reminded me of Phillip's steps, the way he *stalked* around the house.

Becoming a little hysterical, consumed by ancient fear, I forced myself to reach the landing.

Behind me, Jennie whispered, picking up my fear. "Who is it, Mommy?"

Not twice, I thought. *You won't hurt us twice. No damn way!*

I lunged at the threatening figure, striking out at it with my heavy case. I hit the bastard hard.

He toppled unresistingly, and I realized what I had done. "Oh my God! I can't believe it!" I started to laugh, relief not entirely wiping out the dread. "Hooo boy."

Jennie hurried up the final stairs, laughing with me. "Phillip" was a mammoth basket of what had to be a few hundred dollars' worth of long-stemmed roses.

I opened the note that came with them.

TO MAGGIE BRADFORD.

HERE'S TO THE FIRST DAY OF YOUR RETURN TO GRACE. IF YOU REALLY WANT THE JOB, YOU'RE CRAZY, BUT YOU'RE HIRED. YOU MADE MY 'PRECIOUS TIME' PASS LIKE IT WAS NOTHING TODAY. TRUST ME ON THAT.

BARRY

A kind of funny story, in retrospect anyway. A happy ending for sure. But as I write it now, the question comes again, and it's not so funny anymore. Not to me.

When I'm in trouble, is my first impulse always to kill?

Have I murdered, not once, but twice?

A lot of people think so. One of them happens to be a prosecuting attorney for the southern district of New York.

First, there was Phillip Bradford.

And then — *there was Will.*

26

5

San Diego, California, July 1967

Will Shepherd, age six, was dreaming of Indians. Fierce and remorseless, they came at him in waves, their horses neighing and rearing, their arrows as long as spears, pointed at his heart. He loved the excitement, loved the movie in his head, loved the danger.

He heard a splash!

It didn't make any sense. Will opened his eyes, shut them almost immediately, then drifted back to sleep.

Cowboys and Indians again.

No splashes. Not in his movie anyway.

Will woke again at quarter to eight, dressed quietly so as not to disturb his still-sleeping brother, Palmer, and hurried down through the quiet house.

In the kitchen he fetched an armful of Welch's grape jelly, peanut butter, milk, and half a loaf of bread. Breakfast for one. *Who needed a mother? Who needed anybody?*

Will saw his face and uncombed blond hair looking back at him from the side of the shiny toaster. He had to admit it, he thought. *He missed his mother a lot. He missed her terribly. He missed her making peanut butter and jellies.*

He knew that she had gone to live in Los Angeles. He didn't have to suffer through the terrible fights she had with his father anymore, but at this moment he would have preferred the fights to the silence. Sometimes he and Palmer missed their mom so bad it made them cry at the stupidest times. But usually he *hated* her. Usually, but not today.

The splash in the swimming pool?

Suddenly Will remembered. He collected his dish and glass and put them in the sink, then ran out the screen door into sweet, dappled sunshine and the call of sparrows.

He came tearing around the corner of the blue-trimmed white clapboard house, and ran to the edge of the pool. He stopped so suddenly he nearly fell over his own sneakered feet.

And he screamed and screamed, screamed so shrilly he woke his little brother, whose face appeared at the window above him.

Will screamed so bitterly that neighbors came rushing to his rescue. They held him, and tried to shield him from what he had already seen, and would never forget.

What the six-year-old boy saw floating on the shimmering water of the pool was his father in his red-plaid bathrobe and beige trousers. On one foot was a yellow slipper; the other foam slipper was drifting as free as a lily pad.

His father's eyes were open, and staring right at him. *Your fault*, they seemed to tell him. *Bad boy. This is your fault, Will.*

You know what you did!

You know what you did!

At 5:52 A.M. Anthony Shepherd had purposefully walked outside his house and drowned himself in the family pool.

And whatever part of Will Shepherd that was worth saving seemed to drown with his father.

*   *   *

A few days after their father's suicide, Will and Palmer spent their final California afternoon choosing from among all of their clothes and toys. Just enough to fill two suitcases each. *No more than that.*

Their mother had refused to take them to live with her. Nobody told Will or Palmer why. *The stupid cunt,* Will thought, using bad words his father had used when he fought with her. The brothers had spent the days after the suicide with their nanny, who would not take them either, and now they were told they were going to England to people who would. They were to begin a new life with their aunts, Eleanor and Vannie, whom they had never met, but who had made the *two-suitcase rule.*

In loud, chaotic, swarming Los Angeles International Airport, the two look-alike blond boys sat stone-faced and bewildered, awaiting their flight with Dr. Engles, one of their father's few friends. Dr. Engles was telling them about London, and the stupid Queen and the stupid changing of the guard at Buckingham Palace, just like in the poems his mother had read Will before she went away. But Will barely heard what stupid Dr. Engles was saying. He was remembering his father floating in the pool, staring up at him from some dead place.

"*Ladies and gentlemen,*" Will did hear, "*we are now ready to board Pan American flight four-eleven to New York and London.*"

Dr. Engles held out a hand to take Will's. "Well?" Suddenly, Will bit it savagely, as hard as he could, drawing blood.

"Damn it," Dr. Engles said, cuffing him with his free hand. "You little shit! You little monster."

Will opened his mouth. His front teeth were red. "I don't want to go to England," he howled. "Can't we stay here?"

Please, Daddy.

Please, Mommy.

Please, somebody help me.

I didn't mean to kill my daddy. I didn't mean to do it.

Daddy, please stop looking at me like that. Please, Daddy.

6

WILL WOULD NEVER forget his first few hours in England. He and his brother might as well have traveled to the moon.

Aunt Eleanor met them at the landing gate. She was a fat, fussy, powder-white-faced woman who was, Will guessed, more scared of him than he was of her. He disliked her instantly. *She can't hurt me,* he decided. *No one will ever hurt me again, but especially not her.*

She explained that Aunt Vannie had stayed home to cook a special dinner for the boys. *It'll taste like crud,* Will decided. *England is the worst place ever.*

On the way from Heathrow Airport, Aunt Eleanor never stopped talking, and the boys had little chance to observe their surroundings. Whenever they looked away from her, she would jab a finger and remind them to pay attention. Will seriously thought of biting the finger off.

"A great many people who work in London live outside the centre. Close to an Underground stop. We live in Fulham, for example, and we have ever since your mother moved out to make her fortune in America. And I suppose she did, didn't she, marrying your father? She'll inherit all his money, you know, with nothing for you except as she chooses to give it, and goodness knows nothing for us, though we never expected anything from her. Not *her*."

No. Never expect anything from my mother. Will knew Aunt Eleanor taught history in primary school, and that explained why she droned on, but her smell was of sweat, and who was she to be talking about his mother? He could tell Palmer didn't like her either. He was pretending to be asleep, the little faker.

At last the cab pulled up in front of a three-story house, red brick with tiny windows and six steps leading up to the front door.

"Here we are," announced Aunt Eleanor cheerfully, but Will thought about the trees and space and sunshine in San Diego and his chest grew tight.

There were similar houses crowding in on each other on both sides of the street, and the one tree he could see was bent and beaten by the rain, and it had no leaves. Palmer took one suitcase, Aunt Eleanor another, and Will carried his own two up the steps, straining with the effort.

Before they reached it, the front door was flung open, and a woman appeared wearing tight black trousers and a black turtlenecked sweater.

Will gave a little, muffled cry. He felt his heart pound and his face suddenly grow hot.

The woman was young, with ash-brown hair falling halfway down her back. Her eyes were blue and her skin was pale. *It's my mother*, he thought.

Only of course, she wasn't.

She was his Aunt Vannie, his mother's younger sister, but she reminded him achingly of the woman who once, long ago, it seemed, held him, cuddled him, told him she loved him, and then went away. And he was filled with a curious mixture of dread and delight. He wanted at once to fling himself into her arms, and to run away screaming down the street.

"Take off your shoes before you come in," Vannie said. "We don't want dirt trodden all over the house, do we?"

The house. *England*. His new home. His new life. His very own horror story. It was just beginning.

7

THE LEGEND BEGAN early, and it never really varied.

Will is an extremely intelligent and very clever boy, but he seems to be an incorrigible master of the Charming, Audacious, Very Big Lie! So wrote the headmaster of the Fulham Road primary school in the spring of 1970.

If he worked harder, his marks would be much improved, but he seems interested only in sports, where he excels, and in picking fights with his classmates, where he is the acknowledged champion. I personally wonder if he is even aware of the elemental aspects of social behavior or, for that matter, the elemental difference between reality and fantasy.

Will understood the difference — but he had made his choice about which he preferred.

On weekends, Will often took solitary walks around his neighborhood. One day, when he was eleven, he heard shouts coming from a stadium about a mile from his aunts' home. Intrigued, he went to investigate. He paid a week's pocket money to get in.

There, in front of him, was a perfectly dazzling sight: twenty-two men, divided in uniform but united in purpose, were playing what they called "football" in England, but what Will knew as soccer. Only on TV had he seen the game played this way.

He had played the game well at school, but felt it had been haphazard, just a bunch of boys kicking the ball around any way they could.

Here, there was symmetry, geometry, coordination in attack, a beauty as inevitable as the waves of the ocean. One man, controlling the ball with his feet, moved forward; another raced to his side; a third began a run down the wing, received the ball from the second man without breaking stride, and veered toward the center of the field, pursued by an opponent who dived at the attacker's feet and managed to push the ball to one of his teammates.

And then, suddenly, everything reversed, like the tide going out. Defenders became attackers, attackers defenders, a whirling mass; Will was reminded of a kaleidoscope his father had given him when he was five.

And the noise! Each time there was a reversal, each time one team threatened the goalkeeper, the crowd roared, as though they shared the breath coming out of the athletes' mouths, and when eventually a goal was scored, the roaring rose to such a pitch Will thought his ears would burst and his heart explode.

That night his mother came to him in his dream, and while he watched in horror, she kissed his father's open dead eyes, and laughed at Will. Her teeth were red, dripping blood.

You know what you did, Will.

It's all your fault.

One morning, several days later, he found a lost dog on the streets of Fulham. The dog was male, a tan-and-brown runaway. Finally, he had a pal in shitty old England.

"C'mon, dog. C'mon with me," he said and patted the side of his thigh several times. "C'mon, Lassie."

34

Will wandered into a municipal park and the lonely mutt followed like his shadow. He didn't know why he was feeling angry, but he was. The feeling came over him a lot actually, ever since he'd left California. Ever since his father had killed himself. His father's suicide was a really bad deal for Will. He still felt responsible, but even worse, he'd convinced himself that was how he himself would end up.

He sat down by a small pond. The dog was still with him. His new buddy.

Will finally shook his head at the mutt. "Big mistake, staying with me," he said. "Bad luck follows me around. I'm not kidding."

The dog gave a whimper, and put out its paw.

But Will was getting angrier about lots of things. His father, his aunts, Palmer. He felt as though he had a tight belt around his chest. His head was tingling. He was seeing mists of light red.

Will reached down into the cold, shallow water and pulled out a fist-sized stone. Without a hint of warning, he whacked the dog on the side of the head. He struck the dog a second time, and it fell over moaning. One sad, brown eye looked up at him. He kept hitting the dog until it was dead.

He didn't know why he'd done it. He liked the dog. At any rate, Will found that he wasn't angry anymore. He felt okay. Actually, he didn't feel much of anything.

He had even made a little self-discovery; there was a distinctly good part in him, but also a bad part.

There were two Wills, weren't there?

8

WILL KNEW from the start that he had greatness in him, and that he wasn't really impressed by it. But others sure were.

Will Shepherd was the youngest ever to play for the Fulham School's first eleven. When he was just eleven, he persuaded the coach to let him train with the team; he was immediately selected and, oblivious to the jeers of his teammates, who were older than Will by five or six years, he became the team's leading scorer. Their top striker!

When he was twelve, Fulham won the London school league championship, and did not lose again until after Will left the school. As a fourteen-year-old he scored nine goals in a game his team won 12–0.

Will was wispy and long-legged for his age, but surprisingly well balanced. He was extraordinarily fast — he ran, his coach said, "as an arrow flies." He ran like southern California halfbacks and wide receivers in American-style football.

Will practiced every day, every spare hour, until the ball seemed almost an extension of his foot, or at the very least a satellite body attached by an invisible wire. He sometimes practiced as much as sixteen hours on a Saturday or Sunday. The field was his home, not that shitty place where his aunts and Palmer lived.

Local newspaper reporters made him a schoolboy legend around London. They always commented on his reckless style, highly personal and unusual, which they attributed to his being American-born.

But that wasn't the reason at all. What none of them understood was that Will secretly worked on, and perfected, *his individualistic style*. He had. Will decided it was essential to be different, to be noticed, *to stand out*, rather than to be viewed as a loner. Will understood precisely what the game meant in his life: English-style football meant not being lonely and afraid; this new kind of football meant not thinking about his sodding mother and father ever again.

Football was his only weapon. It was going to save him. It had to.

9

Spring 1985

For a year and a half, Barry Kahn worked my piano-playing fingers to the bone. We started with lyrics, and the theories behind them: Bob Dylan's theory, Joni Mitchell's theory, Rodgers & Hart's theory, Johnny Mercer's theory. Barry's *basic* theory was that hard work conquers mediocrity.

He made me write and rewrite, forcing me deeper and deeper into my past until there were days when I wanted to beg him not to push me so hard, to let me rest. But I *didn't* ask for a bit of mercy. I secretly wanted to be pushed even more.

He was remorseless, and so was I. "You're denying," he'd say. "You're hiding in cheap rhymes and phony sentiment." Or: "You're not feeling anything. I know it because I can't feel it. And if I'm left cold, just think what an audience will do. They'll crucify you, Maggie."

"*What* audience?" I asked him.

"You don't *see* an audience? You don't feel an audience that *has to* hear your songs? If you really don't, then get out of here. Don't waste my time."

So on I went until at last we were both satisfied, and I was able to turn to the art of composing. Here too he was strict and unyielding, but music came more easily to me than words. I felt comfortable with it. One day he said I could turn it on and off like water from a faucet. I think he was a little jealous. I kind of liked that — competing with him, being on his level.

Last came the singing, and Barry was a true master of this. He taught me phrasing, accenting, diction. How to sing in front of an audience, how to use a mike in a recording studio. I had, he told me, a natural voice, unlike any other singer's, but it was in this area that it was hardest to judge. "The public alone will decide," he said. "Who could have imagined Bob Dylan's voice capturing an audience's heart — until it did? *Your* voice is edgy, openhearted. Lots of sudden shifts of mood intonation to fit your lyrics. You can sound caring, cold, bored, maternal, loving. I love your voice!"

He did? Finally, a compliment. I memorized it, word for word.

I practiced in the nearby Power Station recording studio, not only performing my songs but acting as a gofer, going on endless sandwich-and-coffee errands. I wore a long black overcoat down to my boots; I wore it *everywhere*. I was "tall blondie with the coat, can you get us sandwiches?" I was "sure, no problem. What do you like?"

I resented being treated like that, figured Barry would never do it to a man, but he insisted it was an important part of the job, and if I didn't like it I could go elsewhere.

There was, I knew, no "elsewhere."

There was Jennie, of course. The "motormouths" were alive and well.

There was Lynn Needham, who had turned into a real pal, an occasional sitter, my official New York tour guide, my shoulder to lean on.

There was our West Side walk-up, the den of iniquity, which had only one really cool feature — a turn-of-the-century

bathtub built right in the kitchen. I *loved* taking hot bub-
blebaths in the kitchen!

There were occasional dates, but nothing even close to anything serious. I began to remember what I'd felt like before
Phillip — too tall, too gawky, a little tongue-tied, inadequate
for all the wrong reasons, not big enough breasts, too many bad
hair days. But really, what it all came down to, was that I was
afraid to get involved again. I didn't want to have to tell anyone
what had happened with Phillip — no, *to Phillip*. I had this
huge scarlet M on my chest, and I didn't think it would ever
come off, wash off, *whatever*.

Nope, there was no "elsewhere."

10

SO, I WAS the coffee-and-sandwiches person, but do you know what — it was so much better than my life had been. It really sucked sometimes, I *hated* those despicable runs to the Famous deli, hated being "blondie with the coat," but I also loved it. It was writing, composing, learning. I was part of something that on occasion could be very beautiful and moving.

One morning at the "music factory," my buddy Lynn Needham peeked into my cubicle/storage bin. "You better drop everything, except maybe that hot coffee. Mr. Wonderful calls."

Barry tried to reserve some time for me at the end of most days, so this was an unusual summons. I hightailed it to his office. His time was still precious.

"I've got good news, and unfortunately, bad news," Barry said as I entered the room where I had once auditioned to be his gofer.

I could feel my pulse racing a little. *Tell me what's happened! Don't drag it out.*

"I sent one of your songs to California," he continued. " 'Loss of Grace.' The revision you showed me last week. Someone likes it out there. Wants to record it."

Impulsively, I ran and hugged him. I don't think I'd ever done that before. I know I hadn't.

He smiled and gently pushed me away. He looked me squarely in the eye. "Now for the bad news. That 'someone' wants to sing it herself."

It was *my* song. "Tell her no," I said. Suddenly, I was crestfallen. "*No*. Barry, please."

"Don't you want to know who that someone is? I *had* to agree she could sing it. That was the deal breaker."

I had a nightmarish vision of some third-rater, some other up-and-comer getting my song all wrong. "Of course I want to know who she is. But if she messes up, I'll murder her!" Bad choice of words, I know.

"I think she'll get it right." He grinned like the sweet person he could be sometimes. "It's Barbra Streisand. She wants to record 'Loss Of Grace.' And she wants you out there with her."

I hugged Barry again. I crushed him and kissed him on both cheeks. Good-bye to shlepping for coffee and pastrami sandwiches — hello to Hollywood!

11

I BOOKED a flight to Los Angeles for Jennie and me. We deserved it; we'd earned it. Once we got out there, I found myself driving a rented Saab Turbo up to the Beverly Hills Hotel. It seemed as though we were a million miles from West Point.

"It's pink!" Jennie exclaimed as we curled up the hotel driveway and stopped in front. "My favorite color. It's pink *everywhere*."

"I had it painted, *just for you*," I told her. "I called ahead. I told them to *think pink*."

"Motormouths!" Jennie yelled as we sat in the impressive hotel carport.

"Forever!"

A handsome, beachboy-blond bellhop carried our beat-up overnighters as if they were Louis Vuitton. He led us to a lovely cottage tucked behind the main hotel — Bungalow Six, our own private pied-à-terre, all arranged by Barry ("so you and Jennie make exactly the right impression"). He would know about that — I sure didn't.

"This is you, ma'am. And you too, little ma'am." The bellhop smiled and swung open the door with a flourish.

I had to take a quick step backwards. Dozens of American Beauty roses were waiting inside. *"Jeez,"* I whispered. The blush-red flowers were everywhere I looked.

"Are there always this many flowers?" I joked. The humor sailed over the bellhop's shaggy blond mop. *The lights are on,* I realized, *but there's nobody home at Hotel California.*

"Oh, no, ma'am. It's a gift. There's a card."

WELCOME TO TINSEL TOWN.
I THINK YOU'RE ABOUT TO HIT IT VERY BIG.
DON'T BE FOOLED BY ALL THE GLITTERY GOLD,
THOUGH . . .
OR A FEW DOZEN ROSES EITHER.

LOVE YA AND JENNIE TOO,
B.

Love ya too, Barry. But I'll never bring you another cup of coffee for as long as I live.

12

MAYBE YOU CAN imagine what I was feeling, or maybe nobody ever could.

This was everything I had dreamed of. All my mind-breaking work, all of Barry's merciless bullying, all the voice lessons and the rewrites. Now, here I was, my stomach tied in sailor's knots, peeking down the semidarkened corridor leading to Recording Room A in the famous Devan Sound Studios.

Famous songs are recorded here. My song could be famous too. Hooo boy.

This was it, boom or bust; that one big shot everybody says they want, but that so many of us never get, and I sure never thought I would.

I knew that different studios achieved a curious mystique, sometimes a superstitious reputation, within the tight clique of major musicians, superstar singers, and their managers. For years, Elton John would record only in an isolated chateau in the south of France. The Rolling Stones had recorded in a ticky-tacky houseboat in Jamaica to get a certain sound. A lot of country singers wanted a specific Nashville studio, and only Chet Atkins could produce their records.

Devan was like that in L.A. I held Jennie's hand. We watched in a kind of dream as a Barry Kahn/Barbra Streisand recording session unfolded before our eyes.

I didn't like it! I hated it, actually. I wanted to scream at the two of them. Barbra's voice was not the one I'd had in my head when I composed "Loss of Grace." Her style was *too* distinctive, too overpowering.

"What do you think?" I asked Jennie. She had heard me sing the song hundreds of times at home. She knew my phrasing, the big emotion shifts.

"Not as good as you," Jennie said after a moment's deliberation, "but I like this one too. It's so pretty." *Traitor. Infiltrator.*

It got prettier as they worked on it though. Each take got better. I began to hear things in my own song I never knew existed. It was my song, but it became hers too. I realized it was a nearly perfect collaboration.

I sat back and quietly ate some crow. Barry kept stopping by between takes. He was being so nice to Jennie and me, so supportive and encouraging suddenly.

After a while, I imagined Barbra Streisand was singing only for me, the way I had sung to Jennie, and I felt transported to a place where the music and all my emotions came together. I was back at West Point, but in happier times, when I used to sing to Smooch the squirrel, and only occasionally let myself dream about moments like this.

I began to feel numb all over, but *nice*-numb.

There were at least a hundred different takes before Barbra and Barry pronounced themselves satisfied, and the tension in the control room dissolved into dumb jokes and contagious laughter. I felt a powerful surge of relief, as though I had done the actual singing. I bowed my tired head.

I felt a hand touch my shoulder. I turned, and looked into the face of Barbra Streisand. She had snuck up on me.

In real life (*if this was real life*) she was striking, but not conventionally beautiful. There was kindness in her eyes, and her smile was sympathetic. I'd already seen that she could be tough, but she had a soft, sweet side as well. Don't believe everything you read in the papers — *trust me on that one.*

"I know what you must feel right now," she said. "A little bit, anyhow. I remember my Broadway debut, *my* first recording session. Butterflies and the shakes, right?"

"Just your basic out-of-body experience," I said.

She sat down next to Jennie and me. "Just remember that you earned this. All the sweat and the tears and the troubles *before* today give you a right to enjoy this tremendously. Your song would be a hit no matter who sang it. Because I did, it'll get the attention it deserves. I love your music, Maggie, and so will everyone else. Write more for me. Please?"

Then she kissed me on the cheek, and gave me a hug. "Thank you," she whispered. "Your song is so true, and the truth inside you is staggering."

For a moment I was tongue-tied, then began to regain my composure. "Shoot, I'm trying not to say anything too stupid," I whispered to her. "You can't imagine what this means to me, to Jennie and me."

"Oh yes," she said. "I can definitely imagine. The first song is the best of them all." Then she looked at Jennie. "Your mom is amazing."

Jennie smiled and nodded. "I know," she said, "but sometimes, *she* doesn't."

13

I USED TO DAYDREAM all the time about stuff like this happening. Everybody does. So this had to be a crazy daydream, didn't it?

I sold a lot of songs in a very short period of time. I was hotter than a ten-dollar pistol. I had the same thought every morning as I woke up in the tiny New York walk-up that I was still too insecure to give up: *None of this can be happening.*

One night, Barry took me to a very ritzy New York restaurant to celebrate "Maggie's greatest hits," as he called them. I continued to be a hot item. Stories about me had appeared in *Rolling Stone, Spin, People.* It was bizarre, unreal, not my style, but I didn't want it to stop. I felt like somebody, probably for the first time in my life.

It was twilight when we arrived at Lutèce on Fiftieth Street in Manhattan. We were seated with a certain amount of pomp and circumstance in the garden room. Barry knew the chef, the owner, the busboys.

"Is this a date?" I asked him. I was kidding — I *think* I was.

"This is my way to make up, once and for all, for our very first interview," he said and smiled. He was in a great mood. We both were. We ordered champagne cocktails, then I had foie gras, salmon with sorrel sauce, a plum soufflé. *None of this can be happening.*

"I could have cooked all that," I said as we finished and ordered brandy and coffee.

"I believe that you could. You know," Barry went on, "nothing has made me any happier than watching you —"

"Come back to life?"

"Blossom," he said. "You know that it's hard for me to talk like this, but it's true. It's how I feel."

Suddenly, I was a little nervous and uncomfortable. I wondered if this really was a date. I didn't think I was ready for it yet. I was also afraid of spoiling the friendship that Barry and I had.

Barry winked at me then. He must have sensed my discomfort. "More and more, people are going to want to hear *you*, Maggie. Your words, your music, your special voice. That sultry contralto of yours. There isn't going to be any stopping you, Maggie. There are no limits to where you can go."

I started to cry. In the garden room of Lutèce. I didn't really care who saw me. I was so goddamn happy, so absolutely thrilled.

Barry used his napkin to dab at my cheeks. We both started to laugh.

"So tell me about yourself. Who the hell are you, Maggie? You're not 'blondie in the coat' anymore. That's for sure."

I had kept everything bottled up inside, but that night I let some of it out. Barry was my friend and I trusted him, which was a big step too.

"There's a small town about twenty miles above West Point. Newburgh," I began.

"Been there. No desire to go back," he said and made a face. "The main street looks like Beirut. *That* Newburgh?"

"It used to be a beautiful city, Barry. Sits right over the Hudson River. Small town America, that's me."

"I hear some of that in your songs, Maggie. Honest, sincere, not too much cynicism. Corny, but what the hell." He grinned mischievously.

I was feeling very self-conscious. "You sure you want to hear this?"

"Stop putting yourself down. *Pleez*. You're going to be a big star now. Everything you say will be considered interesting. You were *interesting* the first day you came to my office."

I punched Barry in the arm — hard — for that one. I shut my eyes, opened them again. This was hard for me. I didn't like to talk about it, not even to Barry.

Finally, I took a deep breath, and began:

"My parents drank too much. Slight understatement there. They were both alcoholics. My father was wild, ran around. He left us when I was four. *My pop.* I developed this horrible stutter that used to embarrass me to tears. I buh-buh-beat it though. Mom died when I was in the eighth grade. My two sisters and I stayed with my Aunt Irene. I moved out when I graduated from high school. My sisters both married and moved upstate.

"Teachers all wanted me to go to college. I just couldn't see myself there. I got a job at a fancy restaurant near West Point. Met Phillip. *He loved me.* Said he did, acted like it. I *really* needed for somebody to love me. I mean — *really* needed it."

Barry frowned. "Phillip was your pop all over again, Maggie. We have a tendency to repeat our worst mistakes, don't we?"

"I guess so. He was a mathematician in the new army. Repressed. Vulnerable. Even needier than I was. Phillip turned out to be a drinker too. Just like Daddy. I wanted to save him, of course. Thought I could."

"He hit you, beat you up?" Barry said and lightly touched my cheek. It was just the right thing to do. My friend.

"I didn't know how to get out of it. Not back then. I didn't know where I could go, how I could possibly bring up Jennie. I used to escape to the attic of our house and write songs all the time. I'd sing them for Jennie. Both of us up in the attic."

"You never performed them around West Point?"

I shook my head. "Forget it! I was much too afraid for that."

"You lied to me during your job interview. You're fired."

"That's okay," I said. I touched Barry's cheek. "I can take care of myself and Jennie now. Thanks for helping me."

"I did nothing. I just watched it happen. You're an amazing person, Maggie. I hope you realize that yourself someday."

I leaned across the table and gave Barry the gentlest kiss. We were such good friends and I loved him. I could *think* that — I just couldn't say it.

"You're the best," I whispered.

"No. Only the second best. I mean that, Maggie. Remember where you heard it first."

14

JULY SECOND of my year of years, the best time in my life by about ten thousand percent. I was at the Meadowlands sports stadium outside New York City. I was there with Jennie and Barry.

I *will never* forget this. No one can take this part away.

A few minutes after eight-thirty the outrageous New York disc jockey, Bret Wolfe, came prancing out onto the Meadowlands' concert stage. He was dressed like a naughty teenager who shouldn't have been let out of the house by his parents.

The first warm-up act was scheduled to begin soon. Everybody in the audience knew that the headliners — R.S.V.P. — wouldn't make their grand appearance until at least ten, probably even later than that.

They were in for a shock though.

Bret Wolfe could barely be heard over the noise of the crowd: "*It is my distinct pleasure to introduce* . . ." The orchestra struck up a familiar melody. Glowing fluorescent flying objects flickered up toward the bland-faced quarter moon sitting over the stadium roof.

". . . My *distinct pleasure to introduce to you — Ladies and Gentlemen . . . R.S.V.P.!*"

Stunned silence followed, then there was chaos in the audience that was still lazily milling into the stadium.

"I can't believe it's *them*. They shouldn't be on for hours!"

"Jesus, what's going on? What is this shit?"

From backstage, I watched as long paper streamers and electric blue fireworks rocketed high above the stage. Billowing smoke and gold lamé sparks erupted and drifted east toward New York. The R.S.V.P. lead singer, Andrew Tone, lithe and very sexy, stepped to the microphone and held it like a live snake. He ran a hand through his long, sandy-brown hair.

"We're Alive and Kicking!" He raised his fist. The band hit its trademark downbeat. R.S.V.P. began to sing the song that was currently number one just about everywhere in the world.

Next came "Champion of Myself."

Then the ballad "Loving a Woman of Character."

The audience was in an absolute frenzy. No one could understand what was happening. Tens of thousands of fans wouldn't come until nine-thirty, when, ordinarily, the local bands and warm-up groups would just be finishing.

The music finally stopped. Andrew Tone stepped to the microphone. He held up his hands for silence.

"Don't worry," he said. "We'll sing those songs over again when everybody's here. You early birds deserved a treat though. You're the *real music lovers*, right?"

Cheers. Some laughter. But the baffling mystery continued for the audience. What was R.S.V.P. doing onstage already?

"We sang those songs for a special reason. 'Alive.' 'Champion.' 'Woman.' I know they're three of our best songs. *You know* they are."

Loud applause confirmed Andrew Tone's opinion of *their* opinion.

"The thing of it is, these three songs were all written by our first — and only — warm-up act tonight. And this is the best warm-up act we've ever had."

Some in the audience might have known my name. Few could have realized I was a singer. Behind Andrew Tone, a bevy of stagehands wheeled out a piano. The stagelights went off and a spotlight hit the keys.

There was a murmur in the crowd, expectant but wary. Everybody's curiosity was up.

"*She* is a real woman of character," Tone went on, speaking softly, away from the light. "It's her first live concert appearance — which is why we came out early. We wanted to introduce her. It's our way of thanking her for her songs.

"I guarantee you one thing! This is the last time the lady will be opening for anyone. So listen. Hold on to your heads. Hold on to your hearts. *THIS IS THE MIND-BLOWING, HEART-STOPPING MAGGIE BRADFORD!*"

15

I LISTENED to Andrew go on and on. *Too much,* I thought. He was raising their expectations way too high. He made it sound as though some scintillating world-class singer were coming onstage.

He wasn't talking about *me.* He couldn't be. The building pressure put a steel band around my chest. I had a contralto voice anyway, and had trouble hitting the real high notes.

I thought I wouldn't be able to play, much less sing. Not only didn't I feel like "a woman of character," I felt I had absolutely no spine.

I could barely breathe.

I made myself walk onto the massive concert stage. There was applause, sincere but scattered.

I remembered Andrew Tone's words: *"It's her first live appearance."*

I got my first full look at the slow-rising mountain of faces; the brightly colored, ragtag quilt of clothes; the streaming spotlight that made the piano look huge and frightening and self-important.

Oh, God, I can't possibly do this. There's an entire city out there watching me.

A wave of panic suddenly swept over me. I felt exactly as I did when I used to stutter and stammer in school.

I knew many of the orchestra players from recording sessions in New York. They were standing now and clapping for me too.

"Cut it out, guys," I yelled to them. "It's only *me*. Stop, stop, stop!"

"Go get 'em Maggie!" a drummer named Frankie Constantini yelled at me. "You're the best."

Somehow, I made it to the piano. I even managed to sit down without fainting, or having a major coronary.

I am considered tall at five feet eight inches, and Barry said I was "striking" that night, but I just felt gawky — the same way I'd felt as a teenager. I'd let my hair grow very long, and it cascaded down my back. At least I liked my hair. If nothing else, my hair was cool.

"I was living in West Point," I managed to say, speaking in a low voice into the gleaming silver microphone. "I was living in West Point, near the military academy there. I was a housewife and a mother named Mrs. Bradford. I loved to sit in the attic, I remember. There was a squirrel there named Smooch, and before my daughter, Jennie, was born, he was my friend. I loved to sit in the attic because there I was safe. There I wasn't afraid that my husband might come and hit me. There I began to write songs."

My mind felt as though it had exploded. Phillip was in it, as vivid as when he was alive. I could hear his footsteps on the stairs in our old house, the menace in his voice: *You can't hide from me!* My hand was trembling.

I willed my fingers to strike the piano keys. I sang with all my heart, everything inside of me:

I used to be a housewife
A new wife
A midwife
I used to live the good life
High in the storm king mountains.
I used to give him haircuts
Fix cold cuts
Mend shirt cuffs
My name was Mrs. Bradford
And I thought I was going to die.
Battery
He hit me!
This can't be me
This can't be me
Battery
I used to be a housewife
A new wife
A midwife
He hit me!
How can he say he loves me
When I think I'm going to die?

The applause grew louder, and then unbelievably louder.
People began to stamp their feet in rhythm to the beat. The
noise was like a physical presence rising out of the stadium. It
carried me higher than I had ever been in my life.

It told me that all these people believed in me. They believed my story.

It was like nothing I had ever experienced, not even in
dreams, and I have to confess, I never wanted it to stop.

Hooo boy, hooo boy, *hooo boy.*

16

THAT WAS THEN; and this is now.

I could never have imagined being *where I am right now*, in prison in New York.

It seems so inconceivable, so impossible. I couldn't conceive of any set of circumstances that would have gotten me here.

This week they brought a top, well-respected psychiatrist to see me, a woman named Deborah Green.

I guess I couldn't blame anyone for thinking that I might be crazy.

The husband killer. That's what I'm called in the newspapers. *The black widow of Bedford.*

I visited with Dr. Green in a small conference room beside the chapel, which made me smile at least.

I was pleased to learn that Dr. Green specialized in physical-abuse cases, rather than homicides.

She made it easy for me. She told me about herself, and why she had been chosen, and that if she wasn't right *for me,* she'd leave. She was my age, soft-spoken, unassuming.

I guess I liked her well enough. Trust? Well, that might come later.

"How's this?" I said to her. "I'll make this easy. I'll tell you everything that's on my mind. I don't see the point in the two of us having secrets."

I was facing Dr. Green, rather than lying on the cot that had been provided. She nodded, then she smiled. She was good at this, getting people to talk.

Of course, I wasn't being truthful with her — there was one important secret I wasn't telling her, or anyone else.

Ironically, it was what might have saved me.

"However you want to do this, Maggie," she said. "If you want to unload a lot of junk, go ahead."

I laughed. "It is junk, isn't it?"

Yes, I wanted to unload.

So, in those first few sessions, I told Dr. Green everything that all the newspapers and TV stations wanted to know, and couldn't get out of me for any amount of money.

I told Dr. Green what made me anxious, ashamed, and also, very angry.

Like about my father, and how he'd left my mother in 1965. Just walked out and left us as though we were some motel he'd visited going cross-country.

Like my terrible stuttering from around age four to thirteen. How it had hurt so much when kids made fun of me; how it had made me feel worthless and small; how I had beat it by myself, *with no help from anyone.*

Like writing songs in my head, to escape from the negative voices in my childhood world.

Like Phillip, who everybody thought was this nice, quiet college professor — but he wasn't, really. He had his black Corvette that he used to *back* out of the drive at about forty miles an hour; he had his gun collection; he had his *rules* to be followed at every waking moment, and probably while I was sleeping too.

I talked for about two hours at a clip, and Dr. Green rarely stopped me.

Finally, though, I was talked out during our third or fourth session.

"I do think you left something out," she finally said.

"What's that?" I asked her.

"Well, what about Will Shepherd? Remember him?"

Oh yes, Will.

The man I was in here for killing.

"I've been working up to Will," I said. "Will is in his own special class."

17

WILL HAD LEARNED to put on a good act in school, and to get by with it. He was already being touted as the best young football player in London. And he was very popular — with the girls anyway. He still didn't have a good friend though.

Early in the summer following his fourteenth birthday, he came down with the Asian flu. Chills and fever possessed him. He actually was afraid he might die, and go join his father.

His Aunt Vannie nursed him through the high fever. She was there for him. This was unusual, for until now, anytime Will got sick, it was Aunt Eleanor who brought him his food and comforted him. Indeed, sick or well, Vannie was a remote figure in his life. She went out almost every night, often on dates with men who squired her for a few evenings, and then disappeared to be replaced by others.

Mostly, Will and Vannie played chess, and they chatted. She was an avid player, but he learned the game rapidly, and by the end of the week they were able to play competitively. He found himself looking forward to the games with increasing excitement.

Chess enabled him to study his aunt up close. He and his

brother, Palmer, had conducted countless, sworn-secret, late-night conversations about her. They wondered about Vannie's men, about her occasional trips to Bournemouth or the South of France. And now, as she studied the board, he was able to stare at her, watch her every move.

He examined her breasts whenever her eyes were occupied with the game board. He imagined kissing them, gently sucking on the soft nipples, which taunted him under every blouse and dress she wore. He imagined biting each nipple clean off.

"You can't fool me the way you do all the others," Vannie told him during one of their tensest games. "I know that you're very clever, Will, and I know that you don't want us to know. But I know. I even know what you're thinking, dear boy."

After six days, Will woke feeling a little bad about feeling so much better. He would have to get up, he knew, and the prospect of being able to play football again delighted him. But the times with Vannie would be over.

There was a knock on his door around nine-thirty that morning. Palmer was already gone — Eleanor was taking him to the Regent's Park Zoo — and Will decided he would pretend to be sicker than he actually felt. He liked to pretend, to act, to see how good he was.

"I'm awake," he said in a weak voice like Tiny Tim's in *A Christmas Carol*. "Come in, please."

Vannie opened the door. She was wearing a gingham dress, cut tightly across her breasts. He noticed her breasts right away — *every time*.

"I'm going to make eggs," she said. "Scrambled eggs. Could you assist in the eating thereof, Master Will?"

"A little," he said, still playing Tiny Tim, acting his heart out. "Maybe a half portion."

"I don't know if I'm up to cooking *that* much." She winked. Which finally got him to smile.

Vannie called his smile scampish. He knew that she liked it. So he smiled for her. *More acting on his part.*

"Just lie there. I'll bring breakfast to you, *Master Will.*"

Trembling, he watched her leave. She returned in a half hour, bearing scrambled eggs and mashed potatoes for them both, and sat on the bed next to him. Now *that* was extremely nice.

Will felt as though he hadn't eaten properly in a month, but her nearness took away his appetite for food.

"Still not hungry?" she asked, finishing her own portion. "Then how about one last game. For the championship of Fulham? You look recovered enough to play."

"You're on. For the championship."

"And what shall we play for, Vannie? What is our championship worth?"

I think I know what you want to play for. I think I know.

18

VANNIE QUICKLY cleared away the dishes, and set up the board on his bed. "The smaller pieces in front, they're called pawns," she teased. "Please move any one of them, so I can begin to thrash you."

Now he concentrated on the game. Her challenge had aroused his huge competitive spirit, and he was determined to win. He even forgot about her breasts, and the rest of her.

The game was their best so far. It was incredibly close — closer, he knew, than Vannie had expected — but at the last minute, in a move he should have foreseen, she took his rook with a knight. She leaned back in smug satisfaction.

"I'm afraid — checkmate, my darling, Mr. Competitive."

"Oh, sod it!" Will roared and struck the game board in frustration. Pieces flew on the bed and across the floor and under the night table.

"Typical loser. Typical man," Vannie said. "How do you think *your* opponents feel on the football pitch?"

They both laughed. Then they scooted around the bedroom, picking up the scattered pieces: queen under the night table;

knight somehow on top of the bureau; king underfoot on the imitation Oriental rug.

On hands and knees, they reached for the king simultaneously. Will's elbow grazed the slick cloth of Vannie's dress; he could feel the warmth of her skin underneath. She didn't pull away. Neither did Will.

Every sound, every tiny movement, suddenly became intensified in the bedroom. Electricity spiraled up his spine, and he could scarcely breathe. *She wants me. I was right. I knew it.*

Vannie stared into his eyes for a long second. She actually *stared* at him. The room was so quiet. He was conscious of the staccato pounding of his heart, and was afraid she could hear it. He wanted to hear *her* heart.

Without saying a word, Vannie's fingers gently traced Will's cheeks. Then, they trailed down over his throat, rode the lump of his Adam's apple. He gave a little moan.

She leaned forward and kissed him softly. Then she nipped his unpuckered lips with her teeth. She wrapped her arms around him, pressing him against her breasts.

Her tongue slid inside his mouth. Her tongue was *inside* him, and it was *hard*.

"Dear, sweet boy," she whispered. "You *are* something else. You're very special, Will."

Will's hands finally reached for her, tentatively at first, as though they themselves barely believed the miracle that was happening. Then more aggressively, up and down her surprisingly well muscled back, her soft face, her neck, and then, blessedly, to those wondrous breasts. *She wants me. Finally, someone does.*

"Not so fast," she whispered. "We have time, Master Will."

"I know that. I've thought about this a lot."

She smiled and her eyes opened wide with amusement. "You *have*, have you?"

His hands slid down along the outside of her legs. Vannie's dress made a sound like light static in the air.

She tugged at her own belt, then pulled him even closer. He didn't know what would happen next — what *could* happen?

He was already taller than she by half a foot, and much stronger, though she *was* strong. Her hands slipped all over him, reaching down into his pajamas. Her dress fell away to the floor. How many hands did she have? Where had she learned all this?

Will's face and neck were extremely hot — on fire; his ears were loudly ringing. His penis felt huge, and he rubbed against her bare flesh with a cry of utter joy. He wasn't sure what to do now, exactly where to go from here, but he would figure it out. He *was* smart, just as she suspected.

Naked, Vannie lay on her back on the bed. She was holding herself open with her hands. Her cheeks were red, blushing, and he loved that look, would never forget it.

"Now," she said, reaching for him. "Now would be a very good time, Will."

She wanted it to happen. She wanted him as much as he wanted her.

Will watched her face — studied her beautiful brown eyes; then her rising breasts; the luscious V of her legs and the dark hair at the center. He was so hard that he almost couldn't believe it was *he*. He felt stronger and more powerful than he ever had. Most important, he knew what to do with her. *He just knew it. Naturally.*

"Don't rush it, Will," she whispered to him. "Take your time, young Master."

"Don't worry. I don't want it to be over either."

When it was, though, when they lay together, and she gently stroked his long blond hair, she said, "You're so very beautiful. You're going to be able to have anyone that you want." She smiled warmly. "You're quite irresistible, Will."

This, Will already knew. He just wasn't sure what it meant. *To be irresistible.* Was that good, or was it very, very bad?

66

19

ALLAN "SKIPPER" THOMAS appeared to be an ordinary fellow, a tradesman perhaps, but Will understood that Thomas was the most important man he had met in his entire life.

Thomas was in his early forties now, manager of the Hammersmith Rangers, but rumor had it he trained as hard as his players, and that he offered bonuses to any on the team who could go past him one-on-one. Rumor also had it that *no bonus had ever been paid*.

He and Will were sitting like proper gentlemen in the living room of his aunts' house. Eleanor and Vannie had tactfully gone out, leaving the men to talk football, as men so love to do.

"I've watched you play, Will," Thomas said, playing everything close to the vest, as Will had expected he would.

"I'm honored to hear that, sir. I really am." *Like hell*. Every club in London had sent scouts to see him play.

"You've got natural talent, no question about it. I could make you into a fine player, over time I could."

Will watched Skipper Thomas calmly, the way Will did most everything. "I'm a fine player already, sir. You know it, or you wouldn't be here."

"You're fifteen years old. Nobody is a player at that age, just a *potential* player."

"I am," Will said.

"And modest too," Thomas laughed heartily.

"No, I'm not modest, sir. That would be false of me. But I am a goal scorer, sir. I have no particular sense of team, of anyone else on the field. I'm a loner, a striker pure and simple. I'm cut from the same cloth as Johan Cruyff, Pele, Gerd Müller. I'm the best at my age that England has ever seen. Fast as any pro, *and* stronger too. All the papers say so."

Thomas smiled broadly at the audacity of this young Turk, but most of all, because he just might be right. "The *local* papers say so, Will."

"And *The Telegraph*. And *The Sun*. Look, Mr. Skipper Thomas, why don't you just get on with it? You want me to play for you; I want to play for you. So cut through it. How much are you willing to pay, sir?"

"Come on, Will, dribble past me. If you think you can. You're the next Cruyff, isn't that right?"

Skipper Thomas and Will were the only ones who stayed on the pitch this late after practice. It was the same thing night after night, practice after practice. Thomas had never seen such maniacal desire in a player, even a young one. Will was indeed an incredible striker, a natural goal scorer.

"What'll you give me if I do? What's in it for me?"

"Twenty pounds," Skipper said and spat.

Will laughed and walked away. He was bare-chested, shaking his long blond hair. "I wouldn't fuck your wife for twenty pounds."

"All right. Fifty pounds. But you have to get right past me."

Will turned back, took the challenge. Thomas tossed him the ball; Will trapped it with his feet. Real casual-like. *Acting* like a dumb, cocky little shit.

Skipper Thomas crouched, but stayed on the balls of his feet. "Whenever you're ready, son."

He was ready now, and he wasn't anyone's son.

Will feinted left, quickly feinted right, headed directly at his coach and then, with fist toward the sky, middle finger raised in the universal gesture of contempt, glided past him as though Skipper Thomas's shoes were glued to the grass.

"Keep your money," he said and laughed at the coach. "I won't need it where I'm going."

Will played two years for the Rangers before his contract was bought by Liverpool, perennial champions of the English League's First Division, for one point five million pounds. He was already the biggest star in England. In his first year he was the League's leading scorer and was barely edged out as Footballer of the Year. He was nineteen years old.

The papers glowingly wrote about his "great inner fierceness," his "uncanny ability to actually fly across the pitch." "He can swoop like a golden eagle, then fly off to his natural aerie — the opposition's goal," the *Guardian* said.

"He is like a Blond Arrow — stretching toward the goal."

"Will Shepherd is the complete egomaniac on the field; he has the consummate scorer's mentality. He plays as though he were *alone* out there."

At nineteen, the Blond Arrow began to make the gossip columns as well. He was "fox hunting with friends in Gloucestershire," "grouse shooting on Lord Dunne's moor near Balmoral," "playing polo at Swinley Forest, in the presence of the Royal Family. The Blond Arrow cuts a dashing figure — *wherever* and with *whomever*."

When he was twenty, Will led Liverpool to the League championship. He was arguably the biggest star in Europe. He was runner-up for FIFA's Best World Player award. "Frankly, Scarlet," he commented on the award, "I don't give a fuck what anyone thinks of my playing. *I'll* tell *you* whether I'm the best or not."

During that same time, Will had been playing international football with the U.S. team. It was his stubborn attempt to keep some connection with America. He quickly tired of being a very good player on a team of donkeys. He quit the team, and thus all international play.

The news stories rapidly became disturbing, and therefore much more interesting to the public. There were hints of alcohol abuse, of drugs, and worse. "Personal reasons" made him miss practices before games. Liverpool transferred him to an ambitious rival for two million pounds. In the off-season, Will began to drive Grand Prix race cars, an avocation forbidden by his contract. "If I live, it doesn't matter. If I die, it doesn't matter," he was quoted on the racing flap.

The Blond Arrow was all the rage — absolutely *irresistible*.

20

Irresistible.

Will drove Melanie Wellsfleet's supercharged red Ferrari sports car to her estate in Somerset. He got the new automobile up to over 115 at one point on the narrow, curvy road, and was seldom under ninety for the length of the trip.

"It's not a bloody *race car!*" Melanie laughed and shouted during one harrowing stretch of high speed and danger.

"It is now. With me at the wheel it is. Hang on, Mel. Ride of your life and all that."

The estate in Somerset was everything Will had expected — and much, much more. The grounds seemed to have been tended with tweezers; the twenty-six rooms inside Ryertton Hall were like a Tudor museum.

"My boss lives very well off my efforts," Will said to Melanie as she guided him through each of the nine bedrooms. Melanie was the thirty-one-year-old wife of Sir Charles Wellsfleet, who owned Will's football team, as well as a stable of racehorses and a well-respected publishing house. Charles Wellsfleet was sixty-nine years old.

"Charles owned this house long before you made the scene,"

Melanie laughed, and gave Will a hug. They had been carrying on their secretive affair for the past four weeks. She couldn't get enough of Will, and was sure he felt the same way about her. *He couldn't be faking that,* the former high-fashion model reassured herself during an occasional "blue" moment.

"I missed you, I want you, I need you," Melanie announced when they reached the master suite with its commanding view of a topiary garden and water terrace. "What do you *need?* What do you *want?*"

He seemed bemused by the question. He wandered around the spacious suite, searching through Melanie's dresser drawers and her huge walk-in closet. He selected several dresses, evening gowns, lingerie, stockings, shoes, and laid them all out on the bed and floor.

"May I ask what you're up to, Will?" Melanie pouted just a little. "I didn't know you had a fetish for my clothing."

"As a matter of fact, I do. Will you model for me? I've never seen you in any of these lovely getups. I'd very much like to."

Melanie smiled. She loved his imagination, his games, his need to play. He wasn't another empty-headed player like so many others she'd sampled in the past. Will had also lived up to his reputation as a sensational lover. She now thoroughly understood this "Blond Arrow" business. She was obsessed with him, and couldn't imagine any healthy woman who wouldn't be. He was *that damn good.*

She tried on Karl Lagerfeld evening dresses, a black dress by Jil Sander, sandals by Chloé. Will sat on the bed, gloriously naked, playing with himself, and watching her every move.

She already knew that he could keep himself hard for hours. If he had a problem in the sack, it was climaxing. So far, he hadn't with her. It was something to look forward to, no?

She was wearing a red gown and a lustrous pearl choker when she found that she couldn't stand it any longer. She scampered across the floor toward Will and his beautiful *arrow.*

"Please, please, *please me!*" she laughed and swooned in a theatrical fashion. "Let me fall on your sword."

Will didn't let her take off the Carolina Herrera, worth thousands of dollars. Not even her Ernesto Esposito pumps. He used the Hermès scarfs and nylons to tie Melanie to the bedposts. Then he made love to her for several hours. He helped her come so many times that he finally lost count. He didn't climax himself.

Sir Charles Wellsfleet arrived at the estate in Somerset around eleven that evening. He'd had a frightfully long day of meetings in London, and expected to find Melanie asleep in the bedroom, as usual.

His wife was wide-awake, however. Her eyes were like huge blue marbles, and she looked as though she had been sobbing for days. She was still tied to the bedposts with the scarfs and nylons, wearing nothing but the choker. Her face was puffy, but as pale as the pearls. The expensive Italian lingerie was strewn about the bed along with the shoes and the torn Herrera gown.

That summer, Will was transferred from Sir Charles's team. The press suspected everything except the truth: Will had tired of Melanie. The Blond Arrow needed to move on to a much larger stage.

21

WILL INVITED HIS BROTHER, Palmer, to his Chelsea apartment one afternoon before the new season began. Though it was expensively furnished, the living space seemed sterile, almost as if no one lived there. A Maggie Bradford record played softly, soothingly, in the background.

"I need your help," Will said, sipping the expensive brandy he had poured for them. Actually, it was his fourth or fifth brandy, and the third time he'd played the same record.

Palmer looked at his brother, surprised. *Will never seemed to need anything, from anyone.* "How could I possibly help *you*, Will?"

"I need a manager. I think you'd be perfect. I've thought about it a lot, actually."

"A manager! I thought Jacob Golding did that."

"He handles my business affairs. I mean a personal manager. Someone to look after me. Keep me out of trouble." *I'm starting to scare myself, brother. If you won't help me, then who will?*

"A bloody nursemaid, Will?" Palmer shook his head and laughed.

Will shrugged. "If that's what you want to call it. Will you do it? The pay is awfully good."

Palmer swallowed his brandy and stood up. "Not a chance, big brother."

"Why? What are you doing now that's so important?"

"As a matter of fact, I've got a good job in the marketing department of Cadbury's. But even if I were out of work, I wouldn't do it."

Will smiled. "Because you hate me?"

Palmer shook his head. His hair was blond, like his brother's, but cut short. "No. Because I hate living in your shadow. I don't hate you, Will. No one can hate you."

"You won't help then? Even if I told you that I'm desperately unhappy? That I'm running on empty? That night after night I think of killing myself?"

Palmer couldn't take his eyes off his fabulously handsome and successful brother. He sat down again. "Are you bloody serious, Will? Or are you play-acting again? Is this another of your mind *games*?"

"*Completely* fucking serious. I want to kill myself right now. Even as we speak. Do I sound like I'm playing a mind game?"

"My God," Palmer said. "I think you are serious. Or mad. Or quite possibly, both."

"I'm no good," Will said. "No damn good. Never have been. You're the only one who can help me, Palmer. We have to stick together."

Palmer stood, a strange, sad half smile on his face. "I'm sorry," he said. "I can't help you, Will. You'll have to find somebody else."

Will watched his brother leave. He refilled his snifter with brandy and drank it in a gulp. "But who is there to find?" he whispered. "Who could there possibly be to really love me?"

22

FACE THE MUSIC, Maggie. It's time to get to Will, to really talk about Will, to get it out once and for all. This is what everybody came to hear.

People ask, especially reporters, how I could have fallen in love with Will? I always want to say — *you would have too, in a millisecond. Don't kid yourself.* That wasn't the way it happened though — not for me.

But Will could be extremely charming. You have no idea! And I was *extremely* needy. I wanted to be loved more than anything else. I'd always wanted that. Doesn't everybody? Don't you?

It happened like this, more or less anyway. This is the truth, and nothing but, so help me.

I began my first European tour in London. It was tense, wild, but quite wonderful. The best of times. Jennie and I stayed at Claridge's. We went to the changing of the guard at Buckingham Palace, and saw *The Mousetrap,* Westminster Abbey, Big Ben. We were fantastic tourists together, and best friends. The two of us never shut up.

I was to give two concerts in London. And I was the honored guest at a costume ball in Mayfair, admission £1000, all receipts given to the fight against children's cancer.

The night of the charity party, I made a "grand entrance" into the living room of our hotel suite.

"Mom, no! You're *not* going out in public like that!" Jennie said, and made a face as though she'd just had a sip of warm stout.

I held a gold lamé vizard, a costume ball mask, up to my eyes. I peered into the mirror and then doubled over with laughter. Jennie was right on. I was straining the seams of my stiff antique ball gown, and my breasts were exposed farther than I'd imagined. *Sheesh.*

"Of course I'm going out like this. I think it's perfect. So would Barbara Cartland."

"Who's Barbara Cartland? Your fancy dressmaker? The costume designer for *Dracula?*"

"You don't know who Barbara Cartland is? Well, that proves you don't know anything about masquerades. You don't get a vote on this."

Jennie rolled her eyes. She buried both hands in her long hair. "But who are you supposed to *be?* Don't leave me in such *terrible suspense.*"

"A queen in the court of Louis the Fourteenth. Who else?"

Jennie giggled. She dropped down to the thick carpet and rolled over a few times.

"You look more like a stripper. *Sorry.* Sorry. Just kidding, Mom."

"You better be."

Anyway, what difference did it make how I looked? It was all a dream, wasn't it? None of this could possibly be real. It was too good, and I was way too happy.

23
***

THIS WAS SO *not-me*. That's why it was perfect.

The grand ball was held in the home of Lord Trevelyan, a four-storied Georgian mansion lit for the evening by enormous searchlights placed on the roofs of the opposite buildings.

When my car arrived, so did the black cab of a boisterous group impersonating the Bloomsbury literary crowd. They were dressed in knickers, suffragette blouses, and long puffed skirts, carrying dusty books and baskets of cut flowers. Jennie would have approved.

I went inside with the Bloomsbury characters to find at least two hundred guests, all outfitted in an array of costumes from all centuries and walks of life, sipping champagne (a glass was quickly served me) and chatting the night away.

Soon a trumpet sounded and the guests grew silent. Down the steps leading to the main foyer in which most of us were gathered came — Queen Elizabeth I! Her crown of rubies and sapphires glistened in the light; her dress, festooned with a thousand pearls, was as regal as its wearer. *This is a dream, right? A neat dream though.*

The "Queen" was, of course, Lady Trevelyan, our hostess.

"Supper is served," a butler announced, and we entered a magnificent dining room. We feasted on salmon, salads, cheeses, fresh fruits, and petit fours. After an hour or so, Lady Trevelyan rose and nodded to two footmen. The doors were swung open to the grand ballroom. Soon music started, a series of waltzes and fox-trots.

A man strode toward me on the dance floor. I would have turned away, but it was crowded, and there was nowhere to go.

He was dressed all in black, a hood over his head, a mask covering his face, so that only his eyes were visible. He had beautiful eyes, I couldn't help noticing. Something moved inside me. *Strange*.

"You're Maggie Bradford," he said. "Please give me your jewels or I'll be forced to steal them."

"You have the advantage," I said. "You know my name, but I don't know yours."

He bowed and raised my hand to his lips. "I'm Raffles, the infamous thief, at your service. And I'd rather steal your heart than your jewels."

I didn't look away from his eyes. "Then let me see your face. I don't let just anyone steal my heart."

I didn't know what to make of him. Lots of men had tried to seduce me since I had become *someone*, but this was a new approach. *Hi, I'd like to steal your jewels, or maybe, your heart.*

He bowed again, and with a single gesture removed his mask and hood.

Before me, without any exaggeration, stood one of the most handsome men I had ever seen. His blond hair hung down to his shoulders, and his green eyes blazed with an all-consuming light. Music came into my head. His tanned skin announced that he spent a lot of time outdoors, but his face was unlined; he was still young. His smile — and he was smiling now — revealed perfect white teeth and the skin around his jaw was smooth and taut.

"Raffles. Really? And what do they call you in the light of day?" I asked.

"Will," he said, "Will Shepherd." He took a step back to study the effect his name had.

It had *no* effect. I had never heard of him. "A nice name." I had noticed his accent. "You're American?"

"By birth. I've spent most of my life in England. I resisted *sounding* like one of them. I'm stubborn sometimes. *Most* of the time."

"And what do you do, Mr. Shepherd? Besides conduct highway robberies?"

If possible, his smile grew even brighter. "I'm afraid that I play football. Or soccer, as you would call it. You could come someday to see me play."

"I'd enjoy that. I guess I would. Although I should warn you, I'm not much of a sports fan."

"Yet I'm an unabashed fan of yours," Will said.

"I love your music," he went on. "The lyrics especially. You seem to *understand*."

Suddenly he took me by the arm. "I play your songs all the time, Maggie Bradford. I want to take you home with me tonight. I'm telling you the truth. I want to make love to you. Let's get out of here. You know you want to."

How could he say that to me? *How could he? . . . You know you want to!*

"How dare you speak to me this way," I shouted over the music.

I slapped him hard, and he stepped back, surprised. My voice must have reached the musicians, for they stopped in mid-melody. Everyone was staring at us.

I didn't care. His touch on my arm was Phillip's touch; his words were Phillip's words.

"If you had *really* listened to my songs, you'd know what I think of cheap come-ons," I said. My voice was shaking, my whole body was. "You've ruined this party for me. I don't give a damn if you're the best soccer *and* football player in the world. To me you're dirt-common, filth, and if you ever *dare* speak to me again, I'll —" I was about to say — *kill you.*

He had already moved away, so I didn't finish. I watched him — we all watched him — walk across the room to the door, his head held high, long hair flowing, his steps measured, manly, but absolutely revolting to me.

I stood very still, fighting down embarrassment and rage. The music started again; people began to dance. Lady Trevelyan came up to me and gently touched the back of my hand.

"I'm sorry," I blurted, and felt close to tears. "So sorry. I didn't mean to make a scene. I'm so sorry."

"Don't even think about it," she said, her voice on the edge of laughter. "You gave Will Shepherd exactly what he deserved, and there isn't a woman in this room who isn't cheering for you right now." Finally, the hostess did laugh. "Of course, they'd all hop into bed with him given the chance. But bravo for you anyway."

BOOK TWO

CALM BEFORE
THE STORM

24

IT WAS ONE *of the earliest court appointments* — I don't re-member which. All I know was that I was so glad to be leaving prison for any reason, even just to travel back and forth to court.

I felt that I was wearing my scarlet *M*, of course. I'm inno-cent, until proven guilty, but not in the *minds* of an awful lot of people, or so I've found. People who don't know me have al-ready prejudged and condemned me.

For some, I'm guilty of murder. For others, they assume that I must have slept around, though God knows, nothing could be farther from the truth. The worst hurt of all, the deepest wound, comes from those who judge me a bad mother. If they saw me for ten minutes with my children — if they asked my kids about their mother — they'd know how wrong they are.

But I am prejudged. *Women*, I think, are guilty until proven *innocent*. And many of the worst accusers are other women. Why is that?

So I wore my scarlet *M* to court that summer morning. I was just glad to be *outside*. The pollen count must have been high, since several people we passed on the streets were sneezing, and the parked cars were blanketed with a thin, green dust.

The guards from the prison knew me, and liked me, and they tried to protect me from the inevitable crowds at the courthouse. A few of the "faithful," "Maggie's mob," had brought their angry placards. "Maggie Is a Murderer" and "Husband Killer" and "Give Maggie a CHAIR, She Looks Tired From All That Killing."

"Keep your head down, Maggie, and just follow us straight in," one of the guards told me.

I had spent so much time inside, cut off from the world, that I wanted to look — but the guard was right. I dropped my head, even though it made me *look* guilty.

The press was clever; they knew the best places to hide in wait at the courthouse. They trapped us on the way in, then they pounced.

There was the usual barrage of insensitive questions. Microphones thrust at me — *did they want me to sing?* TV cameras staring with their large, unblinking eyes.

A woman reporter with frazzled blond hair leaned in close over the restraining ropes at the side door. "Maggie! Over here, Maggie. Please?" she pleaded.

My head rose involuntarily, my eyes went to hers.

"What about Patrick?" she suddenly asked, a TV eye mercilessly staring behind her. "Did you murder him too? Did you, Maggie?"

I have never spit at a human being. I don't spit. Ever . . . but that morning I spat at that reporter. I don't know what possessed me.

The TV camera caught it — the incident, the shot, was on every TV news program, played over and over again. An uncontrollable temper. The *real* Maggie Bradford?

What about Patrick?

Did you murder a third man, Maggie?

Is anybody going to be surprised if you did?

25

"ACCOUNTANTS DON'T KNOW SHIT. So why in hell do we pay them a cent? Now *there's* some cost savings I could live with!"

Thus spoke Patrick O'Malley, standing in the bathroom of the unfurnished Tower Suite of his unfinished, unnamed, unopened hotel on Sixty-fifth Street and Park Avenue.

He was glaring at his accountant, his *C.F.O.*, Maurice Freund. Freund had heard his boss's opinion of accountants before. "But we do know costs," he said, unruffled, "and you're costing yourself an unnecessary fortune."

"Pears soap is necessary," O'Malley raged. "Porthault towels are *necessary*. A Jacuzzi in the Tower Suite bathroom is *essential*."

Freund sighed and shrugged. "The good news is that every room is booked. The bad news is that we're losing money on every booking."

"We'll refigure the damn rates. When you promise the best you deliver the best, and this hotel will *be* the best, goddamnit, or that soap goes right up your ass."

"As long as it's Pears," Freund said, grinning.

O'Malley grunted. "The construction's on schedule?"

"Yup. *Their* schedule. Eight months late at an overrun of twenty percent."

"That's still less than you estimated originally?"

"Ten percent less."

"Then take the soap and the towels from that ten percent."

"No way." Freund took O'Malley's arm and steered him out of the suite toward the makeshift elevator. "Knowing you, there'll be overruns everywhere. The rates go up."

If O'Malley had an opinion, he didn't express it. Rather, he said, "I know what to name the hotel."

Good news, Freund thought. *And about time.* "What?"

"I want to call it The Cornelia."

"The Cornelia. Splendid!" Freund knew his boss was watching his reaction closely, but his pleasure was genuine, his smile sincere. "That's good. The perfect choice, Patrick."

"I don't believe a world-class hotel's ever been named after a woman." O'Malley sounded almost shy.

"Then it's a unique name for a unique hotel. Besides, the time is right."

"She was a unique woman," O'Malley said. "That's for certain. We can finally agree on something, Maurice."

Freund took his hand and gravely shook it. The accountant actually seemed to have *felt* something. "The hotel's her testimonial. Your tribute to the one woman you loved."

26

FOR TWENTY YEARS, Cornelia and Patrick O'Malley were one of New York's most courted and undeniably popular couples. Seeming opposites — he, the gruff, self-made entrepreneur who had parlayed a string of motels into a grand hotel chain in the United States, Europe, and Asia; she, the society beauty who outraged her family, the Whitings, by falling in love with, and then marrying, a *Catholic who had not gone to Princeton* — they were actually perfectly matched. Cornelia's cool tempered his heat; Patrick's passion aroused her own; and in the richest of rich skies in which they orbited like moons, no scandal was ever attached to them. Despite innumerable temptations, he remained faithful to her, and his support gave her strength. Beneath her regal demeanor she let herself grow soft and trusting — only for him, forever for him.

Until forever was cut short by a glioblastoma that took her life in eighteen months, her spirit long before that, and he was left, at age fifty-four, with nothing except wealth, their rebellious son, Peter, and the tremendous sympathy of friends.

*　　*　　*

Now he was building his most magnificent hotel around the shell of an antique mansion, much as Helmsley had done with the Palace. At completion, there would be four hundred rooms, including seventy suites, some with original marble from Witherspoon House. Guests would have a pick of styles: Renaissance Italian; eighteenth-century French; ultramodern American.

And in every room in The Cornelia — O'Malley wondered why he had not settled on the name sooner as he envisioned the hotel — there would be Pears soap and Porthault towels. It was going to be a truly Grand Hotel, the way they used to build them in the best of times, before the invention of accountants.

He spent the entire day at the hotel, meeting with Freund in the morning, personally directing the centimeter-by-centimeter polishing of the marble columns in the lobby, checking the seating and lighting in the Gold Bar, and then, at noon, meeting with the chief architect, Michael Hart.

Their conversation lasted through lunch. Hart went through several crucial items, most important, the gilding of the Renaissance ornamentation of the main lobby and the filigree above the windows at the entrance on Lexington.

Alone once more, O'Malley moved into the kitchen, at last hearing the sweetly satisfying racket of hammering and drilling — the stainless steel stoves, warming ovens, and counters were finally going in after a fourteen-week wait for materials. There were already enough copper pots, O'Malley noted with pleasure, to open the largest supply store in Manhattan.

At seven-thirty, O'Malley found himself once again passing beneath the lobby's antique clock, a timepiece that had once adorned the Winter Palace of Catherine the Great.

At the center of the hotel atrium in the rear of the lobby, an original Bernini fountain, imported from Rome, had been restored to its matchless splendor. That afternoon, plumbing had finally been completed by Timothy Sullivan of the Bronx Local 41, who called O'Malley to announce that all systems were go.

"All ready for lift-off," O'Malley muttered, unlocking the knob that controlled the spigots and spray.

The water rose in gentle bends and bows. O'Malley's face shone like a child's on Christmas Day. "*Damn* but that's fine," he said aloud in the deserted garden.

But the spray had to go higher still, he considered as he studied the fountain. He turned the knob. The water remained at its level. *It would never catch the afternoon sunlight,* he thought. It was like the ejaculation of a ninety-year-old man.

That bastard Sullivan. All systems go my ass! I'll fix it so he never ejaculates again.

Already, Patrick O'Malley had made his first mental note for the next day.

He passed under the lobby clock again, then stopped and checked his own watch. *Eight-sixteen! The lobby clock was three minutes fast!*

He felt murder in his chest. "Slow down, Pat," he imagined Nellie's voice telling him. "Careful, careful." He didn't give a good, flying fuck about "careful." With incompetent kiss-asses all around him — and with Nellie gone — what good was living anyway?

27

WHEN JENNIE WAS THIRTEEN and it was almost time for her to go to high school, I bought a beautiful house on Greenbriar Road in Bedford, New York. It was time for both of us to have a real home. More important, I wanted Jennie settled into a good school.

I wanted stability, and peaceful surroundings, both for Jennie and myself. We picked out the house together. Both of us loved it, the sprawling grounds, and the town of Bedford. We finally had a home again.

I was already infamous for being extremely selective about playing concerts and being on the road. I think I had my priorities straight, and my head screwed on as well. I'd never wanted to think of myself as a star, or live like one either. I vowed not to bring up Jennie that way.

The years with Phillip had made me afraid of hoping for too much more than peacefulness and contentment in my life. *It wasn't so bad,* I kept telling myself.

There was a wonderful school for Jennie in Bedford; we were less than an hour's drive from the city; I could have complete privacy when I needed it, and socialize if I felt like it. It seemed a perfect town for us, peaceful and enduring, the right place to erase the last vestiges of a still painful history.

Jennie dubbed our house Shangri-la, la, la. Not to be spoken — to be *sung*. She had a good voice, and an even better sense of humor.

Most nights were blissfully peaceful at our house. The noises were the singing of birds, the occasional yapping of a dog, sometimes the sound of a radio as teenagers drove by. The "cruising" cars reminded me of growing up in Newburgh, which was only thirty miles to the north.

I was startled one evening in April to hear a pounding on the front door. I was expecting no one. As far as I knew, I was not in trouble with the police. Jennie was in her room doing her homework, and I hoped she was too young for a jilted boyfriend.

I had been careful to keep my whereabouts unpublicized, so the intruder was almost surely neither a fan nor a rival. Someone knocking on the wrong door? Probably.

Curious, and a little nervous, I went to the door. Through the peephole, I could see a man, his body distorted by the glass. He was in a rumpled suit but well dressed, his tie askew, his hair uncombed, his face apoplectic. I sensed he was harmless enough, and opened the door.

"Mrs. Bradford?" he said, somehow managing to sound exasperated.

"Yes. Can I help you? How did you know my name?"

"There's a BRADFORD on your mailbox. A deduction."

"There's a bell on the door. Why not use that instead of pounding?"

"There is?" He seemed genuinely surprised. "I guess I was so angry I didn't notice. Sorry about that."

His anger had evidently evaporated. There was definitely no danger in him. I invited him in. "What's this about?"

He followed me down the foyer to the living room. "If I built hotels the way GM builds cars, I'd be crucified. Yet those shitkickers —"

Ah. That was the explanation. "It's your car, then?"

"A brand-new Mercedes convertible. Not a thousand miles on the useless rattletrap. And here I am, exhausted, minding my own business, happy to be off the highway, when the son of a bitch dies. I mean *dies*. No warning, not even a death rattle. The mother just says to me, 'Fuck you, Pat,' and quits. And do I have a car phone? Of course not. If I had one, I'd use it, and I like the driving time for thinking and enjoying myself in blessed peace. The only reason for a phone is in case the car has a breakdown, and is a brand-new, eighty-thousand-dollar car going to cause trouble? No way. Ha!" Suddenly he stopped and grinned. His smile reminded me of Paul Newman's — *a lot*. "So can I use your phone? I may be the only Irish Catholic who's a member of AAA and not AA."

"Sure thing," I said, hiding a smile. He was funny, and the humor was contagious, at least it was that night. "The phone's in the den. What were you doing on Greenbriar at this time of night?"

"I *live* on Greenbriar. About three miles further down. You must have passed my house a thousand times going to the village. My name's O'Malley. It's the oversized Georgian. I live in it to impress my friends."

I knew the house, or more accurately, the estate. It was one of the grandest on Greenbriar. "You said hotels. Then you must be —"

"Patrick O'Malley. I'm building one on Park Avenue. The Cornelia. Do you like the name? Say yes, and you'll be its first guest as my guest."

This time I couldn't suppress the laugh. "Yes. I might take you up on it. Would you like a drink, Mr. O'Malley?"

He bowed. "You're very, very kind and understanding. Scotch if you have it. Neat."

I showed him to the den, then went to the kitchen to fix a

drink. There really was something about this poor/rich blitzed man that struck me as funny. The look on his face was classic silent-movie comedy. He had star quality.

I didn't get a lot of visitors, besides music-business people, into my safe, comfortable, closed world. I was getting good at pretending that I liked it that way. *I didn't like it at all.*

I poured a Scotch, and went back to the den, knocking gently before entering. I stepped inside the room, then stopped and began to laugh out loud. I couldn't help myself.

Patrick O'Malley had taken off his rumpled suit jacket and hung it carefully over the back of a chair. He had removed his black cordovans and put them neatly beside the jacket.

He lay stretched out on my old, flowered sofa, and he was fast asleep.

28

I WOKE UP EARLY, but Patrick was gone by the time I went downstairs. Jen and I did a three-mile run, then a power drink, and off to school for her. I went into my den and began working, lost in the lyrics of "A Lady Hard as Love."

Around ten-thirty, I walked to the riding stables, noticing that the day had assumed the gauzy look of life shot through a telephoto lens. I felt content. Not a great feeling, but not so bad either. Something was missing from life, but I certainly had a lot, and no complaints.

A florist truck came bumping up the drive and a boy with spiked orange hair and Coke-bottle glasses came hurrying toward me, bearing an arrangement of freesias and decorative ribbons.

There was a note. *O'Malley,* I thought, pleased for some reason.

Dear Margaret Bradford,
 Forgive me for not having immediately recognized your name, but the only singers I've heard of are the Clancy Brothers.

*I don't know for certain if I can face you again. Not after
last night. But I'm going to try. Give it my best.*

*Will you please have dinner with me some evening this
week? Let me try to make amends.*

*You have the most beautiful blue eyes I've ever seen, and
I will spend the time between now and our dinner listening
to Maggie Bradford records until I've memorized your
songs.*

> *The Mortified Sleeper (your neighbor),*
> *Patrick*

My eyes were chestnut brown, and I had a feeling that Patrick O'Malley knew it, and knew I knew he knew it.

Dinner? Why not? I needed to meet more people in Bedford. I left a message on his machine making a date for Thursday night.

Blue eyes — that's Sinatra, not me.

29

THURSDAY was an unexpected and unqualified *hit*. He made me laugh — a lot. He had stories weaved inside of stories, weaved into still more stories. He had a wonderfully warm smile, and a generous nature. I knew I'd made my first friend in Bedford, and it felt good.

Over the next few weeks, I saw Patrick several times. I enjoyed his odd, wry, but honest sense of humor; his unique comic timing; his oversentimental but nevertheless touching stories about growing up in an Irish family of ten; his thrill at putting up his parents in the honeymoon suite of his first grand hotel.

In deference to his globetrotting, I began to call Patrick names that amused him: Padriac, Patrice, and Patrizio. But Patrick had no silly names for me. Sometimes he called me Margaret, the first person to do that since my mother.

"My first love," Patrick told me, "was actually the sea. It's the one powerful image that I still have of Ireland, and when I was growing up there."

Patrick had a modest sailboat, and one weekday morning we took it out on the Sound. Patrick played hooky from his hotel project; I could afford one morning away from the piano, and my own rituals.

Soon, we were out on the water, and I found that I loved it too. Since it was early on a weekday, there weren't many other boats out, even though the day was in the low seventies, with clear blue skies. I could see heavy traffic as we slid away from shore, and watching the cars heading to work reminded me of how lucky I was.

"There but for the grace of God," Patrick said and saluted the commuters. "Suckers!" he shouted into the sea breeze and laughed. He wasn't being mean, just playful.

He and Jennie had obviously conspired, since he'd smuggled some of my power drink onboard, and had made me my usual breakfast. He even joined me for the special mixture of several fruit juices and vitamins.

"So are you finally over the bastard, Maggie?" he asked as we sipped juice. As usual, he was spontaneous and *himself*. I understood that he meant Phillip, who we'd talked about before, but not very much.

"Yes and no," I told Patrick the truth. I felt that I could.

"I think I know what you mean." He gave me a hug with one arm as the two of us stood staring out over the oncoming breakers.

"Sorry I don't have any good advice for you," he said. "I never shot any bastards, though several I know deserved it. Is it all right if I make this light — it's my way, you know."

I nodded. It *was* Patrick's style to be able to joke when things got particularly dark. He made me laugh constantly, and I liked it a lot.

"He *was* a bastard, and I'm sorry I married him."

Patrick waved his free arm angrily. "Awww, he just took advantage. You were very young, and not so long out of your aunt's house. He did his fine officer's act, made his lofty promises, lied to you. I know, let's sail north to West Point. We'll dig up his grave, then we'll pulverize the bones."

I shook my head, but I was smiling. "You make me laugh."

"It's my job. It's what I'm good at."

I looked at him. "What do you think I'm good at?"

He gestured with both hands. "Oh, everything. Everything that I've seen at least. You're closing yourself off a little — that's the only area for improvement that I can see."

"You're funny, and you can be very sweet."

"You think so?" he asked.

"Yes, I do. I definitely believe that. I'm sure of it."

"Well good, there's an object lesson, 'cause I'm not ten percent as sweet as you. The way you talk, the way you think, raise your beautiful girl, Jennie, what comes out in your songs. That's why your music's so popular, don't you know it?"

"I do —"

"I know — and you don't. I have a favor, a big favor."

I tensed a little.

Patrick winced. "See what he did to you, sweet Maggie? I hate it when you're afraid. That *reflex*. Your back is like a washboard."

"I'm getting better," I said.

"I know that you are. Now *don't clutch*. Here's the favor. It's the most wonderful thing I can imagine."

I *couldn't* imagine. I wasn't tense anymore — Patrick had made me comfortable — but I couldn't figure where he was heading with this.

"All right," I finally said, "I'll do anything. That's how much I trust you."

"Excellent. The best words I've heard you speak so far. Now what I'd like, Maggie, what I'd love — would you sing me one of your songs. Any song of your choosing. Right here, just the two of us, would you softly sing a beautiful song just for me?"

It was a beautiful request, and I sang for Patrick.

30

ONE NIGHT, it must have been a week or so later, I had a light dinner with Jennie. Around eight, I drove her to her friend Millie's house where she was having a sleep-over. Then, I went to Patrick's house for a second meal.

Patrick had excused his "chief cook and bottle-washer" for the evening. He said that he wanted to do the honors: roasted lobster with garlic butter, thickly sliced and crisped french fries, succulent corn on the cob. A simple, satisfying *feast*.

After dinner, we took a walk on the grounds to a grove of apple trees at the far end of his estate. There Patrick slid his arm around me and gently kissed the top of my head.

"You smell like orange blossoms. How is that?"

"More like No More Tears shampoo from Johnson and Johnson."

"Whatever. You smell wonderful." He kissed both my cheeks, then my forehead, my nose, the tip of my chin. He kissed me on the lips, and I felt his tongue touch mine.

I pulled away. We had kissed before, though I had never really felt his passion; I always drew back. Tonight was different. *He kisses absolutely beautifully,* I thought. *I just felt his heart and I like the feeling.*

I felt safe with him. The night wind whispered softly through the grove of trees. He kissed me again, and this time I could feel myself responding.

I can't shut myself off any longer. I can't spend my life afraid, even if I am.

"Let's go inside," Patrick said. "I slept at your house once. In the den, and without your permission, as you constantly remind me. Will you sleep at my house tonight?"

I turned my body into his, smiling at the two of us. For once, I was happy about one of Jennie's sleep-overs. "Not in the den, I hope."

I could feel him grow hard against me. "No," he whispered. "Come with me. Please. Trust me."

My reluctance must have been stronger than I imagined, for he had surely sensed it. *Trust him.* Oh, how I wanted to, yet as we turned toward the house I could see Phillip's face, feel the menace of him. I shuddered involuntarily. *Damn* him. We should have pulverized the bones.

"We don't have to," Patrick said, reading my fear. "I don't know everything that happened to you long ago, but we can wait. You're the first woman who's meant anything to me in a while. But I want this to be exactly right for both of us."

He *was* the most considerate and loving man. I did trust him.

"I want to," I said, conscious of how tight my throat felt, how cold my skin. "I do, Patrick. Let's go inside."

31

WE WERE UNUSUALLY QUIET as we slowly undressed in Patrick's sprawling, moonlit upstairs bedroom. In the spun-out silence the beat of my heart was electric, loudly amplified. All sorts of questions and self-doubts began circulating through my head. *I'm too tall for him. He won't like me once he really gets to know me. Do I know enough about him? Relax, Maggie. Please, just relax.*

He looked wonderful in the moonlight. Hard, working-man's stomach. Well-muscled legs. Broad chest lightly covered with silver and light-brown hair. *Sexy,* I thought, and I liked what I was feeling.

Open yourself up to him, Maggie. Don't be afraid. This time it's right.

He held me in his arms for the quietest moment, kissing my hair and my neck. He *held me* as we stood before the moonlit window and waited for me to relax. I sensed that he was willing to wait for a long, long time.

He kissed me again, and I had the feeling that we were falling toward each other. He kissed my cheeks, my forehead, my nose, then both my eyes. Soft, lingering kisses. Finally, I began to kiss him back. I kissed his cheeks, his forehead, his eyes. I continued to fall toward him, at least I had that sense.

"Dear sweet Maggie," he whispered. He *knew* that I was still a little afraid. *He always knew what I was feeling.* He was wise, intelligent, but he never showed off, never seemed impressed with himself.

"You are such a lovely and special woman. I adore you, Maggie."

It was *Patrick's* voice, *Patrick's* arms, and as he lifted me up and carried me to the massive bed, I felt a release, as though he had severed the invisible chains that had held me captive. This was such a sweet, slow dance. It was so new for me — either forgotten, or never experienced. He took his time, and then entered me gently, carefully.

From a fragile place inside me, a place forgotten, pleasure rippled through me, and I shivered. I felt a deep, warm sensation flowing, spreading, rushing out. It was a feeling that had been missing for so long. And it went on and on that night.

"Gentle Patrick," I said finally, and I didn't think I would ever stop *smiling*. I touched his face once again. He was smiling too. "You're so good for me. You're so good, period."

"It will be better and better," he said. "Trust me." Then he whispered, "*Trust us.*"

I did. Finally, I trusted someone again.

32

WILL SHEPHERD should have felt at the absolute top of the world, but somehow he didn't. He was certainly famous, and filthy rich, but he hated it. That night, he was also dangerously high. *The werewolf of London,* he thought. *Beware.*

The cocaine he'd taken as the concert began, and again immediately before the appearance of Maggie Bradford, made him feel all-powerful. And why the hell not? He was a star not only on the football field, but also among the elite attending the special performance at Albert Hall.

Will looked around, grinning, waving. Pete Townsend was there, and Sting, and Mick Jagger — *a new rock group: the Hasbeens* — along with Rupert Murdoch and Margaret Thatcher, *the two people currently destroying England.*

They had come to hear Maggie Bradford soothe their tortured souls. Her ballads did that to people. Her songs were rare, a miracle actually — strong melody, lyric, and mesmerizing. No singer put so many different emotions into one song — all of her songs imitated the dizzying complexity of modern life, or so it seemed to Will.

She came onstage to loud, adoring applause, and yet she

seemed *so shy*. Tickets had been sold out for months. She sat at the piano . . . and simply began to sing.

Will had no memory of the scene at Lady Trevelyan's party, and so he looked at her with a fresh eye. There was her long, flowing blond hair. And the simple beauty of her face.

But she seemed to *glow* on this particular night. He wondered why? What was her secret? What had this woman learned that he hadn't?

Her voice wasn't large or particularly dramatic; there was no melodrama in her style. She sang with a purity that pierced his heart like a sword, and he could actually feel the pain as well as the honest beauty of her music.

She was singing about the sadness of lost dreams, about a fall from grace. Will felt she was singing about him.

Tears rolled down his cheeks. The music moved him in ways he couldn't understand, but it was as though a great light were embracing him from the stage, and then transporting him from the concert hall into a place for only the two of them. *What the hell am I thinking?* he wondered. He was tempted to laugh at himself. He felt like such a damn fool.

God how he loved the sound of her voice though. He could listen to it for the rest of his life.

He had the strange, haunting feeling that Maggie Bradford could save him from himself.

"Did you forget I was with you in there? You did, didn't you, Will? You bastard!"

Will looked at the slender, dark-haired woman who was holding on to his arm as he left the concert hall. He had forgotten about her — hadn't a clue who the hell the beautiful woman behind the dark glasses was. Ah, the werewolf strikes again!

She was stunning, but they all were. Model? Actress? Would-be-actress? Shopgirl? Where the hell had he met her? Christ, this was embarrassing — even for him it was a new low.

"So, how long have you been getting this royally fucked-up on coke? You have, haven't you? Can you play like this?"

Ahhh, Will sighed with relief. *Reporter!* Now he remembered who the hell she was. She was the *Times.* She wanted to do a piece on him. He wanted a piece of her. Fair trade.

He recovered his poise, and immediately went into one of his best Prince Charming acts. He could, he knew, fool the pants off any of them. Even a *Times* reporter.

"No, it wasn't drugs, Cynthia," he said. *Cynthia Miller! That was her name.* He was so proud of himself. "I love her songs. I really do."

"So you said on the way over. Your car is full of her tapes."

"Her music is so damn real, comes right out of her life," Will continued. "Do you like it much yourself?"

"As I told you, *on the way over,* I do like her music, indeed. I also enjoyed the concert, but maybe not as much as you did."

Will pecked her on the cheek — gently, very chastely. "*Now* what shall we do?" he asked. *Careful, Will. She's a reporter.*

Cynthia Miller smiled a sly grin. "I'd like to hear more about the Blond Arrow," she said. She was typical of most reporters, an incredible cynic, a romantic gone bad.

"Would you like to see it?" Will teased. He added a twinkling smile.

He knew that she did. All of them did — except maybe one.

Maggie Bradford! That's who he wanted, he needed — *a real person to understand and challenge him.*

33

THE DOORBELL RANG, and Will stopped reading the morning newspaper. He peered out the window. A showy, silver-blue Rolls-Royce was parked in his driveway. He could hear his maid greeting the newcomer, then footsteps approaching the living room.

"Mr. Shepherd, Mr. Lawrence."

At the entrance stood a smiling, sandy-haired man, perhaps ten years older than Will. Will knew who Winifred "Winnie" Lawrence was. The man was a major force behind the development of soccer in the United States, a man determined to bring the beauty and grace of this refined sport to a nation overdosed on American football mayhem. Lawrence was a lawyer, an agent, but most of all, a hustler par excellence.

Will waited in his chair until Lawrence had entered the room; then he got up slowly, uncoiling as though from a nap, and shook hands with the American. Like so many people from his country, *their* country, Lawrence skipped preamble and pretense, and got right into it. Cut to the chase.

"Tell me, Will, why do you think the Germans remain so powerful a threat to win the Cup?" Lawrence said, his smile seemingly *pasted* across his face. "Year after year, no matter their personnel, they seem to have a powerhouse team."

It was actually a question Will had often asked himself. "Discipline, I suppose," he said. "It's more their team style than any individual, and that makes them strong."

Lawrence beamed, reveling in the obvious, as Americans so often do. "It's a style I've incorporated into the American team. But we need world-class individuals as well. We need a scorer, a striker."

"I figured that's why you came here."

"Yes, that's right. I've come to persuade you to play for the United States. I will not leave your house until I do."

Will laughed at the idea, not to mention Lawrence's gall. "It'll take some doing. There's no way America can compete, with or without me. Why should I do all that training just to go out in the qualifying rounds? What am I too dim to see?"

Lawrence reached into a stuffed briefcase and withdrew a computer sheet, spreading it out on the living room table. The two men bent over it.

"Look here, Will. Suspend your disbelief for just a few moments. *Look.* CONCACAF. Zone Norte. Zone Centro. Zone del Caribe. The official schedule for the American team in the North Zone qualifiers."

"So what?"

"Don't you see? Let me help you then. The Americans don't have to beat anybody worthwhile. Not until they're into the final twenty-four."

Will laughed again. He enjoyed Lawrence's first-class act, but this was simply too much. "Maybe you haven't heard, Mr. Lawrence, *Winnie,* but the American team isn't considered anybody either. Any national team will be absolutely thrilled to play the United States. They'd think the game would be a complete walkover."

"And that's to our advantage!" Lawrence put his arm around Will's shoulder. Actually, he was rather a good salesman, the great American huckster. Very compelling in his way. "We'll have the benefit of *surprise*. What if I tell you that Wolf Obermeier has agreed to coach the American team?"

Obermeier had coached championship teams in his native Germany and in Argentina. He had the reputation of having one of the most brilliant minds in football — and the harshest tongue.

"I'd be somewhat impressed," Will granted. At least now you've gotten my attention. Tell me more, Mr. Lawrence. Maybe I need a challenge right now."

"Or a crowning achievement?" the American said, and grinned.

34

"TRY TO IMAGINE the World Series, the Super Bowl, the Kentucky Derby, and the Democratic and Republican Conventions all rolled into one great event," wrote Mickey Trevor Jr. in the popular American magazine *Sports Illustrated*.

Then you have some small idea of the power and glory of the World Cup.

Next imagine Rio de Janeiro, where soccer may be more important than sex and the samba, and the World Cup makes Mardi Gras seem like a Girl Scout jamboree.

That's where the World Cup final will be played.

And now think of the two teams matched in that final: heavy favorite Brazil, three-time previous winner of the cup, whose lineage is as impressive as the New York Yankees — and upstart, unheralded, pipsqueak America, the miracle men in the red, white, and blue, whose rise from nonentity to heroic challenger has all the elements of a classic fairy tale — only, miraculously and unbelievably, it is true.

Folks, this here is a fairy story to rank with "The Lion King"! You may not have taken much notice when America quietly won the North Zone qualifying tournament, thus reaching the World Cup finals. It might have quickened your pulse a bit when our boys made it past the qualifying round, with only a loss to Germany to mar their record. Good for us, good for my kids, who love soccer because they play it in school, you probably figured, but that's the end. It's all over. And so you turned your attention back to the pennant races, and the wonderful baseball season of Barry Bonds, still a bit puzzled as to why the rest of the world takes soccer so damn seriously, and meanwhile, our team edged past Nigeria into the last eight.

But when the U.S. beat Italy — Italy! — in the quarter-finals (the score was 3–2, and each of the American goals was scored by America's star of stars, Will Shepherd; and then edged Germany 2–11 in the semis, surely your attention returned, and by now if your temperature isn't boiling, if your heart isn't pounding, if you haven't canceled all plans for Sunday night so you can stay home to watch the final, then you're not an American, you don't like sports — or you're dead.

The American team has Will Shepherd and ten other guys who probably couldn't make the starting lineups of any of the leading clubs in the competition.

But Shepherd. Ah, Shepherd!

Soccer is a team sport, but even Wolf Obermeier, the U.S.A. coach, admits that in this case Will Shepherd is the team. "Without Will, we wouldn't have qualified," Obermeier said. "With him — well, look where we are now. Look where we are."

"Bravo! My congratulations to *Sports Illustrated!* Finally something of value, beyond their beloved swimsuit issue!"

Will finished the article and grunted with satisfaction. "Shepherd is the team," he said. "Has a nice ring to it. Accurate reporting for a change too. Bravo!"

"I read it while you were asleep," Victoria Lansdowne said.

The leggy British actress was sprawled luxuriously on top of the covers. Her striking, cobalt-blue eyes admired the physique of the man she had met for the first time the evening before. The Blond Arrow. Right now, the most famous athlete in the world.

Despite the air-conditioning in the Rio Hilton, the suite was hot, and neither of them had put on any clothes after a long bout of sex. They looked every bit as good as their starry reputations suggested. The sheen of sweat glistened on their beautiful bodies.

"What did you think of it? Just another puff piece?"

"I think that if you play football as well as you do certain other things, you'll beat the living doo-doo out of Brazil tomorrow."

He smiled. "Satisfied, I take it."

"Never. Not even close, sweet thing. I'm *insatiable*. Don't *you* read the papers? My 'string of lovers.'"

He looked at her full breasts, the slender, very tan legs that had spread for him so willingly, yet seemed to have a mind of their own. She reminded him of Vannie. Many of them did. Maybe that was why he was beginning to feel a touch angry at *vainglorious Victoria*.

"Want another go . . . on goal, so to speak?" Victoria had followed his gaze down and along her body. She reveled in the power she held over supposedly strong and powerful men. This one was different though. He was smarter than she'd expected him to be.

"I don't think so. Maybe your '*string*' has finally ended here," he said, returning her dazzling smile.

"What's the matter? No more arrows in our quiver? Are we fresh out of joy juice?"

Will fought down the rage, forcing himself to laugh. "There's a game tomorrow, a rather important game. Maybe you've heard? You say you read the papers, dear Vic."

"And sweet Lambkins wants to get up for that, but not for me?"

"Don't," he said. He'd *warned* her at least.

"Don't what?" she taunted him. "Tempt you?" She wet a finger with her tongue, and placed it between her legs. "If you can't do it, I suppose I'll have to do it myself. Now *here's* a juicy picture for the tabloids. *Victoria does herself! Will not able?*"

With a roar, Will was on her, all over her. Victoria *woofed* out air.

"Oh," she gasped. "Oh God, that hurts. That *hurts.*" Victoria Lansdowne tried to push him off, but he pinned her hands to her sides. "Please, dear Jesus, *stop!* Please, please, I'm begging you, Will! Stop it. I'm serious, stop."

But there was nothing that could stop the Blond Arrow.

35

ON THE AFTERNOON of the World Cup final the heat soared to ninety-three degrees on the sugary, white sand beaches of Copacabana and Ipanema. For a while, it was a quiet day, a national holiday in celebration of the World Cup. Rich and poor alike rested, saving their energy for the most popular sporting event in the world.

Then, suddenly, day melted into swarming, jungle-hot night. All of Rio de Janeiro seemed to pour outdoors to witness, and participate in, the national game of "futebol."

The wide avenues of the South American city became a raucous and dangerous carnival. Auto horns honked out *Bra-sil! Bra-sil!* Along the Avenida Brasil and Castello Branco, university students defiantly wrapped themselves in the national flag. All buses and taxis were decorated with bright-colored streamers. Women danced impromptu in the streets, blouses clinging to their breasts, skirts swirling like hoops.

By seven o'clock, the crowd had converged on Rio's legendary Maracana Stadium, police letting no one in without a ticket, though hundreds eluded them and entered the stadium to find what sight lines they could.

Inside, a hundred thousand frenzied Cariocas, waving multicolored banners and placards proclaiming sports victory and social revolution, let out cheers in cadence with the rhythm of ten thousand samba drums, and *twice* that many boom boxes.

At the end of a rampway, standing with the rest of his team amid the deafening noise, Will *listened*.

He could hear his own heart beat against the walls of his chest. He could hear . . .

"*Numero nueve . . . De America . . . Will . . . Shepherd!*" came from the loudspeaker.

There were drawn-out boos at the announcement, shouts of *palhaco*, "clown." But even in Rio, there were cheers for Will Shepherd. Some in the crowd treasured artistry over partisanship, and Will's achievements were art. A quartet of shirtless men ran out onto the field. Each had the numeral nine painted on his chest.

The cheers continued as Will raced onto the field, his fist held high above his flying blond curls. His head was filled with sound and images, fantasies and dreams. He could hardly breathe.

He felt The Thrill travel through every part of his body.

No one could stop him tonight.

He was going to make sports history in front of half the world. No one would ever forget him after this special night in Rio.

36

AT 8:32, THE COLOMBIAN REFEREE set the ball down on a bent tuft of grass.

Brazil versus America! Unthinkable, unpopular, impossible, and yet it was happening.

The World Cup final had begun!

Arturo Ribeiro, the mercurial nineteen-year-old Brazilian star, swept up the ball, passed it to a teammate in a play practiced for hours in the preceding months, and raced forward in a brilliant, weaving dance. The ball was sent back to him. His back to the goal, he cartwheeled and sent the ball flying toward the American net.

The fans exploded.

"*Goool de Bra-sil!*" the PA announcer screamed. "*Goool de Arturo Ribeiro!*"

Time elapsed: thirty-three seconds.

Less than six minutes later, Brazil scored again. Easily, effortlessly it seemed.

Cariocas danced in the stands and let loose black snakes and plucked chickens from hidden baskets. Outside the stadium, flares burst in the night sky; handguns were fired into the air; police sirens wailed on and on as though the long-awaited revolution had arrived.

One would have thought no greater rejoicing was possible. But the celebration of Brazil's second goal was muted, compared to the reaction when Ribeiro scored again in the thirty-third minute of play.

Brazil led 3–0 at half-time!

The game was looking like a rout . . . no, it *was* a full-scale massacre.

Listen to this pompous asshole, Will was thinking as he sat with his head hung low in the visitors' locker area.

"You play as if you are drugged," Wolf Obermeier said. He had already berated his other so-called players, and now he was speaking quietly to Will, whom he had drawn aside as the team left the dressing room to begin the second half. "Something is troubling you? *Are you drugged?*"

"Maybe." Will smiled at the overserious German's consternation. Truthfully, he didn't know what was wrong. He felt refreshed after last night, blurred though the memory of it was; no, it was something else holding him back. He shrugged at the German. Whatever it was, The Thrill had passed through him like a thunderbolt, and he could not recapture it. He felt sullen and slow.

"We need you to become a *madman,*" Obermeier went on. "Three goals. Absolutely impossible to make up. But I've *seen* you do the impossible. This is not the time to play the worst game of your life — you must be hero, not goat." He patted Will on the head, father to son. "Show me you are a man."

A man. Will walked onto the field in total shock. *You're in the World Cup championship, and you're playing like you're still in Fulham. These are the Brazilians. The best in the world. If you beat them, you'll be famous forever. Obermeier's right. Be a man.*

He took a deep breath and trotted toward the bench. He

heard the crowd roaring, but knew it wasn't for him; it was for the Brazilian team emerging from the clubhouse. He looked up into the stands — an ocean of dark faces rooting against him. Well, *fuck them!* He was the Blond Arrow! He did the impossible, *regularly.*

At first, Will's brilliance was all show on the Maracana field. Uncanny dribbling, sudden changes of direction creating paths where none existed, impossible velocity in the smallest spaces — but no support, not even a half-chance at goal.

Then, nine minutes into the second half, Will stepped in front of a bullet, a streaking pass meant for the Brazilian sweeper Ramon Palero.

The white ball dropped like a stone from Will's shoulder. Almost in the same motion, his right leg flew back, and he felt a small muscle tear in his thigh, the pain corkscrewing into his knee socket.

No matter. Will sent the ball flying toward the upper-left-hand corner of the Brazilian goal. The keeper could barely raise his arm, let alone stop the ball as it rocketed past him.

"*Gooool de America!*" Will heard the loudspeaker, and believed the words to be true. "*Gooool de Will Shepherd!*"

The Thrill exploded inside his brain. Adrenaline punched through his body, and the pain in his thigh and knee vanished. He felt all-powerful, the way he had the night before, when Victoria had taunted him. *All-powerful!*

The striker!

The goal scorer!

No one was on the playing field but *him!* The *loner!*

With only three minutes left in the game, he broke free again. He furiously pushed the ball down the left touchline, faked a pass inside but kept it himself, evading a defender who could only look after him in disbelief. His legs stopped suddenly, went forward again; stopped; *accelerated* from the dead stop.

Then he shot, and the ball cannoned forward, a white blur, nearly ripping the net at the back of the Brazilian goal.

"*Gooool de America . . . Gooool de Will Shepherd.*"

Time remaining: two minutes and forty-six seconds.

Still time enough.

37

THE HUGE, SPRAWLING CROWD had grown silent and still, their attention as much on the stadium clock as on the furious action on the field. Less than three minutes to play in what was suddenly a cliff-hanger.

No single player could defeat a great team. Not even Will Shepherd could accomplish such a feat.

Everyone watching believed that; yet none of them could be absolutely sure. He was such a dazzling scorer, perhaps the greatest striker ever. He was a magician, or perhaps he'd made a deal with the devil.

Will intercepted a pass to the Brazilian right wing and, like an eagle, swooped down the field at incredible speed. Everything was concentration now, moves practiced a thousand — no, a million times. He feinted left and went right at nearly ninety degrees, past a stranded defender. He could see the goalkeeper ahead of him, a patch of enemy color.

If he were God he couldn't stop me, Will thought, and saw fear in the keeper's eye. He switched the ball from his right leg to his left.

He used his elbow deftly on a defender. He curled *softly* to the right.

The ninety minutes were up. There would be a few seconds of stoppage time. Plenty of time to be immortal, to join the likes of Pele and Cruyff.

Relax. Let this stretch out. Feel it course through your body like heroin.

The Brazilian goalkeeper moved left, anticipating Will's shot, leaving the right corner of the goal free.

Not much daylight — a tiny sliver.

The referee was raising his whistle. In seconds it would blow and the game would be over.

It was a shot Will was famous for, a curve hit with the left foot that broke from left to right, and Will measured it carefully in his mind's eye. *An opening as wide as the gates of Hell!*

He was aware of so many things: the sudden, chilling silence of the stadium, the sound of his own breath, and even of the ball on the turf, the look of pure horror on the keeper's face, the futile pursuit of the Brazilian sweeper.

His father's face rose up before him. His eyes. His dead, open eyes on the surface of that swimming pool.

And with the force of a whirlwind the furies attacked, demons took possession of his instincts, his legs, his soul. *No! He wouldn't let that control him!*

With a roar and a shudder, Will drew back his left leg and kicked. He hit it smoothly, perfectly.

He wanted to laugh at all those who had ever doubted him — he wanted to scream in each and every face looking down from their precious stadium seats.

The crowd went mad. Literally insane. Strangers hugged and kissed, and a wild dance began, one hundred thousand people participating in the frenzy. From outside and in, horns and trumpets blared, and a thousand streamers flew upward toward the moon.

As soon as he had shot, Will had fallen, all strength gone, and now as he lay on the ground he strained for the sound he didn't hear: "*Gooool de America . . . Gooool de Will Shepherd.*"

He saw the players running off the field, fearful of the crazed mob of spectators streaming toward them. Puzzled, he tried to stand up. Fear swept through his body. He couldn't get to his feet.

But the game is a draw, Will thought. *There's extra time to play. No one but the players should be allowed on the field. Get those assholes off. Get them off the field!*

A stricken Wolf Obermeier reached his side and tried to help him to his feet. "Too bad," his coach said. "How do Americans put it? Tough luck."

"The game's a draw," Will said, but the look on Obermeier's face told him the truth, and at that instant all of his furies emerged, even noisier and more terrifying than the thousands of fans descending on them. *His father was in that crowd, carrying his mother. She was the dead one now. Blood gushed from her open mouth. His father held her out to Will, like a trophy.*

The Haunting.

And Will Shepherd began to scream. Finally, he understood. Brazil had won the World Cup.

The Blond Arrow had missed the shot of his life.

He had failed.

It's all your fault.

It's always been your fault.

38

IT WAS LIKE CARNIVAL in Rio that night, and there was no more sensuous, no wilder time to be had anywhere in the world. Conga lines weaved along every street. Will had rented a red Corvette, and he drove it through the city like a madman. *The football bum, the football loser,* he thought. *The werewolf of Rio.*

"Your name is Angelita, right?" he asked the woman slouched beside him in the speeding car. She was tall and dark-haired; very slender and quite strikingly beautiful. She wanted to feel the Blond Arrow, she'd told him. She wanted the Arrow *deep inside her.*

"Yes, I am Angelita. You keep asking me, as if my name is going to change. Maybe the way you drive we'll both be called Dead On Arrival soon."

"That's cute. That's very funny," Will said, shifting the car into fourth on the wide avenue that ran alongside Copacabana. "A funny and beautiful woman can be very dangerous, no?"

She tossed her black hair back and laughed. "You're afraid I might steal your heart, right?"

"No, not at all, Angelita. I'm afraid that you *won't* steal my heart. I'm afraid that no one will. Do you follow me?"

"Not a word of it, darling."

"Perfect!"

He took her up to his hotel suite. The room was well illuminated by the twinkling lights of the city, so he didn't bother to switch on the lamp. The rhythm from drum-beating bands on the street sounded as though they were right in the room.

"Put it in me right here, right now, Will Shepherd, numero nueve. I don't want to wait one second longer," she screamed at him as they embraced.

That had been hours and hours ago. He had put it in her all right. She'd moaned, then she had tried to scream. Then she desperately tried to pull the "arrow" out of her heart.

"What have you done? Oh my God, what did you do to me?"

"I wanted to steal your heart," Will said in a whisper. "Did I?"

Now, he kept forgetting her name. Who the hell was she? Oh yes, yes, it was Angelita.

Now *Angelita* lay in the bathtub of his hotel room. He looked down at her and knew that he'd finally gone too far, even for him.

He had gone too far — slipped right over the edge.

If my fans could see me now, he thought. Here's the real Will Shepherd. This is the worthless scum I am. Beneath the handsome exterior beats a heart of darkness. Conrad, right? Will had finished *that* book in school. He'd understood it perfectly from the very first pages, until the end.

No one knew him, no one got it — except maybe Angelita. Now, she knows, doesn't she?

The woman's brown eyes were glazed over, looking up at him — looking *sideways* it seemed. He was her god, right? Her savior from the mean streets of Rio. She had wanted so badly to fuck with such a big star. Well, she had been fucked.

In his hand he held a glass filled with red liquid. He toasted Angelita. He saluted the woman with her own blood.

"I'm sorry," he whispered. "Well, I'm not, but I wish I were."

He drank from the glass, and knew he was lost. He had committed a murder. There would be a trial — he would be found guilty. Beads of perspiration formed on his forehead.

Blond Arrow — silver stiletto — vampire — what difference did it make, really.

He was going to prison for life.

39

I KNEW all about "falling from grace," but "falling in love" was something I realized I hadn't really understood before. It was happening though, gradually, beautifully, between Patrick and me. Day by day, our feelings for each other grew deeper and deeper. It was different from infatuation, which we'd experienced as well.

Let me count the ways that I was learning to love Patrick.

There was the way he reminded me, nearly every day, that I was very special, a worthwhile person. I began to believe it for the first time in my life.

There was the way Patrick set out to learn everything about the kind of music I wrote and sang, and how he came to understand and appreciate it better than most music writers for *Rolling Stone* and *Spin*.

There was the way he and Jennie could talk about anything and everything; and the way the three of us could do the same.

There was the way in which he surprised and delighted me with his stories, his wit, his insights.

In fact, during the first half year we were together, the only troubling point wasn't about us — *it was Patrick's son*. Peter was a genuine bastard — the opposite of his father. Peter tried to take over his father's company during that period, but he failed. Patrick mourned his failure with Peter, what he called, *his loss of his only son.*

Which was a good segue for me, I was thinking one afternoon in Bedford. If there could be a segue for this —

This was so hard, so very difficult for me. I was absolutely petrified. I sighed, got myself as ready as I'd ever be, and then said.

"We're going to have a baby, Patrick."

We were sitting in the living room in Bedford. I was about ready to show. Show, I figured — and therefore tell. We had used discretion and protection, but somehow I got pregnant anyway.

Even though I was an "artist" and "music person," I was traditional at heart and the pregnancy shook me to my roots. I told Jennie immediately. She said, "You love Patrick and he loves you. I love you both. I'm happy we're pregnant." That helped me a lot.

Now, Patrick's face registered a half-dozen emotions: amazement, shock, consternation, worry, doubt — but then — joy. Fabulous, unmistakable joy. The smile that I loved so much.

"When's the baby due? My God, tell me everything, Maggie."

"Five months, twelve days. Doctor Gamache didn't specify the hour."

He was smiling very broadly now. He held both my hands. "Boy or girl?"

"A boy, according to the amniocentesis. Allie? Do you like that name?"

"It's a lovely name." He shook his head in wonder. "I'm very happy about it, Maggie. I couldn't possibly be happier. Have I told you lately how much I love you?" He continued to grin.

"Yes," I whispered, "but tell me again. I never get tired of hearing it."

*   *   *

And that night, with a vividness I thought had long ago disappeared, I remembered. I remembered *him*.

Phillip returned to try and spoil everything.

He was drunk, as he often was. He could barely walk. He barged in the front door, yelling my name, and I cowered in the kitchen, not answering him, even when he was only a few feet away.

He had been so different when we'd first met in Newburgh. He'd been an officer and a gentleman, a scholar as well. He had swept me off my nineteen-year-old feet. I had been so needy, so alone. How could I have known that his role as professor frustrated him; that he'd joined the army to fight, but had been ordered to teach instead. He had to follow those orders, and was determined that I follow his.

"When I call you, you say, 'Yes, Phillip,'" he pronounced with a superior smirk.

"Not when you're like this. No, Phillip. Not with me. Not ever."

The back of his hand slashed across my mouth. "Whenever I call, you say, 'Yes, Phillip,'" he repeated.

I said nothing. His wire-rimmed glasses were crooked on his nose. He looked like the effete snob that he was so afraid of being.

"Maggie," he said softly, ominously.

I didn't answer. His hand rose again, this time a fist. He wasn't powerfully built, but he outweighed me by sixty pounds.

"Yes, Phillip, fuck you," I said. I don't swear like that, but I did then.

"What? What did you say, woman? What the hell did I just hear?"

"You heard me."

He stood stock-still. Then he leered. "Okay," he said, "let's fuck."

He lunged for me, swaying drunkenly. I ran up the back stairs to the attic, and slammed the door in his face.

Phillip kept guns up there. There were guns everywhere in the good soldier's house. I took one and cocked it. I pointed it at the attic door, waiting until his wild, angry face appeared.

"Take another step and I'll shoot, I will, Phillip." I was surprised at how calm I sounded, though I didn't feel calm.

He stared at me, tried to stare me down, but he didn't move. Then he began to laugh, a monstrous cackle.

"Oh, sweetheart," he said when he could control himself. *"Sweetheart, sweetheart. You've won this round. But you'll live to regret it."*

I was still regretting it, after all these years.

40

ON A PROMISING BLUE-SKIED MORNING, an uncharacteristically nervous and nonplussed Patrick had to rush me to the Northern Westchester Hospital in Mount Kisco, New York. He was so distraught, so unlike himself, it was charming and funny. Jennie came with us, and she was by far in the best shape, in the most control of the three of us.

As Patrick's car hurtled down narrow, pine-wooded roads, I couldn't keep dark thoughts from my mind though. *Think of the baby*, I told myself, but instead I remembered newspaper and magazine stories that had been tormenting me ever since my pregnancy became public:

"MAGGIE BRADFORD'S GREATEST LOVE SONG: Inside Story of the Not-So-Secret Hold Maggie Has Over Patrick."

How could our beautiful relationship be made to sound so shameful? Who wrote stories like these? Who wanted to read them? I had told Patrick I didn't care what anybody said, but the media could be so cruel. I felt wounded, humiliated.

Of course — at the time — I had no idea of how really savage they could be.

"Patrick, I know you're hurrying ... but please, go a little faster if you can. Please?"

Dr. Lewis Gamache was waiting for us at the hospital.

"Hi there, Mom." He squinted from behind silver-framed bifocals. I had found him months before in the village of Chappaqua. He was a general practitioner who specialized in obstetrics, and I trusted him more than the far more famous doctors who had offered their services in New York.

"Hello, Lewis. I feel kind of shitty." I tried to smile, but felt I was going to faint.

"That's fine. It means you're almost there." He led me to a wheelchair, and I was taken inside.

Almost there, indeed! At eleven o'clock that night, two nurses in white tunics sped me down bright hospital corridors to the operating room. My body was soaked with perspiration. My hair was matted and looked almost brown. I felt clammy and cold. The pain was unbearable, twice what I remembered while having Jennie.

Dr. Gamache was waiting in the operating room. He was his usual wide-eyed and enthusiastic self.

"Hello, Maggie. What took you so long?"

"Ooohh." I shut my eyes as a contraction came again. "I was having too much fun in labor."

"Let's rock and roll," he said. I got the joke, but I didn't laugh.

At 11:19 in the morning, Dr. Gamache said, "Maggie, you've got yourself a little boy," and laid the baby beside me so I could look at him. He seemed to be yawning. *Bored already with planet Earth?* But he was such a beauty.

He received the classic rear-end slap, rather than the foot flick. I could hear his thin, barely perceptible cry.

"I don't think he's got your lungs," Dr. Gamache said. "Nurse, put the baby on the table warmer, please."

"His name is Allen," I said, and promptly passed out.

41

PATRICK NEARLY *FLEW* into my hospital room. He was beaming. He hurried to my bed, and we kissed. He *was* Paul Newman, and Spencer Tracy — all wrapped in one. He really was so wonderful: thoughtful, compassionate, tender, caring. Patrick wanted to marry me — he'd already *asked,* but something about "marriage," and my experience with Phillip, had made me ask him to wait. Patrick said that he understood. I hoped he did. I also hoped he would ask again — *soon.*

Something crunched in his sport jacket pocket as he hugged me. Curious, I reached inside.

"You've gone too far this time, buster," I said and smiled and rolled my eyes. "Cigars? How corny can you get?"

"I'm a corny guy." Patrick shrugged. "The cigars are for my friends. I bought Irish whiskey for the unwed father."

"Did you see Allie yet?"

"You bet. The *testicles* on him. Bigger than his feet. I'm so impressed."

I laughed. "That *would* interest you."

"I thought it might interest his mother just a little."

"To know that her son is well equipped for the world."

"Exactly right, and very well put."

Patrick reached out and held me gently against his chest. I could feel his heart beating. I loved that feeling, more and more so each day.

I can't think of a better father, I thought.

Then I said it aloud for Patrick to hear. I had never been happier in my life. I would marry Patrick soon, I knew. We were already a family though, and happier than most that I knew.

That night, I sang for little Allie for the first time.

42

THIS IS how it happened, dear readers. The third murder you've heard so many horrifying rumors about on TV and in the press. This is my confession, and it's never been printed anywhere before.

Patrick loved his work, the grand hotels he had built; I was sure that he loved Allie, Jennie, and me; and he loved the sea, loved to sail. The only trouble in his life was the continuing fights with his son, Peter, over control of his company, and particularly The Cornelia Hotel. In the process, Peter also made it clear that he despised me. Patrick and I decided we had to live with Peter's attacks. So be it.

I will never forget that day in early May. It was the first sail of the new spring: some time together for the two of us.

We were dressed early that morning, sharing hot chocolate by five. My new and absolutely wonderful live-in, Mrs. Leigh, appeared and wished us a happy day off. "Don't worry about anything here, Mrs. Bradford." With Mrs. Leigh, I didn't have to. She had brought up two beautiful children of her own, and she was already part of our family.

Patrick and I drove out to Port Washington on Long Island. *We had a whole day off to be together. What a special treat that was!*

By six-thirty, we were sauntering down the sun-spotted deck of the proud, Victorian Manhasset Bay Yacht Club. The air was cool, but the morning promised pleasure and relaxation. I stopped Patrick halfway down the walkway and gave him a hug and a kiss. I couldn't resist.

"I love you," I whispered. "Simple and uncomplicated as that might sound."

"Hard to come by," he smiled, "but so spectacular once you find it. I love you too, Maggie."

We reached the *Rebellion* a moment or two later. We would be sailing due east, Patrick told me, "into the sun, away from the earth."

"The storm last week beat the hell out of these boats, ours included," Patrick said, as he began a quick inspection. "Still water in here. Motor battery's probably dead. Antenna for the ship-to-shore broken. Shit. Remind me never to build a luxury liner. It'd be another *Titanic*."

The *Rebellion* made it out of the yacht club around quarter past seven. We were on our bright and merry way. As much as I loved spending nearly every waking moment with Allie, as much as I missed him already, I needed a morning off. I had been missing Patrick.

It was a blue-skied morning, the kind of day that automatically made me feel good. I could see Patrick relax at the helm. On the horizon, a forty-eight-foot ketch moved slowly, probably toward the Caribbean.

By noon, our boat was gliding through tiny whitecaps, miles away from the madness of New York. The hotel, Peter O'Malley, even Jennie and Allie, were forgotten. We were together on the privacy of the sea. I wondered if this was the day Patrick would ask me to marry him again.

Smoky, soot-black clouds appeared suddenly from the northwest: a storm, rushing toward us rapidly. The temperature fell at least ten degrees within five minutes.

"Oh *shit*," I said. "Plan a parade, right? Boo, hiss! I can't stand it."

Patrick looked at the clouds with anxious eyes. "I'll call the Coast Guard for a weather check. Maybe we can wait this out."

He walked toward the cabin, then stopped in midstride. "Hell, I can't call. Ship-to-shore's busted. Guess that means we head back in. Take the wheel, Maggie. Hold on tight."

"Aye, aye."

I wrestled with the steering wheel while Patrick reefed the mainsail. The pull was still too heavy at the helm. Patrick decided to change to a smaller storm jib from the sail locker. As a last resort, he'd take the jib down and motor back to Manhasset.

Then the storm hit! A chilling fog curved around the high-peaked sailboat, and rain poured down, soaking us. The wind howled. Seawater splashed across the deck like a flash flood. The frightening power and force of nature were in evidence everywhere.

My hand slipped on the wheel, and I had to fight to keep us on course. There was an exhilaration in the action, but beneath it, like a coiled snake ready to strike, fear had begun to lurk. This wasn't fun anymore.

Patrick cursed loudly, then he *really* cursed. He ran, slipping and sliding, to where a loosened sail flapped like a wet bed sheet.

He seemed to hesitate as he reached the sail, and drag his left leg. That was the impression I had, of his leg *dragging*.

He paused, as if he'd forgotten something, then fell to his knees, as though someone had hit him on the back of his head.

"Patrick!" I called out.

He tried to stand. I saw him raise his hand to his chest. Then he collapsed.

"*Patrick!*"

I rushed across the slippery deck to his side. His face was as white as the mainsail, and his breathing was irregular. He lay on his side, and winced in pain as I moved him onto his back. Suddenly, I couldn't breathe. A tight fist clenched in the pit of my stomach.

I found wool blankets and a strip of greenish tarp. I covered Patrick as well as I could. I took his hand in mine. I was having trouble focusing my eyes.

"You went away," he whispered. "Please don't do it again. Let me look at you, Maggie."

I tried to keep his body quiet as waves rolled over us, soaking us.

"I'm here. And don't you go away either. Everything will be fine. You're going to be all right."

I believed it, at least part of me did, but the fear-snake inside me uncoiled, and I had to turn my face away so he wouldn't see it. Then I looked back at him.

Patrick's face had turned an ashen gray. Beads of perspiration appeared on his forehead and upper lip, though the wind was cold. *Oh please, God. Oh please,* I kept thinking. *I love him so much. Please don't do this.*

"Just in case I'm not around for last call," he said, "I want you to be happy. And make our son Allie happy, which I know you will. And make sure Jennie doesn't marry an Irishman. *Promise,*" he whispered in the voice I loved so.

"I promise," I finally whispered, fighting back the tears.

"I love you, sweet one," he said. "I love you, Maggie. You are the best."

Patrick had that familiar, wry look in his eyes, but suddenly they changed. He stared past me.

Then a strange sound rose up from deep inside his chest. He let go of my hand. He just let go of me. *Simple and uncomplicated, as our love had been.* I screamed as I stared into Patrick's eyes. *Oh, God, please don't let him die.*

I held him tightly and began to cry. I put my head on his chest, now silent and still.

Oh, please ... please, don't let this happen. Whoever's in charge, show us mercy.

Patrick couldn't hear me. He was gone. As swiftly as the storm that swirled about us had come up.

43

I MUST HAVE HELD HIM for an hour, not caring what would happen to me or to the floundering boat that bore us.

The storm had traveled due east, and the waters were calm again, though I barely noticed. A feeble sun cast streaks of amber light on lapping caps of grayish-green water.

I sat helpless beside him on the lonely, quietly rocking deck. I thought of the times we had shared together, and each time I did, I started to cry again.

Don't go away. Let me look at you.

Don't go away, Patrick. Don't go away and leave me ... oh, Padriac, oh, Patrizio, I moaned.

Sailors from the Coast Guard found me drifting at the reddish edge of sunset. I was still cradling Patrick in my arms.

So there you have it — *that's how I killed him. That's my confession.*

BOOK THREE

WILL

44

WHEN WILL HEARD loud and persistent knocking at the door of his suite in the Rio Hilton, he shivered. He staggered from his bed, and hid himself in the bathroom.

He was barely able to navigate the few steps without falling. *Go away, whoever you are. Get the hell away from here!*

He heard the front door of the suite open and the sound of voices. A maid, and someone else.

Jesus Christ, they can't come in here — whoever it is. Not now!

"Thanks for letting me in," the voice said. "I can manage from here."

Palmer!

Who in hell invited him?

Nobody can be here — not even my brother Palmer! I'm out of control and I don't know if I can ever get it back!

Palmer Shepherd's eyes took in details of the puzzle: the closed bathroom door; the mirror laid flat on the night table bearing a razor, a rolled up hundred dollar bill, the remnants of God knows how much cocaine. An empty bottle of tequila on the floor. A half-full glass of a red liquid on the other night table. Port? Cinzano?

But where was Will? Where in hell had Will gone to?

Here I am, little brother!

With the howl of a werewolf, a naked Will was on him, wrestling him to the ground, pinning his arms. Then Will was sitting on his stomach as he had when they were boys.

"You lose. I win!"

Only this time Will's eyes were scarily wild, and his body — God, his body! — was covered with blood.

Palmer stared up at his brother in disbelief and horror. "Jesus, Will, what in hell did you do to yourself?"

Will laughed loudly, manically. "Cut myself shaving."

Will sprang off him and appeared to dance across the room. He picked up the half-full glass and offered it to his brother. "Cut *her* shaving too. Blood actually goes with tequila. Taste?"

"You cut *who* shaving? What the hell happened here? What are you on?"

"Angelita. I've got her body in the bathroom. She's just a whore." Once more he held out the glass of dark red liquid. "I'm afraid I drank most of it myself. Breakfast of *champions*."

"You didn't," Palmer whispered. He rose to his feet on unsteady legs. "You couldn't have."

"Didn't *what*? Couldn't have *what*?"

"Kill her."

"Well, I don't know." Will's eyes were easily as large as silver dollars. Mad eyes. "Let's find out. Let's have a look."

Will opened the bathroom door, and shared his secret life with his brother.

"What's the verdict, little brother? Did I, or did I not? Are you going to help me this time?"

45

FOR ONCE the outrageous stories in the fan magazines were mostly accurate and true, and maybe even understated. Will knew this, and so did his brother.

Will *was* dangerous, even more dangerous than the tabloids suspected. He *had* spent six weeks in a private New York hospital, recovering from a "breakdown." There had been a "substance problem" in Rio.

He'd done much worse things than a little cocaine — but he'd gotten away with them. It had cost him — a sizable bribe every week to his beloved brother — but at least he was still free and on the loose. He wasn't in prison for the rest of his life.

Will and Palmer had decided he ought to live somewhere other than London for a while. The little bastard Palmer had insisted on it, actually. It was a part of their "deal." For some reason, Will found himself drawn to New York anyway.

He sublet an apartment on the East Side, and loved it so much he went looking for a house. He happened to read in the *Times* that Maggie Bradford had a place in Westchester. So did Winnie Lawrence. Will decided to look in Westchester first.

He was still a huge fan of Maggie's songs. Her music was

healing; he was convinced of it. He'd even talked to his hotsy-totsy Fifth Avenue shrink about the songs, especially the lyrics. The doc was also a Maggie Bradford fan, so he understood what Will was talking about — at least he thought he did.

Will fantasized about meeting Maggie one day in Westchester. He was certain it could be arranged somehow. He was clever enough to accomplish that, wasn't he?

46

THIS IS THE PART that doesn't make much sense. Maybe that's why it fascinates so many people, holds their attention over weeks and even months as the murder trial approaches. This is the real mystery — even for me it is. My time with Will Shepherd, my dark night of the soul. How could it have happened? How did it happen?

After Patrick's death, *his heart attack,* I kept to myself, with only Jennie and Allie, and stayed miles away from the media, whom I had come to dread and despise during my pregnancy. On a lushly green spring morning nearly a year after Patrick's death, I was working in the garden. Allie was playing by my side. We were interrupted by the security guard, hired to keep away unwelcome visitors — which meant, just about everybody.

"There's a Mr. Nathan Bailford here," he said. "Knows you don't want to see anyone, but says it's very important."

Nathan was a neighbor I didn't know well. I did know he was a high-powered lawyer, and that he was instrumental in keeping Peter O'Malley from interfering in the completion of

The Cornelia. What could he want? Why was he here now? Was there more trouble with Peter?

"Let Mr. Bailford come up," I reluctantly told the guard. "We have company," I told Allie. "Let's go get pretty."

The lawyer was in his late fifties, but looked about forty-five. He smiled in greeting, but his charcoal gray suit, white shirt, and a crimson-and-gold rep's tie were lawyer-serious, and not one silver-and-black curly hair was out of place.

Nathan Bailford took my outstretched hand in both his own. "You know, I've driven by I don't know how many times since the funeral. I've thought of you often, didn't know whether to barge in or leave you alone."

"I'm glad you finally decided to come." *Patrick's friend is my friend,* I thought, and tried to be hospitable.

"So, are you okay?" he asked.

"Oh, it comes and it goes," I told him. "The nights are the worst. I'm kind of having a bad decade."

Nathan Bailford didn't know how to answer. Finally, he just smiled. Good decision. I liked him for that.

"Actually, I'm here on business," he admitted, when coffee was served on the patio. "It's something — well, it just couldn't wait any longer. As you know, it's been almost a year since Patrick died. I *had* to stop by today."

He sipped his coffee and I noticed that his hand shook. He loosened his tie. "Patrick's will is finally scheduled to be read. It's been an incredible mess. Never seen anything like it. My staff and I have been preparing everything according to his explicit and typically complicated wishes. Maggie, I've got to tell you. It's going to mean a bad fight. Peter O'Malley is not a happy camper right now. Patrick was right about his son — Peter can be a real bastard. He is one."

I wasn't ready for this. I had given no thought to Patrick's money or his estate, and Nathan's edginess frightened me. The idea of a fight with Peter was disturbing, but the thought of the media hearing of it bothered me even more.

"What's that got to do with me?" I asked. "Nathan, I really can't get involved in all this."

Nathan Bailford stared into my eyes. "Patrick's left controlling interest in the corporation to you, Jennie, and Allen. He's bequeathed Peter a flat sum, a tremendous sum, of course, but twenty-seven percent of the business is yours and your children's."

I couldn't believe what I had heard. *I couldn't believe it!* "H-how much is it worth?" I asked. I *actually* stuttered.

"Over two hundred million dollars in cash, stock, and real estate holdings. Give or take a few mil. A lot, Maggie."

I felt a crazy burst of anger. "Oh, Nathan, why? I don't need twenty-seven percent or any percent. I've got money, more than I need. I don't want anything to do with it. I really don't."

All of a sudden, I found myself laughing, which made Nathan Bailford sit back in his chair.

But God, it was *funny!* It really was. I had just inherited something like two hundred million dollars, and I felt as though I had been put in prison.

47

HE WAS CARRYING JENNIE! How could that be? I couldn't believe what I was seeing, but I *was* seeing it. There it was. Ba-da-boom.

Will Shepherd, the soccer player who had tried to pick me up at the Trevelyans' party in London, was at my front door, carrying *my daughter!* It definitely was he. No mistaking that. I'd never forget the long blond hair and his face, and a few other things about him as well.

The guard had called from the front gate saying that Jennie had hurt herself and that a man from the neighborhood was bringing her up to the house. When I saw who it was, I was absolutely stunned.

This was insane.

I didn't ask about Jennie — she looked *too* comfortable, dressed in a sweatsuit, her legs dangling from his arms.

"Put her down! Please put Jennie down," I loudly told him.

"Where, ma'am?" Will Shepherd said in a soft, calm voice. Jennie was no more difficult for him to carry than a pillow.

"There. On the couch in the living room is great. Please, put her down!"

He looked at me with troubled eyes, which gave me pause. "Hey," he said, "she was hurt. I nearly hit her with my car. Lucky thing she jumped aside and only twisted her ankle. It happened right in front of the Lawrences'. That's where I'm staying. I was just going out. Didn't see her."

"It's kind of you to have brought her. Thank you," I managed. My voice was cold. "Now please leave. Thank you though. I mean that."

Jennie sat up on the couch where he had placed her. "You could at least offer him some coffee," she said. "Something?"

"I'm sure Mr. Shepherd's done enough for us and wants to get on about his business."

"You know who I am?" he asked. Now he looked even more puzzled. *The bastard.*

"We've met," I said. Curt, just like that.

He seemed surprised. "Really? Where? I don't go backstage, though I've heard you sing. It was at the Albert Hall. The Queen was there."

"Not at a concert. At a party." Curt.

"If so, I don't remember, and I'd remember meeting you. I'm quite certain of that."

He knelt to check Jennie's ankle. "Doesn't seem like there's anything broken," he said. "I've broken enough bones to be a decent judge of that. Still, you should probably call a doctor."

"As soon as you go, that's what I'm going to do. Thanks for the advice."

He rose slowly. "Nice to meet you, Jennie. Hope you feel better soon." He turned toward the door.

"Good-bye, Mr. Shepherd," Jennie said. Suddenly, I suspected some shenanigans on her part in this. She and her friends occasionally "stalked" rock stars, so why not a sports celebrity?

"I don't want you talking to him again," I told her when the door had closed.

She stared at me, her face red. I'd never seen her this angry. "How could you act that way? *Mother*," she cried. "*God!*"

She leapt from the couch, gave a small cry, and collapsed. She *had* been hurt. Maybe Will Shepherd had done the right thing in helping her home. Maybe I had been wrong about him this time.

48

MY HOUSE was next door to one of the better Westchester country clubs, the Lake Club in Bedford. The members of the Lake Club paid astronomical dues and fees to ensure that the finest chefs and groundskeepers were employed there. Its carefully manicured lawns and private gardens reminded me of Gstaad, Lake Forest, Saint-Tropez, places I had visited on my concert tours of Europe.

I was at "the club" for a party in late September. It was one of my first forays back into the real world.

I had to stop to catch my breath at the top of the steep fieldstone steps that led from the driveway to the main clubhouse. The last big party I had been to was for the opening of The Cornelia, and a memory of Patrick came back so clearly that tears welled up in my eyes.

"Damn," I whispered. *Get a grip, Maggie.*

The beautiful lawn was filled with people. Dimly, I became aware of a wet bar, and a jazz combo playing quietly beside it. I said hello to a few Bedford residents, smiled at others whose names I should have known but didn't. A Broadway producer took me aside to insist that I name a price and the talent I wanted around me for a show. I told him that the offer was flattering, but really premature, and that I would call him when I was ready. I was pressured by his intensity though, and began to feel an all-too-familiar anxiety building.

The recluse of Greenbriar Road strikes again! I thought. It was too much too fast. I shouldn't have come. *Damn it, damn it!*

Soon I excused myself, and went to be alone in the gardens that branched off the Lake Club's riding ring. I felt like such a fool; a loser, outcast, freak. I remembered being that way all the time when I was younger; too tall for most boys, and a stutterer as well.

The gardens were empty, and I inhaled the fragrant air, relaxing into a kind of hazy satisfaction. This was better.

" 'The loss of grace is the saddest trip . . . but grace can be rewon, Maggie.' "

My words, whispered close behind me. I wheeled to face the man who spoke them.

Will Shepherd was standing next to me.

I actually *jumped*.

49

I TOOK A STEP BACK, but not too far. Somehow, he didn't seem quite as threatening in the colorful gardens and in broad daylight.

"I came to find out why you were so cold to me when I brought your daughter home."

My eyes rolled involuntarily. *He couldn't be that thick*, I thought. "You really don't remember, do you?"

He shook his head. Sunlight bounced off his blond curls.

"What are you talking about? Please tell me," he said.

"The costume ball at the Trevelyans. You asked me to go home with you — be with you. You were very crude. Worse than crude, actually."

"I don't remem—" He stopped, and slapped his forehead. He actually blushed. "Oh my God," he said. "Oh shit. You have to forgive me. I was drunk, maybe drugged, and completely crazy."

"And disgusting," I added. "Don't forget that. Well, nice seeing you again. Good-bye."

I turned and began to walk back toward the party.

He ran to catch up with me.

"I'm not drunk now, not drugged, and I'm just a little crazy. Please talk to me for a moment. It's important. To me it is. Please? I think I can explain my behavior."

"But do I want to hear it?" I said to him.

"Fair enough. I'm sure I deserve that, though I still don't remember much of what I did."

I studied him for a few seconds. He was dressed in a rumpled white linen suit, and the color of his hair seemed gold. He was tan, and definitely handsome — I had to give him that.

"I only want to tell you one thing," he said, affecting a sincerity I couldn't believe was genuine. "You're an inspiration to me, to a lot of people. I heard you sing at the concert for the Queen, and I thought you were singing to me. I know you weren't, but that's what I felt. You touched me, so thank you. That wasn't so bad, was it?"

Despite myself, I turned toward him. I saw pain in his eyes. " 'Loss of Grace'?" I asked.

"That song more than any other, though I loved them all, well, most of them. I was going through a bad patch at the time. You reminded me that grace could be rewon."

"Yes. Well. Have you rewon it?" I asked.

His expression grew sadder. He suddenly seemed very genuine, almost human. "No, I'm afraid not. Not in this lifetime. Not after . . . my performance in Rio."

I shook my head. I was lost.

"In Rio? I'm sorry."

For the first time, he smiled. I hadn't seen him smile before, and it was something to see. "You mean you don't know?"

"I'm afraid not. I seem to remember that when we first met I told you I knew nothing about sports. Sorry, but I don't keep a little scrapbook of your clippings. We have one Michael Jordan mug from McDonald's at the house. That's about it for our sports collection."

"Well thank God about that," he said. The smile remained. Turned down, but still present.

We were silent for a moment. *He's shy with me,* I thought. *He doesn't know what to say next.*

Oh boy, Maggie, don't start this. You won't, of course, but don't even think about it.

"I ought to go back," I said. "My date —"

"He can wait a few more minutes, can't he? Take a walk with an old retired gent first."

I hesitated. "I was about to leave."

"Don't leave yet. Please. We were talking about you last night at dinner. Winnie Lawrence, June, and I."

"Oh?"

"They told me about Patrick O'Malley. I'm very sorry."

"Yes. It was terrible." There was nothing I wanted to add.

We walked through a tunnel of drooping pine trees, a lamp-lit watercolor undercourse. We began to talk of all sorts of un-expected things: the old Harlem River Railroad line (Will was a bug on railroads); how rural Westchester compared with rural England; a recent Jeffrey Archer novel we both had read. He was as correct with me as a schoolboy, and I felt my own shyness coming back.

I did fear I was being conned. But I figured he was trying so very hard . . . and he was sweet that day. And, I have to admit, *to be truthful,* he was gorgeous to look at.

A patch of laughter, scattered party applause, snuck through the blackthorn bushes. I looked at my wristwatch.

"I don't believe it. We've been talking for over an hour. I do have to go. It's my night to cook. Will, I'm sorry."

"I'm not. Not a bit. I'm some terrific guest of honor though. This could be my last retirement party. I'd better go back too."

As we walked back to the clubhouse, he took my arm for a second, a gentle touch on my elbow, then let it go. "I needed that," he said. "I haven't talked to anyone like this in a long, long time."

"I haven't either." I admitted. I smiled. "There — we've shared a secret."

"Could we see each other again? I'm really not the way you think."

I knew he would ask, and I knew my answer. "I'm afraid not. It's too soon for me."

"You're right," he said. "Besides, there are far better men for you than a retired football bloke."

I liked his self-deprecation, at the same time suspecting it might be part of his seduction routine. *It must be terrible for an athlete to retire, to be finished with a career so young. How would I feel if I had to give up singing?*

"And there are younger and more beautiful women for you," I said to him.

"I'm looking for something a little deeper than that now," he said. "And besides, you are beautiful. Don't you know that? . . . You don't, do you, Maggie?"

"I really have to go now," I said.

But I already realized he was different from what I had originally thought. He had substance, but he was very complex. Interesting.

50

MAGGIE BRADFORD was everything that her songs promised, and maybe even more, Will thought. She wasn't aware of it, but she was very attractive as well.

She was the one who could save him. He was convinced of it, and he began to be obsessed by her. He had to see her again. He listened to her songs constantly, at home, and in his car.

He planned everything carefully, beginning with a long letter asking not for a meeting, but for her understanding. Another time he wrote of his mother's desertion when he was a boy, then of his father's suicide. He told Maggie how her songs soothed and helped him, and asked only that she respond in some way.

There was no word from her, and, as was the usual case, he turned to other women. He lashed out at one of them. Nothing as bad as Rio, but scary anyway. The werewolf of New York.

But out of the blue, Maggie wrote him a letter. She told him that the first step was to face his pain, as he so obviously had. He finally called her and asked for a meeting — just once, in New York, and only for lunch.

They met at one o'clock, November 12, at the Oak Room in

the Plaza Hotel. The locale was meant to be as nonthreatening as possible. He had it all figured out. He was going to win Maggie over. He couldn't bear to lose again.

He planned to seduce her.

He planned to win.

He had no doubt that he would.

51

A MONTH AND A HALF passed before I saw Will again. He *wrote* to me several times. The letters revealed even more than talking with him had. He was deep, and also sensitive. When he finally called, I was ready to see him again. Just a lunch. Harmless enough, or so I thought.

This was lunch with Will Shepherd! Even if it was in the dark, gloomy Oak Room. I was sure a lot of women would have died for the opportunity. A few of them were actually there, it seemed, checking us out from nearby tables.

I must admit, he was nice to be with. Will was personable, articulate, warm, and he continued to be sensitive. As I look back on the meeting now, I have a terrible suspicion though: I wonder if he *rehearsed*.

"I like to talk to other people who've been in the spotlight," Will admitted. "As long as they have their heads on straight."

I grabbed at my neck. "My head okay?"

Will laughed. We both did. I knew exactly what he meant about talking with people who had experienced "star treatment." There definitely was a bonding that could happen.

"Tell me about Rio," I said to him about midway through lunch. "No, tell me some good stuff, first."

"I don't want to talk about me," Will said and waved off the question. That was unusual, and refreshing. The thing I *didn't* like about talking to most "stars" was that they loved talking about themselves. I'd have bet that Will was like that. Now I saw that I'd been wrong.

"Leave it at this," Will said. He took a sip of his wine and stared into space. "I'm changing now. I'm looking for grace re-won. Just like in your song."

"You'll find it," I said gently. He had touched me a bit. He was clearly vulnerable, and needy. I secretly liked the fact that he enjoyed my songs so much. I guess I wanted to be a part of his conversion.

"Help me, Maggie." He said the words softly.

"How? How can I possibly help you, Will?"

He looked at me so intensely I felt my cheeks burning. "Include me in your songs," he said.

I did better than that. I included him in my life. It was as though I couldn't help myself. As though the planets had conspired to do this to me.

He asked me out, hesitantly, and I found it not so much charming as riveting. He had a way of being attentive that told me I and I alone mattered. He shut out all distractions when we talked. He looked only at me, listened only to me, made me believe I was wise, and *worthy,* and special.

And so, I went out with Will Shepherd again.

It was very romantic in the beginning. It all came very slowly. It felt right.

We didn't even kiss until our fourth "date." It came naturally, at my front door, as he was saying good night. The kiss had gentleness *and* passion, and I felt myself responding almost despite myself.

I pushed him away, gently. "This will take time."

Will kissed me again, a longer kiss that was amazingly tender. For me, it was half pleasure, half pain. I wanted him and I was afraid of the need. I'd heard the stories about him; I was skeptical that he could change. And yet, he so desperately wanted to change.

This time Will moved away voluntarily. He opened the front door for me, and was gone.

My driveway was lit at night, and I stood there for a moment, watching him walk to his sports car. Long after it had disappeared into the darkness, I stared after him, my emotions confused, but definitely heightened.

52

WILL DROVE straight to Manhattan that night. He pushed his sports car to over a hundred on the Saw Mill River Parkway. Jesus, he was good! But he was also frustrated, and incredibly, painfully horny as a goat. He didn't know how much more of this slow-dance courting business he could take. He wasn't used to it.

Maggie was as straightforward and honest as her songs — but he was beginning to wonder if she was worth the challenge. He was having trouble, well, being so fucking nice all the time. Sometimes, he felt he couldn't possibly be good enough for her.

Cat and mouse, he thought as he crossed from Westchester into New York City. That's what it amounted to with women. He almost always caught them — some were just more trouble than others. It was another game really, a substitute for football, and *whatever* football was a substitute for.

Rebecca Post was an art dealer who had a big co-op on East Sixty-first Street overlooking the bridge. *Rebecca was such an easy little mouse to catch,* Will thought. Maybe she was too easy, but he could probably think of something to spice that up. Sure he could.

Will used his key to let himself into her luxury apartment. It certainly hadn't been hard to get his own key — he'd just asked, *once*.

The Blond Arrow tiptoed when he was inside the darkened apartment. He felt like an intruder. A digital clock in the living room *clicked* the time — twenty past one.

An intruder — he rather liked that. He thought he could get into it. He was an intruder — wasn't he? He *intruded* into the lives of a lot of women, and they seemed to welcome the diversion.

The werewolf of London, Paris, Frankfurt, Rome, Rio — and now New York. So be it.

He peered into the master bedroom and saw Rebecca. The dear girl was sleeping in the nude, spread out in a comfy, sexy pose on top of the sheets. Her long auburn hair fanned out across the pillow. Beautiful. Desirable as hell.

Will knew exactly what he wanted to do — *rape her, without saying a single, solitary word.* And then just leave her apartment.

That's what the Blond Arrow did — exactly what he felt like doing.

Same as it always was. Love was just a game — to be won, or lost.

53

WILL HAD TO FLY to Los Angeles for a couple of screen tests at the beginning of January. I found that I missed him more than I wanted to admit, or thought that I would. Sometimes, I feared that he was a sorcerer, a sleight-of-hand artist, a seduction artist like no other. Barry counseled me that Will was exactly that. "He's not that way with me," I told him. It was the truth.

Will came back on a Thursday, and took me to dinner in Bedford. I wore heels and a beaded black dress, a little glamorous for me, and was glad when he noticed. "I love the way you look," he said. Simple, but nice to hear.

He was in a wonderfully expansive mood. I enjoyed seeing him this way.

"The good news," Will told me, "is that the camera loves me. The bad is that I can't act." It was a funny line, and we both laughed.

He talked nonstop. He seemed genuinely amazed by his reception in Hollywood. I found that I was really happy for him. We laughed a lot over dinner. I felt completely relaxed around Will now. People kept pointing us out, but they were considerate enough to stay away. Maybe they thought that we were in love?

By the time dinner was over, it was snowing. Wind whipped the trees so they bowed like exotic dancers; the flakes bit into our eyes as we dashed for the car. Even as we ran, I wanted to reach out and hold him. I just did. It was how I felt.

Will drove home carefully, and walked me to the front door. I still wanted to be held so badly. He had on a very nice, subtle cologne. He'd only worn a sport coat and looked dashing. His cheeks were rosy red, and when he smiled, it was quite something.

"Good night," he said. "Thanks for going to dinner and listening to me talk way too much about the new career."

I didn't want him to go. *Sorcerer*, I thought.

"Hold on," I said. "It's a mess out. I don't want you driving in this storm." *There had already been too many accidents in my life.*

There was a strange, soft light in his eyes. His smile was soft and kind too. "It's only a few more miles. I think I can make it, Maggie."

"Please?" I said. "Just come in for a bit."

Will nodded, and followed me inside. He seemed reluctant to stay.

He said he had to make a quick phone call — that he was supposed to have a drink with the Lawrences and had to let them know he wouldn't be coming.

When he returned, we settled down in the living room. I'd checked on Jennie and Allie, and they were sleeping soundly. Unless someone set off a cannon in their bedrooms, they'd both be dead to the world until morning. Then I'd need the cannon to get Jennie up and ready for school.

I am a single woman, thirty-eight years old, I told myself. *I'm in control of this situation. I can handle it. I'm not doing anything wrong. I enjoy this person I'm with very, very much. Of course, he has cast a spell over me!*

"I never would have imagined *this* happening," I told Will as we sat and watched the snow fall. "The two of us like this. Snowflake watching."

"Truthfully, neither did I. I didn't think you'd give me a chance to prove that I'd finally come to my senses, become a grown-up, that I could change for the better. How am I doing? Do you see any improvement?"

"You're doing just fine. Don't push it," I said, and we both laughed.

I put my head on his shoulder and enjoyed the moment. I liked feeling his back and shoulder muscles. I really would never have imagined myself with Will, but I was so comfortable now. I even allowed myself to admit that he was an incredible hunk. I loved the clean, fresh smell of him. His hair was thick and amazing. I wondered what he liked about me.

He turned his head, and kissed me. "Not *too* grown-up," he whispered. His kiss made me a little dizzy.

It was my decision, my choice. I took Will's hand, and led the way to a guest bedroom near the pool. I was conscious of his fingers curled around mine. I'd straightened up the guest room earlier in the day. Fresh linen. Aired the space out. *Just in case.*

I guess I wanted this to happen. No, I knew that I did. *And that night, it did.*

Cut to train going through very picturesque mountainside tunnel.

Again, and again, and again.

54

SPECIAL MEMORIES — so confusing now. Like photographs that don't really tell the whole truth, like photographs that can lie.

The blue-and-white-striped Land Rover flew up the imposing rock face at the famed resort hotel in Las Veides. Will and I had three unbelievable days to ourselves. Just the two of us.

Our Mexican driver rounded a curve so fast that the Rover nearly skidded off the narrow road; a fall would have hurtled us a thousand feet down to Acapulco Bay. I held Will tightly, wanting to be as close as I could. I was into all the tiniest details: how I fit up against him, the contours of his body, every little scar and its origin; how fast his light blond beard grew. I wanted to know everything there was to know about his life, not the exaggerated stories in the tabloids.

"How about a swim, Maggie?" he asked when we got to our room. He sounded shy, and I liked the sound of his voice. "Let's throw on our suits and explore the deep blue sea."

Will and I were gently rocking back and forth, hugging each other under a revolving teak ceiling fan in our suite.

"Maybe a little later," I murmured. "We're alone right now,

and I think I want to enjoy this. I'm sure I do. Can we . . . just . . . do nothing?"

He laughed. "Okay, no deep blue sea. How about no suits, and an exploration of the intimate, private pool that management has so thoughtfully provided?"

"That sounds better. I like that idea a lot."

We kissed softly, for a long, long time, the way we often did. I had the thought: *Am I losing myself, or am I finding something I've lost along the way?*

Will slid the glass doors that opened onto a spectacular terrazzo. We continued to undress until we stood in front of the small pool that glittered with hundreds of sun diamonds and stars. Yellowbirds and colorful parrots chattered in the surrounding brazilwood trees. This was paradise, wasn't it? Or so it seemed at the time.

Through a curtain of royal palms and bougainvillea, I could see the red roofs of other cottages, but not the other private swimming pools. I liked that touch. *No one could see us either.*

With a tiny whoop, I jumped into the pool, pulling Will after me. We weren't being silly — just playful, like a couple of children.

He grabbed my arm, drew me to him. He was already hard. I slid my hands down his slender, muscular body and stroked his thighs. He was always so warm and tender with me; he was nothing like what I had expected.

We kissed again — soft and long.

Will raised me from the tile floor of the pool, and turned me so I could brace myself against the pool's edge. He slowly, slowly entered me. I closed my eyes, becoming aware of new sensations, relishing the warm sun on my face, and an even greater heat building inside.

I had never been with anyone like Will. He made me feel so special. I have to say that, because it's the truth.

55

THERE IS a powerful, powerful image that never fits for me, that will always be a mystery, a beautiful and sad and troubling mystery.

After Will and I returned from our quick trip to Mexico, we spent a long weekend doing everything the kids wanted to do. Doing *some* of the things Jennie and Allie wanted to do anyway. They were so excited, and Will was wonderful with them.

We went to New York for one day, and we played out-of-towners — the Trade Center, the Statue of Liberty, the museum mile, even the Hard Rock Cafe. But then, we spent an even more special day on the grounds around the house — as a family, seeing if that's what we all wanted.

I watched Jennie and Allie with Will, and I could tell they adored him. I was almost certain he liked being around the kids, that he ached to bring up children just right, the way it ought to be done, not the way it had happened to him. He had told me as much.

I remember seeing him with Allie that afternoon at the house. The extraordinary picture sticks with me, one that will always play on my mind.

It was an Indian summer kind of day, brilliantly sunny, in the high fifties. The two of them were riding on one of our tamer horses, a sweet mare Jennie had named Fleas. Will and Allie rode across a wide field of tall grass that looked sea-green in the light.

They had their winter jackets on, but open, acting *very manly,* both of them strikingly blond. They were laughing uproariously as Fleas loped on, seemingly in very slow motion.

Will held Allie tightly and very securely in his arms, and he was beaming with joy. I knew the happiness was real, and I loved what I saw. I loved the look on their faces.

Jennie came and stood beside me. "Aren't they just beautiful?" she said. "They look like a real dad and his boy. Oh, I love it now, Mom. I feel so good inside, so right."

"Me too," I said and hugged Jennie.

56

WILL TOLD ME everything; we told each other everything, until *I believed that we had no secrets.* One night he shared a terrifying story of his father beating his mother, then of his mother's words to him: *"Only Mommy loves you. Only Mommy does."*

Listening to Will talk, I'd never felt closer to him. Maybe I'd never felt close to anyone. Certainly, I'd never had so much pain revealed to me.

"But she left me anyway," he said. There was a faraway look in his eyes. "So she didn't really love me, you know, Maggie."

He could be so sweet, and at those times, I imagined the way he must have been as a boy. I could picture Will as a boy, as a beautiful, blue-eyed boy.

"You think it was your fault she went away?"

"Yes. But I'm getting better about it. I'm almost there. I couldn't have done this without you, Maggie. You, Jennie, Allie, just being around all of you has made all the difference."

I reached to hold Will's hand. His pain, his *love* for me, seemed so clear. It was very touching. I could identify with his sad family history, and *maybe*, I was trying to help convert my own angry father through Will.

"I'm not going to leave you," I whispered to Will. "Not ever."

"Marry me, Maggie. Don't give up on me. Promise."

In the morning, I told him I would marry him to prove it.

57

CAT AND MOUSE: *the glorious game of love.*

A wanna-be model, Cam Matthias, took Will in her mouth and rolled her long tongue slowly over and around, eliciting a groan and a tightening of his hands in her flowing red hair.

God, he was such a fabulous, untamed animal, Cam thought. *He might actually be the most exciting man on earth. Someone had to be, right?*

"Oh," Will said. "Jesus, Cam. That feels wonderful. *You* feel wonderful."

They had been going at it for hours. He was insatiable, and made her feel the same way. When she knew, or thought, he was about to come, she released him and lay on her back, placing his cock between her breasts, and once more increasing the pressure until she thought he could stand it no longer. He kept going though, on and on, like some kinky version of the Energizer bunny. The image made her howl with laughter. They both howled.

Next, she knelt in front of the wall. She reached behind and spread the cheeks of her perfect bum.

"Take your time, as if you wouldn't anyway," she said.

It was the night before Will Shepherd's wedding.

58

AT ONE O'CLOCK, three hours before "the wedding of the decade," two dozen policemen in their finest navy blue uniforms and dress-white gloves took up their positions at the main and service entrances of the Bradford home, as well as down along Greenbriar Road. Their first assignment: clear Greenbriar of the people from New York, Yonkers, and as far away as Tennessee and Texas, who had come to catch a glimpse of Will and me on our wedding day.

They would all be disappointed, I was afraid. Neither of us was interested in any publicity on the day of days, or even after, for that matter.

By three o'clock, Greenbriar Road had been officially closed to the public by the Bedford police. The entire street was off-limits to everyone except those bearing the silver-engraved cards from Cartier that simply stated: *Wedding Guest*.

I had carefully selected one of the out-of-view rear bedrooms as a dressing room, as well as for getting my head together before the madness started in earnest.

Jennie (who treated my wedding as the greatest day in *her* life), the dress designer Oscar Echavarria, and two of his young associates were fussing over me that afternoon. Allie was content to stay close to our nursemaid, Mrs. Leigh, and watch the excitement. I wore a beautiful gown of creamy satin. Both the veil and train were of understated Belgian lace. A single strand of pearls encircled my throat. I couldn't have been any happier. I *felt* beautiful inside and out. Not only was Will healed, but so was I.

"Elegant. Lovely. Perfection." Echavarria pronounced approval, eyeing me as though he were Leonardo and I the Mona Lisa. I found it hard to keep from laughing at his forgivable grandiosity.

"You look cool, Mom," was Jennie's assessment.

"Give me a few minutes alone," I finally said. "I just need a little time to take it all in."

"Sure," Jennie said matter-of-factly.

"*C'est ça,* everyone out," said Echavarria, clapping his hands like a ballet master.

They left, but I held Jennie aside. "Thanks for putting up with me these past few weeks," I told her. "Now go get pretty. Only not too much prettier than the bride, okay?"

"Don't worry about that. That couldn't happen even if I wanted it to, which I don't."

"I love you," I whispered.

"I love you even more, Mom."

"Couldn't."

"I do. Get it? I *do.*"

The wedding list read like a who's who. Will's manager and friend, Winnie Lawrence, would be there, of course. Nathan Bailford, Barry, my friends from Bedford, my sisters and their families from upstate, musicians and singers, soccer world people. And reporters and photographers from all the metropolitan papers, the local TV stations, the networks, *People, Time* — I swear, there almost seemed more strangers than friends.

One of the final cars to arrive, I found out later, was a gleaming burgundy Maserati. Behind the wheel sat Peter O'Malley.

Somehow, Peter had gotten an invitation.

The door to the back bedroom suddenly swung open without so much as a knock. *Now who could —*

"*Will*, you're not supposed to be —"

"— Getting married so young?" Will smiled. He looked gorgeous in a black Brioni tuxedo, but he also looked refined. "True, but with a woman as beautiful as you, I couldn't resist. Do you know how much I missed you last night? I could probably show you."

He took a step toward me. "Out. Don't you dare." I started to laugh. He could always make me laugh. "Out. I mean it."

He continued on undaunted, and took me in his arms. His hand gently touched my breast. Nothing too provocative — and thus *very* provocative.

"Ummmm," he said. "You *are* an eyeful. A handful too."

"Will!"

"Yes I am."

"I love you so much. Now, *go.*"

"Enough, enough. I respect your wishes. I shall honor and obey, from this moment on."

Obediently, he left the room, humming "Always." I smiled and thought it was the perfect prelude.

59

A YOUNG PIANIST from Juilliard sent the first notes of "The Wedding March" crescendoing across the picture-book back lawn. The music, *everything,* sent a shiver up my spine. I loved my wedding day even more than I thought I would.

Latecomers were hurried to their seats. Pesky radio and TV station helicopters whirled through the blue skies overhead, while television cameras never seemed to stop shooting. What seemed like a thousand photographers snapped photographs of the guests and the groom.

I finally appeared.

The bouquet of white calla lilies that I carried trembled in my arm.

I was used to large crowds, but I felt a little nervous here. I spotted my few remaining relatives from upstate, smiling tentatively. Jennie, my bridesmaid, stood solemnly near the altar. Mrs. Leigh sat in the front row, holding Allie, who wriggled in her arms. Will's aunts were there, Eleanor and Vannie, one matronly, the other strikingly attractive.

I did a double take! Will was standing next to them instead

of at the altar . . . no, it wasn't Will, but Palmer. A smudged carbon copy.

I was escorted down the flower-strewn grass aisle by Barry. He looked somewhat rumpled in his tuxedo, his flower already drooping from his lapel.

"You're so beautiful. You actually have a glow," he whispered as he let go of my arm and turned to find his seat in the front row.

I lifted my eyes to the white altar trimmed with pink and white roses. It was a bit too much, but it was beautiful. Will stood beside his best man, Winnie Lawrence. He was smiling at me.

Never, for a single second, had I thought of turning back.

"I now pronounce you husband and wife," the minister said. Will lifted my veil and gently kissed me. I could feel him through the tux. He always felt so good to me. The guests applauded. Camera flashes popped like yellow daisies all over the cascading lawn. Helicopters fluttered overhead. What an unforgettable scene!

Stiff, comically correct Day Dean waiters burst from the rear of the main house, with silver trays bearing glasses of champagne. Others circulated iced shellfish and caviar, canapés of crabmeat, tea sandwiches, cheeses, fruits, pâtés. A great orchestra led by Harry Connick Jr. began to play from a highly polished pinewood platform installed at the entryway to an enormous yellow-and-white-striped tent, which would later serve as the ballroom.

Maybe not the wedding of the decade — but quite the blowout, I had to admit. I smiled, felt incredibly warm and fulfilled inside, and started to get into it.

A huge, striped tent shaded half an acre of lawn between the main house and the duck pond. Inside, bands of children ran between the dining tables covered with pale yellow linen cloths, and graced with wicker centerpieces filled with bachelor's buttons, baby's breath, and yellow rosebuds.

The music ranged from Strauss waltzes to Carly Simon to Patsy Cline. After a formal, sumptuous sit-down dinner, and just before dessert, Barry got up and sang his "Light of My Life" to a standing ovation from the guests, Will, and me.

Then my friend Harry Connick spoke, his voice cutting through the continuing murmur of the crowd: "The bride will now cut the cake. Maggie, get your butt up here. C'mon, shy girl. Time to be the center of attention again."

Waiters arrived bearing three gargantuan wedding cakes. On each stood a marzipan man in a soccer outfit and a marzipan woman leaning against a piano. Will and I mashed cake into each other's mouths, photos of our messy bites eventually making the covers of *People* and *Paris Match*, and all sorts of other ridiculous magazines.

After dinner the tables were quickly removed. The band began to play. Will and I danced the first waltz (to "Starglow," one of my songs), then the other guests joined us.

I was dancing with Barry when a man cut in, and two-stepped me away. "Are we finally happy now?" Peter O'Malley said. His speech was thick, whiskey-slurred, and he was as gray-faced as Patrick had been in death. Physically, he was a caricature of Patrick: recognizable features, but small beads for eyes, and fifty pounds heavier than his father had been.

"Let go of me," I said. "Please, Peter." He was holding my arms so tightly I could feel his nails digging into my flesh.

He was actually like a madman. "You cheap slut. Think how much you hurt *me*. You had my father, now you've got his house, his money, his death on your hands, a handsome new husband."

I tried to pull away from the drunken man, but I couldn't. He wouldn't let me. "What do you mean, 'his death on my hands'?" I finally said as quietly as I could.

He shouted in my face. "You know fucking well what I mean!"

"You think I killed him?"

"I think his death was convenient for you. Let's leave it at that. Let everyone draw their own conclusions. I know I have, and I'm not alone."

"He died of a heart attack, Peter. Please leave. You're drunk."

"A heart attack induced by who? What did you do to him, Maggie? *Fuck his heart out?*"

I pulled my right arm from his grasp and hit Peter as hard as I could. An open-hand slap. A wake-up call.

His dark eyes blazed in thin slits. "Quite the little bitch, aren't you?" He suddenly let go of my arm. "You're nothing but a whore! Then you're probably used to *this!*"

Red wine from a crystal goblet sprayed my face, blinding me momentarily. "And Shepherd's nothing but a stud. The whole world knows it." I heard Will's roar of rage, but I didn't see him throw himself at Peter, knocking him to the ground. He punched Peter again and again. Will was all over my tormentor.

Winnie Lawrence finally pulled him off, separated the two interlocking bodies like a referee.

"Maggie! Oh Christ, poor Maggie!" Will cried. "Are you all right?"

Peter was struggling to his feet. His face was coated with blood, one eye already half-closed. "You took my father's money. His hotels. Everything! He was my father, *and you killed him*," he yelled.

Two security men finally led him from the tent. Peter went unprotestingly, too weak to fight back. I could already imagine tomorrow's news headlines. *Damn.*

Will took me in his arms, and gently wiped my face with his handkerchief. "Oh, Maggie, I'm so sorry," he whispered. "Forget about Peter O'Malley. We have a life that's just beginning. I love you," he whispered.

"I love you, Will."

I really did.

60

"WILL? Is it you? The old married man? The reformed ex-bachelor?"

" 'Tis indeed, Winnie. What's the good news from the Left Coast? Do I have an acting career or not?"

"You're not going to believe this, but Michael Caputo said yes. He loves *your ass*, and your mind. He thinks you're a natural."

The Thrill. It returned in an exhilarating rush for Will. He sprang from his chair with a loud whoop, though there was no one home to hear it.

"Tell me everything," he said.

"Well, for starters, it's the lead in *Primrose*. That's right, *the lead*. The character's named North Downing, but despite that it's an okay script. More important, it'll be a huge hit at the box office."

Primrose was the country's number one best-seller, a hundred plus weeks on the *Times* list, a saga of passionate love set in the early part of the century. Michael Lenox Caputo was the director who had bought it for a small fortune; he was producing it himself. As Selznick did with *Gone with the Wind,* he had instituted a very noisy, nationwide search for an unknown to play the lead, this time a male. Box-office draw was guaranteed by the novel's phenomenal popularity and also its female star, Suzanne Purcell, a tempestuous actress whose on-screen fire was reportedly matched in her private life.

"Good going. Jesus," Will said. "I didn't think we had a chance. Maybe I am an actor, after all."

"It was *you*. You look hot on film, and you can *act*. Caputo saw it instantly. Even the novel's asshole author likes you."

"Still, if you hadn't pushed me, I'd never have had the nerve to screen-test for the great Caputo. When does the damn thing shoot? Where? I'm stir-crazy anyway."

"Australia. And it starts soon, very soon."

"Australia? For an American epic? What's that all about?"

"It's winter in Australia when it's summer here," Winnie said, as though that explained anything.

"So what?" Will asked.

"So . . . welcome to Hollywood!"

61

THE CAST of *Primrose* had been assembled, all except for Suzanne Purcell, who was not to appear in the first scene and would make her own entrance, in her own style, on her own time schedule. She was, after all, *the star.* It was 5:30 A.M. on the gentle, rolling plains of Perth.

This was the start of principal photography: scene one, take one; cameraman, Nestor Keresty; director, Michael Lenox Caputo. Everyone had huge hopes for the film. Maybe four hundred million, worldwide. The novel was *still* number one.

Will, Caputo, and several technicians were huddled inside the poorly heated trailer that served Will as a dressing room. They were all waiting for the temperamental genius Nestor Keresty to settle on his lighting — the proper play of fill, and front and back lights, to capture the feeling of early morning in a Texas farmyard. High art, indeed.

In the film's first scene, North Downing was to deliver a baby mare, by lamplight, inside a dilapidated barn. The scene had hooked book readers, apparently by the millions. North Downing was the "last American cowboy," but a sensitive lover and husband as well.

"I want you to make me a promise," Will said, drawing Caputo aside. "This is a serious fucking promise, Michael. I'll hold you to it."

The director frowned. He had been asked to promise weird things by actors, and this boy was a neophyte. Still, he was a very large and powerful neophyte, who reportedly had quite a temper. "Shoot. Anything at all, Will."

"I want you to make me grunt and sweat bullets out there today. When I carry that baby horse, I want it to look *hard,* as though I'm in as much physical pain as the mare was. I want you to turn me into an *actor.*"

Caputo smiled, and tried not to laugh. He bit his lip, *hard.* No one had ever asked him anything like this before. "So you don't think good looks are enough?"

"No. Not even close. Christ, Tom Cruise *looks* good."

"That's all the audience will care about, Will. Trust me. Style is reality these days."

"I don't give a damn about the audience, never have. I was the best there is in football. Now I want to be the best there is on the screen. I will be too. Count on it."

Michael Caputo stared at Will, stunned by his preposterous, naive request. *He's like a boy,* Caputo thought, but all he said was "I'll try my best."

"That's all I ask. I'll do the rest. You're going to eat that condescending smile you gave me a minute ago."

"I'll be happy to do it," Caputo said, then he smiled again. Actually, he liked Will Shepherd, and wanted to see him do well.

The very first scene called for North Downing to deliver the foal, then carry it across the barnyard to his young wife, Ellie. This morning, they would shoot only the birthing sequence and North's walk across the farmyard. Later, they would film the actual presentation to Ellie.

It took them twenty-two takes. Will was awkward at first,

despite numerous rehearsals, concentrating more on Caputo's instructions than on the subtle emotion necessary for the potentially mawkish scene.

Caputo drove him mercilessly, trying to pull out real feeling, and Will found himself sweating so much he had to have new makeup after every take. They got it right on take twenty-one; they got it perfectly.

"One more time," Caputo said. "For insurance."

Will stood behind the horse, delivered the foal with a grunt of pleasure, and, smiling, picked it up lovingly in his arms. Staggering, he left the barn, made his way across an icy patch, and entered a door in a facade meant to simulate the front of the Downing house.

Will stopped. He started to smile, then to laugh out loud. *Jesus, this was rich. This was the best.*

There was a woman standing at the back of the facade, just out of range of the cameras. When Will entered, carrying the foal, she ripped open her blouse, exposing her breasts to him.

He nearly dropped the foal. There was incredible amusement and invitation in her eyes.

Maggie, he thought. *She'll never forgive me. Screw this woman, and you're screwing yourself. She'll ruin your life.*

But he couldn't stop looking at her. She was beautiful. Breathtaking, actually. And he had seen enough of the world's famous beauties to know.

"Welcome," said Suzanne Purcell, "to *Primrose.*"

62

I COULD STAY with Will in Australia for only a week. Barry kept pleading with me to finish the new album, and eventually I had to agree to come back to work.

As my car pulled up to 1311 Broadway, I thought back to a storm-blown morning years before. *Look how far you've come,* I told myself, and I had to smile. *A singing star. Happily married. Occasionally a sex junkie. Not bad. And not the same unsure and frightened Maggie who came to Barry for a job, any job.*

Today, Barry popped out of his office to greet me. He brought *me* coffee. "Come across the street with me to the studio. I've been working on several arrangements for 'Just Some Songs.' Wait till you hear them."

"Barry, I've got two new songs. From Australia."

"The arrangements first, then I'll listen. You look great, Maggie. Still glowing. Marriage is obviously agreeing with you."

"I'm happy, Barry. Really happy," I told him. Of course, Barry would never admit that he might have been wrong about Will, or anything else, for that matter.

Once in the studio, it was business as usual between the two of us. Nothing had changed; we loved our work and the chance to be together. The tough challenge was to make each album — each *song* in each album — different and better. We didn't always succeed, but we always tried like hell.

The work went extremely well that day. I was pleased with Barry's arrangements (I almost always was, though I was far more critical than I had been when we first met); he loved one of my songs and liked the other. The album was going to be a very good one.

It was midafternoon by the time we knocked off, and I decided to do some shopping. A reward. A splurge. Then home to the kids. I was cooking tonight. Then we planned to watch *Forrest Gump*, on video. We'd seen it only six times already. Maybe I'd make Bubba's Shrimp for dinner. That would give Jennie a laugh.

I found a little doodad I wanted at Bergdorf Goodman and left the store a little after three-thirty. Fifth Avenue was filled with taxis, buses, the usual pedestrian parade. I didn't see my car and driver right away.

Then, *trouble*.

A TV camera suddenly surfaced like a submarine scope out of the street crowd. Two young bearded apes from Fox News jockeyed up to me. Bad-looking guys. Real neanderthals from the look of them.

"Maggie. Maggie Bradford," one of them shouted. Instinctively, I moved away, desperately searching for my car.

"Maggie. Over here, Maggie. Is it true you and Will were having difficulties in Australia? Is that why you came home?"

I could hear the whirr of a camera. Pedestrians stopped to look at us. *Oh, damn these TV people,* I thought. *Get a life. Let me live mine.*

"No." I was curt with them.

"We hear he's gotten real close to Suzanne Purcell. That's the buzz. Know anything about that?"

My stomach spasmed. "No." Will and I knew there would be rumors about him and Suzanne. If there weren't, the studio would probably start them.

"So you didn't see this photograph?"

"No. No comment. Bye now. Nice sharing vicious rumors with you."

I couldn't push through the crowd and get away from them. *Where was the car, for God's sake?*

"The photograph, Maggie." A pushy, little bald man from Channel Five was shoving a microphone in my face. "It was in all the papers. Will and Suzanne Purcell. *Very* cozy. You didn't see it?"

I shoved him aside, pushing him back into the cameraman. I saw my car finally, and I ran and shut myself inside.

It wasn't until we were gliding through the green woods near home that I began to relax. *The nerve of those insensitive bastards!* It wasn't the first time I had clashed with a reporter. It had happened in Rome and once in Los Angeles. *What happened to privacy?* I asked myself. *Who do they think they are?*

I wished Will were home right now. In the car with me.

Oh, Will, forget about being a big movie star. Let's just disappear and be nobodies for the rest of our lives.

Will and Suzanne. The picture. Could it possibly be true? No, I didn't believe it. Wouldn't believe it. I felt that I knew Will by now. I was sure that I did. The picture was just more paparazzi crap. It wasn't the first, wouldn't be the last.

In the car, I dismissed the thought. But it came back to me when I went to bed that night. It kept me awake through the witching hours, two and three in the morning.

Will and Suzanne Purcell.

No!

Damn the paparazzi anyway.

63

THERE WERE NO PAPARAZZI for this particular moment.

> SCENE: *Ellie's bathroom. Beautiful morning light everywhere. Ellie is soaking in a tin tub, covered with thick suds, occasionally brushing them aside so she can look at her stomach. North enters, looking concerned.*

> CUT TO: *Ellie's reaction. She looks at her husband with shame. North kneels next to the tub. He's not like most men. He understands the way his wife thinks.*

NORTH: Why have you been avoiding me, Ellie? Ever since our baby, you won't let me come near you. This isn't the way we wanted it.

ELLIE: 'Cause I'm not pretty now. That's why. (She begins to cry.) I'm never going to be pretty again. That baby ruined my body. It's made me an old woman.

NORTH: Nineteen isn't old. You're as pretty as ever. You're my beautiful wife. (He starts to brush away the mounds of suds.) You're Ellie, and that will never change.

ELLIE: Don't! Please . . . oh North, please.

NORTH: Hush. (He swipes away the suds, revealing her breasts.) See, you're very pretty. You're so pretty, I almost can't stand it.

ELLIE: I'm swollen, like a suckling pig. I ache and I *feel* old, even if I'm not.

NORTH (Picking up a washcloth and tenderly caressing her body with it, his hand hidden by the suds as it goes beneath her breasts): Not here, you're not. Or here . . . Or especially *here*.

CUT TO: Ellie's reaction. She is obviously excited by his touch. She smiles, and the smile is beautiful. Ellie is as beautiful as North says she is.

NORTH (Continuing to caress): My beauty. My Ellie.

ELLIE (Breathing hard): Am I still? Am I?

NORTH: Yes, you are. You always will be. I told you that, and it will never change. Even when you do become an old woman.

CLOSE UP: Ellie and North kiss, more and more passionately. Suddenly the room is extremely steamy.

CAMERA: Moves down to show the bathwater moving as North's hidden hand gets more and more agitated.

"Cut!" Michael Lenox Caputo's voice knifed through the stillness of the scene. "Great take. Wrap it. I have to go masturbate now!"

Neither Will nor Suzanne Purcell stopped though. The technicians kept their cameras rolling, and would soon have film of the two stars that they could sell to any of the tabloid TV shows.

Will and Suzanne seemed to notice nothing around them. She had stepped out of the tub and, naked, unashamed, was laughing and pulling at his belt. He picked her up and, mouth on hers, in a kiss no patron of *Primrose* would ever see, carried her to his trailer. Will slammed the door behind him with his foot.

The werewolf of Perth.

64

"WHAT HAPPENS NOW?" Will asked. Principal shooting on *Primrose* was finished; only editing and dubbing remained to be done.

He and Suzanne were walking together on the dusty plain. He hadn't meant to get involved, but as they say, shit happens. Suzanne was truly one of the most beautiful women in the world, and Will had always appreciated the very best.

"I go back to California, you become Mr. Maggie Bradford, just like you were."

Will blinked. The words stung. "And what we had out here?" he asked Suzanne.

"We had some fine times, didn't we? You're good, Will. One of the best."

"*One* of?" He snorted out a laugh. "You're beautiful *and* you're a comedienne."

Suzanne laughed as well. "Yes, I have a brain, Will. Oh, sweetheart. *I've had* the best! Actors, other athletes, ski bums. But you are very good. No worry there."

He could feel ancient demons. Roused from sleep, they began to claw upward, from the pit of his stomach to his brain. Jesus, he hated to lose. He couldn't bear failure.

"This picture will make me a star," he said, fighting to keep his voice level. "Then I won't be 'Mr. Maggie Bradford.' "

"*I* made you the star," Suzanne Purcell said. "Don't forget that. You really shouldn't let this insane business get to you anyway. It can, you know."

Destroy her, he thought. *But not now. Take it easy, Will. Go slow. You learned your lesson in Rio.*

He kept silent. They turned back toward the hotel. "One last time?" he asked.

Suzanne grinned and reached for him. "Now that's the proper spirit. Your room or mine?"

"Yours," he said. "We'll use your toys."

Suzanne Purcell had no idea how she had gotten herself into this mess. She felt as though she were having an out-of-body experience.

The moment she'd stepped into her hotel room, Will had hit her from behind. Not that she could tell what had happened at first. She'd felt a hard wallop between her shoulder blades. Then the blue shag rug seemed to be rushing up at her face. She hit the floor hard, and lost consciousness.

And she awoke *like this.*

He'd tied her with jump ropes that she used as part of her exercise routine. He'd gagged her with her own bra, and more rope.

Then he'd put her in the bathtub.

That was when it started to get bad, unbelievably bad.

He cut both her wrists and watched her blood flow into the tub and down the drain.

He just sat there and watched her bleed.

Suzanne struggled wildly against the ropes, and made strange, muffled sounds.

She had tried to scream, but the gag was too tight. Finally, she decided to plead with Will — using her eyes.

"Oh, I see," he finally spoke to her. "*Now* you want to talk things through. You probably even want to take back some of those nasty remarks you made outside? Am I right, Suzy? You see, *I have a brain too.*"

She nodded her head as best she could. She was losing a lot of blood, and she was starting to feel woozy — as if she might pass out.

"I know this isn't an authentic suicide, but it's like one. The next best thing," Will said. "It's fascinating to watch someone die. You can't imagine. Your eyes are amazing to watch right now. About a thousand thoughts coursing through your brain, right? You can't believe that you, the great Suzanne Purcell, are about to die. It's too weird, right? Your life can't just end like this, right? *It's all in your eyes, Suzanne.* Extraordinary."

Will suddenly stopped talking.

He just watched her — bleed. It was definitely like a suicide. Like his father's.

When Michael Caputo came to Suzanne's hotel the following morning, he wanted to wish her a safe trip home, and thought, maybe, he might get lucky. Suzanne didn't answer the house phone or respond to his knock.

He finally got the manager to open her door. *Drugs,* he thought. *Damn her. Why did nearly every beautiful woman have to be a head case?*

He found Suzanne naked and badly cut, unconscious but still alive. She was handcuffed to the hotel bed. It would be half a year before she could act in another movie, and her close-ups would never be the same.

Suzanne swore to Caputo, and then to the police, that it hadn't been Will. She would say no more than that. She wouldn't press charges.

Not a word to anybody.

He had scared her that badly. She believed that Will was capable of murder, of anything.

BOOK FOUR

DARK SIDE OF THE MOON

65

I AM NOT A MURDERER.

I never murdered anyone. Or so I've begun to tell myself, over and over again.

As we entered the courthouse everyone was staring at me, and I couldn't catch my breath. I felt I must be going mad. Maybe I am.

Policemen from the prison, as well as my faithful cadre of expensive lawyers, had me surrounded, penned in, claustrophobic. I remembered how it had been in the crawl space under the house at West Point. All the horror stories seemed to be coming together.

It was pouring, and hundreds of people, mostly with black umbrellas, but a few with blue and red ones, had turned out to catch a glimpse of the so-called famous murderess.

It destroyed me to know that my children would see me like this — *in handcuffs, wearing my scarlet* M.

We marched into the courthouse and upstairs to a room where Judge Andrew Sussman was waiting. The judge was a large man, about six foot six, with a salt-and-pepper beard that he allowed to grow in wild and bushy. He was probably in his mid-forties, and reminded me of a rabbi. That was a good sign; it made me think that he would be just and fair. That was all I wanted.

Justice. Fairness. The American way, right?

Judge Sussman was holding the formal murder indictment in a solemn-looking black folder. My lawyers had told me what to expect — but I couldn't get used to it.

What in the name of God was I doing here? How could this be happening to me?

I wasn't the bad person in all of this — I was the victim. How could I be on trial for murder?

The press who would be covering the murder trial were already in the courtroom. Not one, but several artists were on hand to draw versions of the way I looked today. How goddamn *artistic!*

I stood with my chief attorney, Nathan Bailford, in front of the bench. This couldn't be happening to me. None of it seemed real.

"Good morning," Judge Sussman said in a civil tone, as though I'd come about a parking ticket, or a violation of the Bedford town code on keeping the grass cut short at the curbside around my house.

"Good morning, Your Honor." I was surprised that I could speak so confidently, that I could get the words out, that I could be civil too.

Judge Sussman held up the black folder for me to see.

"Mrs. Bradford, I have here the indictment from the grand jury. You've seen it?" he asked. He talked plainly and simply, as though I were a young child, but accused of something very serious.

"Yes, I have, Your Honor."

"You've read it, and had time to discuss the indictment with Mr. Bailford or your other attorneys?" he asked next.

"We've talked about the indictment."

"You understand the charge against you? That you are accused of the murder of your husband, Will Shepherd?"

"I've read the indictment. I understand the charge against me."

He nodded, like I was a good student, or an especially good defendant. "And do you plead guilty, or not guilty, to the charge of murder?"

I looked him square in the eye. I knew it didn't matter, but I needed to do this anyway.

"I am not guilty of murder. I plead *not guilty*."

66

NEW YORK CITY. Central Park. Will and I had been married for nearly a year.

"Maggie, can you see anything? I can't see a damn thing. Too many bloody trees in this bloody park."

Will, Jennie, and I were sitting in the fuzzy-gray darkness of a stretch limousine. Nervously, Will lit a cigarette, the match flaring blue and gold, lighting his face. He raked his fingers back through his thick curls.

How pale he is. Tired. Scared, I thought as I watched him. *This is his World Cup all over again, isn't it? He needs to prove something tonight. Well, I can understand that.*

"What are they doing at the head of this blasted, interminable line?"

"I can't see," I told him. "Clearing away pedestrians, I suspect."

"See how popular your movie's going to be," Jennie added support.

The limo was stuck, engine idling, at the Columbus Circle entrance to the park. We were fifth in a shadowed row of

Rollses, Bentleys, and Lincolns bearing dignitaries, the producer/director, and the stars.

Finally, the caravan began to move, making its way down Central Park South, then onto Seventh Avenue and across Fifty-fourth Street to the Ziegfeld Theatre, and the world premiere of *Primrose*.

With each turn of the limo, Will's anxiety increased; his hand, when I took it to comfort him, was sweaty, and as soon as he finished his cigarette he lit another. He rarely smoked, but tonight he couldn't seem to stop. He wasn't himself.

"It'll be all right," I said. "It's just pregame jitters."

"*All right?* In fifteen minutes the critics are going to watch me on the screen, thirty feet tall, nowhere to hide, saying 'Top of the Morning, Ellie. That's a wonderful name for your horse. You take care of her, girl, just as you would your very own child.' "

"It's just a story, Will. People want it to sound like that. They want to escape from real life sometimes."

"Not the New York critics. They'll see it for the abominable shit it is, see *me* for the fake I am, and — poof — there goes my short-lived acting career."

"No way," Jennie told him.

"Way," Will joked with her at least.

The caravan stopped. Suddenly there were chubby, hairy fingers rapping at the limousine's side window. I recognized a chubby hairy face and released the door lock. "Trouble," I whispered, "always comes in pairs."

"Caputo!" Will grinned as the director squeezed his wide body into the backseat.

"They're going to crucify us," Caputo said, his face mournful. "I just know it. My instincts are always right. Aren't my instincts right, Will? Comes from growing up in Brooklyn. People from Brooklyn have great instincts."

He was so comically miserable I had to laugh.

"People are expecting big things from this film," Caputo said. "As well they should for fifty mil — but Will and I both know they're getting sheep shit. *Australian* sheep shit. Not even the good stuff."

Will laughed at the director's humor, which was nearly as dark as his own.

"Where's your wife?" I asked. "She doesn't seem to have had any more luck calming you down than I've had with Will."

"Eleanor's in the car ahead of us with my saintly mother. They can't stand me when I get *meshuga* like this. They kicked me out of my own car. So I'm here. *Somebody's* got to take me to the theater."

I opened the car door, and pulled Jennie along with me.

"Where are you going?" Will asked.

"To join Eleanor, and Michael's mother. You two artistes deserve to be alone together."

67

I REJOINED WILL when we reached the Ziegfeld, and we got through the searchlights, the screaming crowds, the reporters, the studio executives, and settled ourselves into our seats of honor.

Neither Jennie nor I had ever been to a world premiere. It was actually great fun. Everyone looked so wonderfully inappropriate in their tuxes, dark suits, and party gowns — just to go see a movie.

In about fifteen minutes, the picture started and the credits rolled. WILL SHEPHERD. There his name was, as large as Suzanne Purcell's. Even before the title appeared the crowd applauded, and I heard Will grunt. I'm not sure whether it was from fear or pleasure.

Then the movie started, and I was caught up in the gorgeous shots of the American West. Nestor Keresty had seen beauty in the landscape that I had not and had made his art come alive on the screen.

Will delivered the foal, carried it to his young wife (*she looks closer to thirty than nineteen*, I noted with satisfaction), and delivered his dreaded line.

The audience was quiet. No one snickered. Will finally relaxed in the seat beside me. Jennie flashed him a thumbs-up. "See?" she whispered. "Told you so."

The movie went on for a little more than two hours. It was fast-paced, hokey, lush, romantic. I found myself enjoying it — until North came up on Ellie in the tub and began to wash her.

The way Will looked at her was the way he looked at me when we made love. It didn't look as though he were acting; it was desire in his eyes, lust. His hand disappeared under the suds, but I sensed, just by the way his arm moved, what he was really doing.

My heart clutched. Suddenly I couldn't breathe. I had to sit up very straight in my theater seat.

They've been to bed together, I thought, and a dull ache spread through my body. I remembered the rumors in the press, and Will's firm denial of them. *They were lovers offscreen, weren't they? Oh please, don't let that be true.*

I made myself look at Will then. He was watching the screen intently, his mouth half open — *reliving it!*

When the interminable love scene finished, Will leaned over and tenderly kissed my cheek. "I was acting, Maggie," he whispered. "I know what you're thinking, but you're wrong. Maybe I am an actor."

I sighed, breathed deeply, and began to feel a little better. Yes, maybe Will was an actor, after all.

68

THE GLITZY premiere party for *Primrose* was held privately upstairs at the Russian Tea Room on Fifty-seventh Street. A hundred or more people came over to shake Will's hand and tell him how superb he was. He recognized none of them, and only acknowledged their praise with an abstracted nod.

He was somewhere else, actually. *He was looking for his mother and his father. Their ghosts, he knew, would not miss an opportunity as grand as this.*

He was losing it big time, wasn't he? Yes, this was Rio all over again. It had all the makings of a disaster. He realized that he still hadn't learned how to live with defeat.

A Caputo public relations flack came running into the restaurant around eleven-thirty. Everyone looked up. This was the moment they had been waiting for.

"A hit!" he shouted, waving a copy of the *New York Times*. "A serious rave. Well, close enough."

He handed the paper, already folded to the Entertainment Section, to his boss, then stood in the crowd which had gathered around Caputo to hear the producer/director read the important review aloud.

"*Michael Lenox Caputo, that master of blockbusters, who alone among our current crop of directors can still produce an engrossing, even enthralling, entertainment, has surpassed himself with Primrose, sure to be one of this season's biggest box-office successes. . . .*"

A cheer went up from the guests, especially the studio executives. A small band hired for the party played "Hail to the Chief." Caputo read on silently as the noise continued, then, when the room was once again quiet, flung the paper aside.

"Modesty forbids me from reading more," he said. "You'll all have your copies in the morning. Meanwhile, let's have a celebratory drink! Let's have several drinks! We've earned it tonight."

Waiters served expensive champagne. The paper, which had landed on a table near the entrance, went unheeded by everyone except Will, who picked it up with a casual air, and began to read, wondering why Caputo had not gone on.

He found his own name almost immediately:

Caputo is wonderfully served by his female star, Suzanne Purcell, who radiates innocence and sensuality in equal measures and, in her love scenes, manages to be both nineteen (which in real life she is not) and a woman comfortable with her sexual appetite. Her male counterpart, however, the former sports star Will Shepherd, is patently more comfortable on a soccer pitch than the beautifully photographed plains of Texas. He treats her as though she were some luscious morsel, no more important than a slice of New York cheesecake, or maybe even Texas cheesecake. Both stars look great without their shirts, but when Mr. Shepherd is actually called upon to act, whatever emotion is generated by the raw sex disintegrates into a pout, a forced smile, or glycerine tears applied by a makeup man, but not produced by the heart. Mr. Shepherd seems not to have much of one. He should not have been so hasty about giving up his athletic career.

Will read no further. He turned toward the guests. He was feeling crazed and frantic, absolutely wild.

He looked around the room, searching desperately for Maggie. She was standing by Caputo's side, smiling at something the director said. *Well, fuck her.*

She was supposed to be my salvation, my soul mate. That's what her songs promised.

But she told me I was wonderful in the film.

She lied to me, goddamn her.

Bitch!

He hurled the paper down, and disappeared into the night. He feared that he was going mad, or maybe that he was already there. He needed to hear the cheers of the crowd, to feel that kind of absolute love, but there was nothing for him here.

Will turned onto Seventh Avenue and he started to jog. Soon he was running at almost full speed. And still there was no cheering, no love anywhere in sight.

The werewolf of New York, he thought.

69

WILL HAD BEEN MISSING for two days, and I felt as though my heart had stopped.

Winnie Lawrence and I looked for him frantically, checking local and New York hospitals and police stations, calling everybody at the party with whom he might have left. The kids were in a panic too.

No one had a clue as to where Will might have gone. I remembered stories he'd told me about Rio — his disappointment. Something had happened down there that had changed him.

I had read the *Times* movie review, of course, as soon as Will had left the room — read it with horror and anger as I realized what it would do to him, how it would hurt. I'd been there myself. I'd suffered through mean-spirited reviews, some deserved, some not.

Another high-profile failure. So many failures in his own eyes.

I knew about that feeling too. I wanted to be there for him. *But where was he?* How could I help if I couldn't find Will?

On the third day I called Barry again, and asked him to

come to the house. "I feel a little out of control," I told him once he arrived. "I think I should be doing something more, but I can't think what it might be."

"He'll come back," Barry said. "He has something good to come back to. Don't forget that."

"You always overestimate me, and underestimate Will. He could have killed himself, Barry. I'm really afraid for him. His father committed suicide."

"People like Will *don't*," Barry said. "He knows what he's doing."

"How can you say that? You don't know Will. You don't know how hard he takes things."

Barry shrugged. He didn't believe it. In a way, neither did I. I thought that Will would come back. He loved me, and he loved the kids. He had to come back.

"I fantasize finding him in a ditch somewhere. Just because the police haven't found him —"

"They haven't because he doesn't want to be found. I understand how terrible this is for you, but you're overreacting, Maggie. He's probably on the bender of benders. He'll come back when it's over."

Would he? I was afraid that maybe I didn't know everything about Will. I hadn't been with him in Rio. Who had? What furies drove him then? Which were driving him now? Perhaps he wasn't telling me the truth.

And how could he just disappear?

I saw a picture in my mind — Will and Allie riding Fleas across the lot in back of our house. He had to come back. It was inconceivable that he wouldn't.

70

AND EVENTUALLY, he did.

I was awakened by a familiar hand touching my cheek, then lightly stroking my hair. *Will was in the bedroom!* I knew his touch so well. My heart jumped. Terror came over me.

"*Will!*" I finally managed to whisper, my mouth dry with fear.

I pushed his hand away and twisted myself out of bed. I faced him with a fury that had grown all the time he was away, and now was at its height.

"Where have you been? Why didn't you call us? Oh God, Will. You think you can just come back like this?"

There was something in his eyes that night — something so different, so strange. It was subtle, but I picked up on it. He didn't look like himself.

He was dressed in unwrinkled black slacks and a black T-shirt. His hair was casual, the windblown look. His jaw was covered with a day or two's light growth.

He smiled at me the way I'm sure he did at every woman in his life who had been angry at him, and whose forgiveness he needed. I wanted to scream at him, lash out at him with my fists.

"I've been in London. I went to visit my aunt. She's like a second mother to me. Only she wasn't there, off on holiday with Aunt Eleanor, so I came home."

Yes. Of course. To another mother. To me.

"I'm sorry, Maggie, I shouldn't have done it, definitely should have called. You can't *imagine* how upset I was at that dreadful premiere. You have no idea what goes through my mind."

No, I didn't, I couldn't, I didn't want to, but I tried to be patient, and to understand. Maybe, I tried too hard.

71

WILL HAD BEGUN to wear two-hundred-dollar dark glasses almost all the time now — at night and inside the house. He called it his "film star phase."

He used any and every excuse to be out of the house. In truth, he was afraid to be around Maggie and the kids. Maybe he didn't love them anymore, couldn't *feel* what he wanted to, but he didn't want to hurt them either.

He didn't want to hurt them.

He drove his new Mercedes convertible into New York one obnoxiously sunny afternoon. He felt hollow, as though there were absolutely nothing inside him. He'd spoken to his brother that morning, but of course Palmer wasn't any help. Palmer didn't want to have anything to do with him anymore.

He wanted to end it all — maybe in a spectacular car crash. He pushed the Cabriolet to over a hundred on the narrow, winding Saw Mill. He was much too skillful a driver to crash though; his reflexes were perfect. Or maybe he didn't really want to die — just yet.

Why the hell should he want to die?

Primrose was fucking soaring at the box office. The absurd movie had made it to number one, and had stayed there for weeks. Even more absurd, he was being touted as the next Eastwood, or Harrison Ford. What a goddamn idiocy. Hollywood made him ill with its amateurish reading of public tastes.

In a single week, he'd gotten over a hundred loathsome scripts to read. He'd finally selected another best-seller, a powerful psychological thriller called *Windchimes*. He'd negotiated a contract for four million up front.

Principal shooting was set to start that very day with the famed British director Tony Scott. It was going to be another hit movie, everyone was sure of it. It had all the "ingredients."

Well, Will was sure it was going to be another piece of commercial garbage. He knew what was good, and what wasn't. He knew when he was fooling the world, and that it would catch up with him sooner or later.

He couldn't stand the fucking reviews — *because they were true, his critics were right. He was dog shit on a stick.*

He couldn't stand it anymore.

He couldn't bear being Will Shepherd: the barely living legend, the ex-football great, "the incredible Hunk," "Mr. Maggie Bradford."

As he entered New York City and saw the road signs for Broadway and 242d Street, Will floored it and took the convertible to over a hundred again.

Traffic was thick, and he swerved from lane to lane as other drivers angrily honked their horns.

I don't want to be Will Shepherd anymore, he was thinking as he maneuvered the car with one hand, then one finger, then *look, ma, no hands.*

I don't want to live like this.

I can't.

Was that what my father was thinking when he first went underwater?

72

HE WAS GOING UNDERWATER. Down, down, down. The water was cool and dark. It wasn't so bad to drown.

It was as "Will Shepherd" that he began the early evening at the Red Lion Inn in Greenwich Village. As Shepherd he consumed seven Scotches, neat; as Shepherd he was now playing out, for an audience of mostly inebriated admirers, his greatest triumph in a Manchester United uniform.

Since he was buying drinks all around, the audience was with him, hanging on every word.

"Will, Will," one of them chanted. An Englishman. A genuine fan, probably.

"The Blond Arrow!" Will shouted back, his voice thick with irony that none of them seemed to appreciate.

"The Blond Bum," another voice called out from the back of the barroom crowd.

Will stopped in the middle of his story. It was just some punk wearing black leather and black jeans, acting the macho man. He glared at the asshole, thinking *Euro-trash*, thinking *let's get it on.*

The punk made his way through the crowd. There were two

friends with him. Will saw tattoos on their arms: falcons or eagles.

"A stinking bum," the punk repeated, now facing Will as the spectators stepped back. His accent sounded German.

"A pansy," one of the friends added. "A British fag." Definitely German.

Anger, which had struggled for days to escape, now roared from Will's mouth. A string of curses exploded.

The Euro-trash punk stepped forward, beckoning to Will. "Come get me, bum," he said. "Come get me, you has-been."

Where he got the chain he held, Will couldn't imagine. It really didn't matter. He charged the German anyway.

The Blond Arrow charged blindly. He wanted a fight; any fight would do.

He got out of the Red Lion with only cuts and bruises. Nothing important. Nothing fatal.

He remembered that he was supposed to be on a movie set. *Well, fuck that. This was a better psychological thriller anyway.*

Now came a series of white explosions in the shadows of an abandoned storage warehouse just off Hudson Street. A gang was beating up on him; *he didn't know why. Could it have been something I said, mates?* He was aware only of the intense pain of their kicks — to the head, to the stomach and groin, to the ribs — of the relentless agony each hard blow produced in his brain. *Punishment,* he thought as he was falling to the pavement.

Fair and just punishment for his crimes, his sins, his entire life.

His arms and legs were pinioned. He couldn't move a muscle. His face was smashed down onto the gritty concrete of the sidewalk. His nose was leaking blood. Then his legs were lifted off the ground like meat on a hook.

And he was really pounded. He was battered, kicked, butted, until he was sure that every bone in his body had been broken. Strangely, he welcomed the physical pain. *It told him that he was alive, right?*

His entire world was suddenly spinning out of control. It was all bright liquid red. Will felt he was falling, pitching forward into a black hole.

He was being left to die on the New York streets, wasn't he?

It wasn't so terrible, really.

He was just following in the footsteps of his father. He'd always known it would end like this.

Will Shepherd found dead in the street.

Strange, weird — his last thought, his final image was of the dog he'd killed years ago. He had loved that dog.

73

THIS HAD TO BE a nightmare. It couldn't be anything else. I wasn't really awake, was I?

The Manhattan police came to my home around midnight. They broke the news politely, but their good manners and tact couldn't ease any of the pain. I had to sit down immediately. I thought I was going to pass out or maybe be sick. I was in a state of shock.

I finally was able to call Winnie Lawrence. He lived close by. The two of us went to St. Vincent's Hospital in New York.

I was permitted to see Will only briefly — he was sleeping, heavily sedated, his face swathed in heavy bandages. He looked horrible.

I felt as though I were in a dream. Whatever was happening, couldn't be. What had happened to the man I had married, the person I loved? *This badly beaten person couldn't be Will!*

We were approached by Detective Nicolo, the police officer who had come to Bedford with the news. I didn't want to talk to anyone, to see anyone.

"He's pretty beaten up, but it looks worse than it is," said Nicolo. "The doctors say it'll be a couple of weeks before he can get out of the hospital. I'm sorry, Mrs. Bradford. We don't know how it happened. Or who did it. No witnesses have come forward."

"He was supposed to start shooting a film yesterday," Winnie Lawrence said.

"Good luck." The detective smiled wryly. "If the part is *Rocky V,* he might be able to manage it okay."

"Jesus!" Winnie said, and headed for a pay phone.

Detective Nicolo turned to me. He looked like Al Pacino, only with a larger hooked nose. His white hair was slicked back. "Do you have any idea why he might have been attacked, Mrs. Bradford? Do you know if he was with anyone last night?"

I shook my head. "I'm sorry. I don't, detective. I'm not myself right now. Sorry, sorry." I fought back tears.

Nicolo clucked and nodded sympathetically. "He wasn't home with you last night then?"

"I expected him. He didn't show up."

What was the detective implying? Why am I protecting Will? I wondered. *Because he's my husband, and I love him.*

"It'll be hard to find the men who beat him up." Nicolo had taken out a black notebook; now he put it away. "If Mr. Shepherd can't describe them, there's not much we can do. I'll come back here as soon as he's able to talk. I'll stay in touch with you."

He shook my hand and left, telling me to call him if I had any information. An agitated Winnie joined me in the waiting room.

"They're going to replace Will," he said. "They say they can't afford to wait until he recovers from this. Whatever the hell happened to him?"

I shrugged, feeling numb and cold all over. It was neither good news nor bad. A frightening thought crossed my mind. *I didn't know who my husband was.*

"He'll be devastated about the film," Winnie said.

"I don't know, Winnie." I felt a wave of sadness, an overlay on my fatigue. "I think maybe he'll be relieved."

74

I DROVE BACK TO BEDFORD with Winnie Lawrence. Our nursemaid, Mrs. Leigh, was there with the kids. Fortunately, everyone was still sleeping when I got home.

I didn't want to explain about Will; I wasn't sure that I could explain, that I understood.

I loved Will, but maybe he'd fooled me; maybe he was a good actor when he wanted to be. I had thought I could help him, that I was helping him. My mother had made the same mistake with my father. Oh God, I didn't know what to think. I wanted to go up into the attic — and just write songs again.

I sat in the den, staring out onto the grounds. The morning sun was up and birds were chirping everywhere. But unpleasant images were flying inside my head — bad ones. I remembered a movie with Julia Roberts called *Sleeping with the Enemy*. I felt as though I were in it, or maybe this was *Gaslight*. Or maybe I *was* dreaming. Please. Let this be a dream.

I don't know who my husband is, I kept thinking. *Is that possible? Is that what's happening? What is Will doing to himself? What is he doing to all of us?*

Allie wandered into the den and found me there. I did my best to act as though nothing were the matter.

"I've been waiting, waiting, waiting for you to get up and come see me," I said to him. I patted my lap for him to come sit. He ran to me and jumped into my arms.

I held Allie, and kissed and hugged him. He did the same for me. He had no idea how important that was to me right now. I felt as though I might start stuttering again. My chest seemed to collapse in on me. I loved holding him like this though. We'd done it every single morning since he was born. I don't think we'd missed a day.

Suddenly Allie turned to me. He squinted as he looked up into my eyes.

"What's wrong, Mommy?" my little boy said. "What's wrong?"

Later that morning, I returned to the dreary hospital in downtown New York. I was allowed to see Will again. He was sitting up, still incredibly dazed, and sipping juice through a straw.

The part of his face not covered by bandages was purplish; his eyes were horrible thin slits, his lips puffy, as though they had been stung by a swarm of bees again and again. He looked like one of those poor men who sleep on sidewalk gratings all over New York. *My husband looked like that.*

Will reached a hand toward me when I came in. I felt my heart soften. I couldn't help it. "Maggie . . ." he whispered.

I didn't take his hand, but instead stood looking at him. I hated holding back, but I had to.

"Maggie . . . forgive me. Please forgive me."

"How can I, Will?" I finally spoke to him.

He began to cry like a little boy. Will curled himself into a tight ball, a fetal position, and he wept. He seemed so pathetic, horribly alone, and I couldn't imagine what was the matter with him.

My heart nearly broke, but I didn't reach out to comfort Will. This time, I couldn't.

222

75

BAD THOUGHTS had been drifting through Will's head ever since he'd come home, but while he was in the hospital as well.

It frosted him that Maggie was still a huge star, and he was a nothing. But most of all, it incensed Will that she was *happy*. Maggie, Jennie, and Allie were a self-contained unit. They didn't need him. They functioned beautifully on their own.

Bad thoughts. Constantly. Morning, noon, and especially at night.

Like the one about Allie having an accident while they were out riding horses.

Or pretty Jennie — lots to fantasize about there. Jennie was sweet on him anyway. She was like all the others, wasn't she? They wanted him, desperately, until they discovered who he really was.

Palmer was as bad as the others, maybe worse. His own brother was taking money from him to keep a few harmless secrets. Well, at least Palmer had always been up front about being a worthless bastard.

Maggie was the real problem, and he didn't know what to do about her.

Lots of bad thoughts though.
Lots of possibilities. None of them very nice.
Like?
What if I killed myself, as my father did?
What if I took it one step further?
What if, what if, what if. . . .

76

WATCH CLOSELY NOW. *Please.* Try to listen to each word, to every nuance. This is where the ride starts to get real tricky, where I began to seriously question my sanity. Just thinking about it made me feel tense and uncertain and sick to my stomach.

Am I guilty? Am I the murderer they say I am? Or am I the victim here?

"I'm going to San Francisco. I have to go, Will," I told him a few weeks after his "incident" in New York. He was still acting strange, but he was good around Jennie and Allie, so I didn't complain too much.

"What?" Will barely glanced up from the TV. He seemed to get lost in whatever he was doing lately. Sometimes he looked a thousand miles away, spaced out, when I tried to talk to him. I didn't understand what was happening. How could I? There was an invisible wall between us.

"They've asked me to do a benefit concert at Candlestick Park, and I've accepted. I need to sing again, Will. It's been too long."

He clicked off the TV and turned to face me. He'd been watching the game in a T-shirt and shorts, which always made me think that he was waiting to be called in from the bench. He was still amazingly fit, and looked ready to play. "Without asking if I wanted to come along?" he said.

"It's probably best if I go alone. Barry'll be there —"

"That asshole."

"— and we'll be releasing the record as soon as we can after the performance." I had no inclination either to sugarcoat my plans, or to say what I really felt, which was "at least I *tell* you when I'll be gone."

"So you *decided* to go to California, just casual-like." His face was turning red. His eyes protruded, wild. *One of these times, he's going to go off, isn't he?* I said to myself.

He turned on me in a fury. "What am I anyway? Some bloody footman in this house? Is that it, Maggie?"

"Who said you were? I don't feel that way. God. What's happening to you? Can you please explain that to me?"

"I say where you go, and don't go! Got that?" *Suddenly, I could hear Phillip. Almost the exact same tone of voice.*

But I managed to stay calm, at least on the outside. "No you don't, Will. You can decide about your life, not mine."

He rose from his chair and walked toward me. I held my ground. He stood motionless and glared at me with dark, suspicious eyes.

I didn't like this. Not the look, not the threatening body language. I had never seen him like this, and suddenly I was afraid.

His hand flashed out! There was no way I could avoid it. With a roar, he struck my cheek, strafing across the left side of my face. His backhand caught me a second time and sent me reeling backwards.

It was as though two explosions had gone off inside my head. *I couldn't believe it!* He'd never hit me before. Never raised a hand, never threatened.

"You're *not* going to San Francisco!" he screamed. "*You're not leaving me, you bitch!*"

He drew back his hand for another blow, but then he stopped and let both hands fall to his sides.

It was as though he'd had second thoughts, or come to his senses, almost as though he were another person.

"Okay," he said. "Go to San Francisco. I don't care what you do, Maggie."

I began to shake all over. I wouldn't let myself cry. Then, I began to tremble, badly. My legs felt useless. My arms too.

"I'm taking Allie and Jennie," I told him. I could barely speak, or even look at Will. "You can't stop us. Don't try."

77

BATTERY.
  He hit me.
  This can't be me.
  The lyrics to my own song played in my head. I was staring vacantly through the jet's oblong window, my eyes climbing a mountain range of snow-white clouds. Beside me, Allie lay asleep, his furry head nudging my lap. Across the aisle, Jennie was listening to something with her airplane earphones.

  Both of them were happy to be going with me. They had no idea about my trouble with Will. The concert coincided with Jennie's vacation. Allie *always* wanted to be at my side, and usually was. The three of us were so close that we'd come up with the acronym *JAM. Jennie, Allie, Maggie.* We'd never changed it to include Will.

  Coming off the plane, I was aware of the usual stares and hellos from total strangers. Some tried to get my autograph, nearly trampling us with their efforts; others reached out to touch me, as though the contact would somehow grant celebrity status to them as well.

  Celebrity!

If only they knew what it really meant to be famous . . . to have so many eyes always watching.

There was a fax from Will waiting for me at the Four Seasons Hotel in town:

> GOOD LUCK, MY SONGBIRD
> FORGIVE YOUR WILL HIS TRESPASSES
> PLEASE FORGIVE ME
> HURRY HOME WITH THE CHILDREN
> I LOVE YOU — *ALWAYS HAVE, ALWAYS WILL.*

> I crumpled the paper.
> *Always Will*, indeed.

78

BARRY, JENNIE, ALLIE, and I were cuddled inside a big red-and-silver Bell helicopter. Beneath us were the bright lights of Candlestick Park, the dark waters of the bay. I was dressed in my usual outfit: a loose white peasant's blouse, long skirt, flat shoes, so I wouldn't be a millimeter taller than I was.

But was I really ready for this? I wasn't sure, but I had to try it, really wanted to.

In less than an hour I would be making my first major concert appearance in almost three years. The networks had sent film crews. This was *news*, right? — *hard copy*. A live album was being recorded tonight. There had been over five hundred thousand requests for tickets; there were fewer than eighty thousand seats.

Yet we were sealed off in the helicopter, a private family: my children, my best friend. This was better than being down there, I was thinking.

"Let's not land," I said.

Barry raised an eyebrow and made a face. He put his hand over his mouth as though he were speaking into a mike. "Uh, Earth to Maggie, Earth to Peter Pan."

"I mean it. Can't we just stay up here till tomorrow?" I was feeling a little giddy.

"What'll we use for fuel?" Jennie asked.

"They can refuel us in midair. Like long-range bombers. It'll be cool."

"We'd be hungry," Allie said, always thinking of eats.

"They can pass in sandwiches with the fuel. No problem." Jennie laughed. She liked it when I talked nonsense.

"I'm hungry *now*," Allie announced. He was always the most practical member of JAM.

"We're about to land," Barry told him, "no matter what your mother says. I'll get you some food at the Park. All-beef franks, mmm-mmm good."

I suddenly felt a wave of sadness, and also unbelievable fear. Stage fright. "I don't know if I can go on," I said. "Really, Barry. No joke."

He took my hand. "Preconcert jitters. Go with the fear. Use it."

"More than that. It seems so safe here, so *right*. Down there is danger. First the fans, and then —"

"Will," he said. I had told Barry nothing about the fight, but he'd guessed something was wrong. He knew me too well.

"Life," I said.

Okay, so I'd sold close to twenty million albums; I'd won eleven Grammy Awards.

But I could still get scared, couldn't I?

My singing style was the personal confessional mode, right? I could do that now. Just go out there in front of all those people and be myself. Be very up front and personal.

The trouble was — I was starting to feel like *my old self*. I remembered the Maggie who had existed in West Point. I even remembered the little girl who broke into tears because she couldn't stop stuttering when she had to answer questions in school.

I knew exactly what my performance was supposed to be — edgy, but also heartfelt. My songs were supposed to be succinct and catchy on the surface — infected with all kinds of influences: rock, Broadway, classical, French art song — but under the surface, complex and psychologically true.

I knew all this as I walked out on that big stage in San Francisco, as I looked down on all those expectant faces.

So why was I afraid? No, absolutely petrified? Why was I scared that I wouldn't be able to sing at all?

I sat down at the piano, and I started to mouth lyrics against the stiff, chilly breeze off the bay.

I almost got through the first song —

Then I went to pieces.

With all those strangers watching — but also my children, with Jennie and Allie right there in the stage wings.

BATTERY, I sang.

HE HIT ME

THIS CAN'T BE ME

I started to stammer, then to stutter again — something I hadn't done in so many years, something I'd fought so hard to overcome.

I couldn't sing anymore. I couldn't go on.

I finally turned and *talked* to the huge crowd — "I'm having a little trouble up here. *Whew.* I'm sorry. I'm in trouble."

I was beginning to have heart palpitations. I felt faint and thought I might fall off the piano bench.

Then Jennie and Barry and Allie were there for me. So were a couple of the musicians. They helped me offstage. I could barely walk.

"Poor Mommy," Allie kept saying. "Poor Mommy. Mommy got sick."

79

WILL HAD ALWAYS been a night creature. Now, more than ever he needed to get out and around. *The werewolf of Bedford.*

He whipped his black BMW coupe approximately five hundred yards down Greenbriar Road. He turned from one tree-lined, shadowy driveway — his own — into the next.

The main entrance to the Lake Club was marked by ten-foot-high fieldstone pillars. An uneven fence of like stone ran the length of the property, and Will drove past the entrance to a designated spot near the fence.

He parked and got out. The fence swung open; a path led to the rear of the clubhouse and a service door that would be virtually invisible to anyone who wasn't looking for it.

Inside the club, there was a tangible stillness in the air that signified privacy and privilege. It reminded Will of the silence of cathedrals and European banks. He maneuvered his way past deserted billiard and smoking rooms to yet another door, on which he knocked, paused, and knocked again.

The door was opened from inside. Will blinked at the sudden bright light assailing his eyes. Then he took in the mahogany paneling, the long oak bar, the Tiffany lamps, and the Renaissance paintings that hung on the walls of the room.

The group of men clustered at the bar had watched his entrance. They said hello once they saw it was he, and that Will belonged there.

Peter O'Malley was one of them. Strangely, he and Will had become friendly at the club. They had Maggie in common, didn't they? Maggie had brought them together, and they frequently talked about her. Peter dreamed of bringing Maggie down.

That evening, they were both attending a late-night get-together at the country club. The meeting was strictly unofficial.

Once, or sometimes twice a month, after the club closed, a few members brought in special entertainment. It was a way for the high-powered men to let off steam and have some social, and certainly politically unacceptable, fun. God knows, they couldn't seem to get it at home with "the wives."

The room was lit by the gold and red flames from an ample fieldstone fireplace. *The fires of Hell,* Will called it. *A sample of what's to come for the lot of us.*

Standing in front of the fireplace in a more or less orderly row, stood six girls. They were all young beauties. Their bare skin and long hair gleamed in the burnishing firelight.

The eldest looked twenty at the most, the youngest might have been sixteen. Each was wearing a black sleeping mask. The girls were never permitted to see the members, or even the location of the club.

The exclusive Lake Club of Bedford Hills, Will thought to himself. *It was a facade, like everything else.*

Later that night, Will picked out one of the young girls. She was tall and blond and reminded him of Jennie.

80

I THINK I KNEW in my heart, for some time, that the marriage was over between Will and me. It was a matter of timing now. What would be best for the children, then for me, and finally for Will. I didn't want to hurt him, just leave him.

Will was there to greet us when we got home. He was also his old self. Our arrival revived him. He became almost giddy with joy. He seemed genuinely concerned about what had happened to me in San Francisco, my minibreakdown. He said he understood "the jitters" very well, and I believed Will did.

He promised me there would be no more anger, no more fights, no more disappearances. His fear of desertion had made him desperate. He was in touch with his feelings once again.

I listened to Will and everything he had to say. I heard the words. I had already made my decision though. Will had shown me, however briefly, a side of him that I couldn't possibly be around, or deal with.

An uneasy calm descended on the house in Bedford.

It was calm sometimes too with Phillip, I thought.

*　　　　*　　　　*

I was getting everything in order, talking to Nathan Bailford and taking care of the legal aspects as best I could. I just needed another day or so, then I would talk to Will. In the meantime, I saw a very good psychiatrist in nearby Tarrytown. I was, as the papers would later say, *"under a doctor's care,"* whatever that is supposed to convey.

Something came up unexpectedly. I received a call to come to Jennie's school. They said it was important. The Bedford Hills Academy's administration building was a small, neat Victorian-style house that looked like a thriving country inn. As I hurried inside, students and office staff recognized me and tried not to stare. I waved to the kids I knew, and even to some I didn't recognize.

I ran up the stairs, stopping long enough in a bathroom to comb my hair, put on lipstick, check to make sure that my head was on straight.

I was going to meet Dr. Henry Follett, Dean of the Academy, and I wanted to look no different from other mothers with children at the school. For some reason, I was already more upset than the occasion probably required.

Dr. Follett's office was small but pleasant, with a picture window looking out over the campus, and school memorabilia everywhere — pennants, championship banners, photographs of Follett with students or local officials.

He was a likable man in his fifties, compact and natty, and I guessed he had a sense of humor, though his expression was serious and his smile was professional. Still, his eyes were kind. And he had a nice handshake.

I didn't know why he had summoned me. I was busy at home, distracted with Will, but I had come to the school right away. My stomach, my back, my neck were all in knots.

"It's about Jennie," he said, as soon as I was seated in front of his large, cluttered desk.

"Yes. I figured as much. Is she in some kind of trouble?" I

asked. I was trying not to show what I was feeling inside. I had to be strong here — for Jennie. I could do that.

"I'm not sure, Mrs. Bradford. Maybe you can tell me."

I hadn't noticed anything too unusual about Jennie. She *was* a teenager though. "She seems fine. Rebellious at times, argumentative, mimics Butthead and Beavis around the house to drive me crazy."

"Acting the same at home though? Not sick lately? Not depressed or unhappy?"

I shook my head, and continued to feel both confused and worried. What was he getting at? I saw Jennie every day. Of course she had her own life and her own friends. I operated on the principle that the best thing a mother can do for her teenage daughter is to give her a reasonable amount of space to grow up in. That, plus love.

"Certainly not sick," I said. "What's going on, Dr. Follett? Please tell me why you called."

He drummed his fingers on his desk. "This semester, Jennie has skipped seventeen days of school."

Bombshell! I felt suddenly cold all over. "Skipped seventeen days?"

"Cut her classes. Didn't show up at all."

"My God! I had no idea. I almost don't believe it, but of course I do. It isn't like Jennie."

"No, it isn't like Jennie," he agreed.

He handed me some papers from his desk. A report card and several illness notes. "Is that your signature?"

I looked at the notes and the report card. My hands were shaking. "My name, not my handwriting." *Another bombshell.*

"Jennie's?"

"I'm not sure. Could be." My head was spinning too. This was the last thing I'd expected. Jennie had never been in trouble.

"We think she was trying to forge your signature," Dr. Follett said, bringing me back from my reverie.

"Jennie wouldn't do something like that." I winced. Obviously, she had.

"Are you sure? If it's not your signature, and it's not Jennie's forgery, then whose could it be?"

My brain whirled. "I really haven't a clue." Suddenly, I was angry at Jennie though. We had always trusted each other. I'd made time for Jennie no matter what else was going on.

"Mr. Shepherd?" the dean asked.

"No. He's her stepfather. He'd simply sign. And this isn't his signature either."

"Look at the latest report card," he said. "Have you seen this?"

I looked. B's and C's. I wanted to cry. Jennie had always been an A student. Maybe I hadn't been paying enough attention because of that?

"Mrs. Bradford, Jennie is one of the best students at Bedford Hills Academy. Then suddenly, just this semester, she gets very bad marks. For her anyway. That sometimes happens in the senior year, when a kid's been accepted at college and feels she deserves a break. But Jennie's a sophomore. Just the time her grades should be highest."

"I know. *Jennie* knows," I said. I didn't understand what could have happened. This had come out of the blue. I didn't think she had picked up on Will and me, but maybe she had. Kids can tell.

Dr. Follett stood up from his desk, and extended his hand. "We all love Jennie here at the Academy. Faculty and her classmates both. If you find out anything, please call me. It wouldn't be betraying her secrets. This isn't the first time something like this has happened to a student, and we're pretty good at fixing things."

I shook his hand, then I headed out — to try and find Jennie. She had skipped classes again today.

First though, I sat in the school's visitor parking lot and tried to stop my body from trembling. My world seemed to be falling apart again.

81

JENNIE ARRIVED HOME around three-thirty, her knapsack full of books, looking innocent of any wrongdoing. I asked her to take a ride with me.

I drove to the Pound Ridge Reservation, a nature preserve in the heart of Westchester. At around four, the two of us hiked up a hill toward an antique fire tower, from the top of which you could see Long Island Sound, and even the New York City skyline far to the south.

Jennie, of course, wanted to know what was going on. I asked her to wait. All in good time, my sweet darling.

We walked silently — I didn't know where to start — and stopped, breathless, when we reached the crest. I was feeling maternal, angry, hurt, optimistic — just as in the songs I wrote. *True songs out of life, right?*

"I've been to see Dean Follett," I finally told her. *The first shoe drops!*

Jennie had been looking at me. Now, she turned her head away. Not a word.

"He says your grades are falling. He also says you've been skipping school." *The second shoe.*

"School's boring and I hate it." Jennie's tone was surly and defiant. Not like her at all. It was Jennie at her absolute worst, and not something I saw very often.

"You didn't used to think so," I said to her.

"I do now. There's nothing worth learning. The teachers there aren't very bright, you know."

"So you don't go anymore. That's interesting, Jen. Quite a revelation. What do you do with your days?"

"Nothing much. But nothing is better than my classes."

"You're not home."

"How would you know that for sure? You're shut up in your study most of the day."

Now she was being completely unfair, but I kept my cool. "I'd know, and *you* know I would. I love you, Jennie, and if you're in any kind of trouble —"

"Nobody gives a damn about anybody else. Don't fake it. Don't condescend to me now."

Even without touching her, I could sense an awful tenseness in her body, the effort she had to make to speak at all. When had this happened? How had it happened? Why?

"I love you," I said, my voice unsteady. "You're the most precious thing in my life. It's always been that way."

Her composure finally broke. So did mine. "Don't say that," she suddenly wailed. "Don't say you love me, Mom. I don't deserve it."

I could barely speak. I was holding back great, racking sobs. "Why? I *do* love you. Why shouldn't I tell you what's true?"

"Because you *couldn't*. You don't know who I am, and it takes something like this to get your attention. *Failing grades!* I mean — *who cares?*"

I finally bowed my head, and I started to cry. I thought that I could handle anything, but not this.

Suddenly, Jennie flung herself at me, burying her face in my neck. I could feel her hot tears, her body's warmth.

"I can't tell you," she sobbed. "I'm not even sure that I know.

I'm fifteen and it's all a little nuts. So what's new?" she finally choked out a laugh.

"My God, Mom," Jennie said to me then. "You're shaking all over."

We sat on the ground and held each other for a long, long time. A breeze came up, and I wrapped my sweater around her. *My baby,* I thought. *My friend for so many years. My sweet Jennie.*

But I could think of no way to comfort her, and make it better for either of us. I blamed myself, of course. I'd tried so hard to be supermom, but it wasn't enough. It never is.

82

I SPENT a blessed hour the next morning, which was unseasonably warm, working in the garden behind the swimming pool. The time alone, the feel of sunlight on the back of my neck, the physical exertion — all were exactly what the doctor ordered. I began to regroup.

I needed time to think things through in a straight line. The worsening situation with Will. Jennie's problems at school. My own bad experience in San Francisco. It was a lot to take at one time; I was afraid that I wasn't handling it very well.

There was an explosion in the woods beyond the pool.

I stopped digging, stopped thinking, stopped breathing, and listened with total concentration. And dread.

A second explosion came from behind a thick wall of evergreens. The trees masked my view.

Gunshots? Oh my God.

I was on my feet, running at full speed toward the thick pocket of trees. A scream was stuck in my throat.

Oh God, dear God . . . what's happened?

What's happened now?

I plunged into the woods, heading for the sound of the

shots. My heart was pounding and there was a sharp pain in my chest.

Instinct drove me; I didn't even think of calling for help. Whom would I call to anyway?

Gunshots? Near our house? How could that be?

My ankles were stabbed by rocks and thistles. There were no more shots, just a frightening, desolate silence. Finally, I came to a clearing. I stopped running.

Will was standing there. Will was holding a rifle in the crook of his arm.

He turned at the sound of my footsteps. He looked at me as though I didn't belong there.

"What are you doing?" I managed to speak.

"Target practice," he said. He motioned to a row of beer and soda cans set up on a log. "Care to give it a go, Maggie?"

He flashed his best North Downing smile. "I'm getting quite good. I'm a natural it seems. Great hand-to-eye."

Phillip had a gun too. I had used it to kill him. I remembered dark blood pouring from his mouth, saw his look of horror, heard his grunt of surprise as the fatal bullet struck him.

"Get rid of it!" I screamed. "I don't want it anywhere near my house. Get rid of that gun!"

Will looked at me coldly, but then he grinned. "*Our* house. But it's your call, Maggie. If it disturbs you, it's gone. If you don't trust yourself around guns, I understand."

83

THIS WAS THE DAY. I just couldn't have known it. I wouldn't have expected it. This was the day.

Having been unable to sleep, I slipped out of the house at dawn. I was wearing a terrycloth robe and my rattiest sneakers. My long hair was in knots. Hopeless.

I figured the air would be good for me, give me a fresh start. I hoped no one would see me like this. No paparazzi sneaking shots through the fence.

I walked to the partly crumbled fieldstone wall that divided my property from the grounds of the Lake Club. My sneakers stamped defiantly through damp leaves and creepers. Chattering blue jays and robins darted among the high trees over my head.

"Oh, shut the heck up," I grumped at the birds.

I was startled to hear another kind of sound in the woods. A human voice.

"Who's there?" I called ahead. "*Hello?*"

J. C. Frazier appeared. He was coming out of a meadow that belonged to the Lake Club, where he worked as head grounds-keeper. J.C. was always outside, so we met from time to time. I knew that he was seeing Mrs. Leigh, and she thought he was a good man. *Yes, and they are hard to find,* I was tempted to tell her.

"Mornin', Mrs. Bradford. You the one responsible for this fine weather?" he asked. Not a care in the world, and why should he? His grounds were in perfect order.

"I thought *you* were in charge of the weather, J.C."

"No way, ma'am. I'm charged with the grounds only. I believe *you* have the upper atmosphere. And a real good job you've made of it today. Blue skies everywhere I can see."

We stopped to talk over a mossy stone wall. J.C. probably knew more secrets about the residents of Bedford than anyone around, but his discretion was as much responsible for his keeping his job as was his skill, so our talk was of seasonal flowers and the approaching summer. Harmless small talk, but it hit the spot, and took my mind off my problems, if only for a little while.

I remembered something I'd been meaning to ask somebody at the club, or maybe something I'd been afraid to bring up before.

"Sometimes at night I've noticed lights on in the club. I'd say around one or two in the morning."

J.C. thought about what I'd said, then shook his head. "That's not possible. No, I'm afraid not, Mrs. Bradford."

"I've seen the lights. I'm positive that I have."

"No, ma'am. I don't think so. Couldn't be. The club closes at eleven. Always. That's the golden rule."

I thought of arguing with him further, but gave up. If J.C. didn't want to talk, he wouldn't talk.

He tipped his ballcap, a blue one that read "N.Y. Giants." "Got to get back, plenty of work to do. You have a pleasant day, Mrs. Bradford."

I watched J.C. make his way back toward the large estate house of the club.

Strange, I thought. *Why wouldn't he know about the lights? Or why would he lie to me?*

I finally went back to the house determined to talk to Will that morning. It had to be done, however painful for both of us. This seemed like as good a day as any.

Jennie and Allie were toasting Pop-Tarts in the kitchen. They were both dressed. Jennie looked *ready for school*, which pleased me.

"Is Will up?" I asked, trying to make it sound as though it were a big deal, nothing special.

"You just missed him, Mom," Jennie said. "He had to go to the city on business. Said he'd be back around four."

I groaned. Will was almost never out of the house this early. Just my luck.

This was the day.

84

WILL DIDN'T COME HOME at four that afternoon.

He still hadn't arrived at seven-thirty when we sat down for dinner.

Or at ten, when we went upstairs to get ready for bed. He never called to say he'd be late, or maybe that he wouldn't be coming home at all.

I lay in bed with the lights off, but my eyes wide open. I was blaming myself, and I knew I shouldn't do that. Will had been so incredibly romantic and sensitive in the beginning of our relationship, and then he had just switched it off. Completely.

I wondered if he was having an affair now, or maybe more than one. I guess I shouldn't have cared about that, but I did.

I don't know how I finally got to sleep, only that I did.

"Damn! Damn it to hell!" I heard.

Will's curses woke me. *He was inside the bedroom. He was home.*

I could see him standing near the door, examining his toe. He'd stubbed it in the darkness. *Well, good. Serves him right.*

The bedroom door was half-open and light from the hallway silhouetted his body. His face remained in shadow.

He turned to look at me, but I pretended to be asleep. I held my breath. Then he crept out of the room.

He pulled the door awkwardly behind him. The door slammed shut. More of his stupid head games? *Damn him.*

I looked at the luminous face of the bedside clock: 12:45.

Where had he been tonight? Maybe I should get up and talk with him now, while the kids were asleep.

I got up, walked to the window, and looked outside. I saw Will. What was he doing? Where was he going down there?

I put on my robe and left the bedroom. The hallway was dark. On his way out, Will had turned off the night light we kept on for Allie.

I hurried downstairs.

The lights were off in the living room and den. There was no sound, no movement.

Something seemed wrong to me! Why were the lights off?

What was he up to?

The downstairs rooms were dark and quiet too. There was no one in the kitchen, or in Mrs. Leigh's room. Fridays were her night off, I remembered.

I went back to the foot of the stairs and peered up. *Nothing to see. Was Will back inside the house?*

I started to climb the stairs again.

Halfway up, I saw something standing against the wall. My heart almost stopped. My legs nearly went out from under me.

It was the rifle! I'd finally found it. *In the middle of the stairway, where Will had left it!*

My head was filled with loud noise. Chaos and confusion. None of this made sense to me.

What was going on?

Was Will upstairs again? What was he planning to do with the rifle? Where had it come from?

I started to run up the stairs. I reached the top step and stopped. At the far end of the corridor a line of light showed from beneath a door.

It was Jennie's door. The light hadn't been on just a few minutes before.

I was suddenly terrifed that Will was in there. *He's taking the children,* I thought.

I ran to get the rifle, then I hurried back. At least I had the gun now, not Will.

Had he planned to murder us all? Disturbed men did things like that. It wouldn't be the first time, would it?

I had a flashback. Phillip!

I ran down the corridor and yanked open Jennie's door. The rifle was ready, at least I thought it was. *I really didn't know very much about guns. Next to nothing, actually.*

What I saw inside the bedroom drove me absolutely out of my mind.

85

THIS IS THE DAY! Oh, Jesus God, Will!

Don't shoot him. Don't do it. Maggie, don't! a voice inside my head screamed at a deafening level.

Jennie was on the bed, wearing short, white pajamas. Her long, bare legs were exposed. Her eyes were closed; she seemed to be breathing normally. There was a glass of milk on the night table, half-finished.

I took in every tiny detail, understanding nothing yet.

This was so bad. This was so bad.

Will stood at the foot of her bed. He was dressed in khakis and a sport shirt. What he'd worn for his business meeting in New York? He looked too casual for business. *What was Will doing in Jennie's bedroom?*

"Maggie!" he said, as cool as could be. His film star persona. "I thought you were asleep. Were you trying to fool me?"

My heart was pounding so hard and fast it was difficult for me to breathe. "What are you doing in here?" I gasped out the words. *"What is going on?"*

Jennie suddenly sat up, and rubbed her eyes. She looked

frightened. "Mom? Will? What's the matter? What's happening? Is that a gun? *Mom?*"

Will smiled at the horrifying scene. It was the most scary and evil expression I had ever seen. I didn't know the person I was looking at. *What was he doing in Jennie's bedroom? I thought that I knew.*

"Jennie and I were just getting ready for some fun," he said. "Care to join us in bed? *Ménage à trois?*"

Ménage à trois? I was too scared and stunned to speak. For a moment my body was paralyzed. My pulse was racing crazily. I felt my mind implode. *Will and Jennie? Oh, my God, no!*

I raised the gun and aimed it at Will. I didn't care about the consequences.

I couldn't pull the trigger though. I couldn't do it. I couldn't.

"Get out of this house, and don't you ever come back," I said in a steady voice.

Will pushed past me and with his great speed rushed down the corridor. I could tell by the sound that he took the steps two at a time. He was laughing in a loud, braying voice, the kind you heard in horror movies.

I went after him, hampered by the unwieldy gun. I didn't want to shoot him, just make sure he was gone — forever. *Gone from all of our lives.*

He went out the front door, and I ran after him. I could see little at first except the outline of overhanging trees, but I heard his footsteps retreating toward the back of the house.

I pitched forward. Hit my knee. Caught myself with one hand.

Suddenly I couldn't hear steps anymore!

I pushed myself up. I listened intently, as I have never listened before.

I was frightened. I thought I might be going into shock. I felt cold all over. I was *freezing* cold. *I couldn't forget seeing Will in Jennie's bedroom. The look in her eyes.*

251

It was too quiet. I couldn't hear Will, or see him either. What was he doing out here?

The moon had disappeared behind a cover of clouds. It was nearly pitch dark. I couldn't stay outside. I knew I should get back in the house.

Perhaps he had tricked me. Gone back to Jennie. I didn't know what to do.

I stood uncertainly, squinting my eyes and looking around, trying to penetrate the darkness. I remembered hiding in the crawl space beneath the house near West Point. My nightmare had completed a full circle.

Silence.

Darkness.

The cold. I was shaking all over again.

"You stupid, prying bitch! You betrayed me."

With a roar, Will attacked from behind. His strong hands struggled to grasp my throat. I fought free from the stranglehold. He struck my face, a glancing but jolting blow. It brought me to my knees. I fought to get up. Couldn't. Not even close.

Will swung his leg. With a powerful kick, he broke my rib, maybe several ribs. The pain was sharp, and unimaginable. The shock, the terror of that moment, was beyond belief.

I fell toward the hard, cold ground.

The rifle went off with a roar louder than any of my screams, louder than a clap of thunder. I rolled onto my stomach, then everything went black and I fell unconscious into the cold, wet leaves.

86

I DON'T KNOW.

I don't know.

I honestly don't know what happened on that fateful night of December 17. Did I shoot Will? Did I lure him outside and then blow him away? They say I did. Am I guilty of murder? Two murders? And if two murders, why not three?

Are they right when they call me a killer? The black widow of Bedford?

Maybe I've finally gone crazy. It feels that way. It feels so awful, so unfair. But life isn't always fair.

I woke in my own bed with my face buried in my pillow and an agonizing pain throbbing across my left side. I felt as though I'd been beaten with a work shovel. Everything was crashing loudly inside my head.

In my mind I tumbled and tumbled but couldn't stop the images of violence and horror from coming at me.

Who had fired the rifle?

Jennie, I thought. *I've got to get to Jennie. And Allie.* I was conscious of a great buzzing noise. At first I thought it was in my head, but then realized it came from outside.

Why were there voices outside my house? What in the world was going on?

My eyelids felt unnaturally heavy. Pain, like a razor cut, was behind them. Another kind of pain, particularly sharp, knifed into my ribs.

I forced my eyes open, then quickly closed them. The light was too bright. *Who had turned the lamp on?*

I heard footsteps on the stairs. Will!

I tried to sit up but couldn't. *A flaming yellow bolt crossed my vision like heat lightning, like a bold graphic on MTV.*

Again I opened my eyes.

I could barely see the heavyset black man in a dark suit, white shirt, and tie. He was standing by the side of the bed, looking down at me. He seemed seven feet tall. His horn-rimmed glasses appeared too small for his giant head.

He was *staring* at me. An odd look on his face. *What was he doing in my bedroom? Or was I in a hospital? This felt more like a hospital actually.*

"You're Maggie Bradford?"

I tried to nod, tried to understand what could possibly be going on, *wherever I was*. Maybe I was having a flashback.

"We found you outside, carried you up here," the man said. He passed some sort of badge before my face. A gold and blue insignia.

"I'm Emmett Harmon, Chief of the Bedford Police." His solemn voice boomed inside my head. *The Chief of the Bedford Police?*

Oh, dear God. What's happened? Jennie? Allie?

"What are you doing here? Please, where are my children?" I whispered. My throat was raw and ached when I talked.

"Maggie Bradford, you're under arrest for the murder of your husband, Will Shepherd. You have the right to remain silent."

BOOK FIVE

TRIAL AND ERROR

87

"MS. NORMA BREEN?"

"Yes. Who is this I'm speaking to?"

"My name's Barry Kahn."

"You don't say. My, my. The *singer* Barry Kahn?"

"The same."

"I think you're terrific! Your songs are anyway. What can I help you with?"

"It's not for me that I'm calling. We need your help."

"We?"

"Nathan Bailford and I."

"Nathan! How the hell is Nathan?"

"Up to his ears in the Maggie Bradford defense."

"Yes. I'd heard he took it on. Tough duty."

"We'd like to hire you for our team. Nathan says you're the best investigator he knows."

"I'm very good, but what difference does it make? Isn't this case pretty open and shut? That's what I hear."

"We don't think so, not at all. Nathan thinks it's anything but open and shut."

"You could have fooled me. The media has her drilling the son of a bitch, blowing his head off."

"There's more to it than that, believe me there is. You interested in finding out what?"

"He was shtupping someone else?"

"We'll never know. Probably. But Maggie wouldn't kill him for that."

"Abuse?"

"Far as I know, he hit her once. No, I'm sorry, *twice*. She wouldn't kill him for that either. She's a good person. Just like in her songs."

"Then why'd she do it?"

"That's what we're hiring you to find out, Ms. Breen. We're not entirely sure that she did."

"You need a defense, or you want the facts?"

"We need a defense."

"Ah. My thanks for your honesty. I like that in a famous singer."

"But we're sure the facts will lead to the defense. Maggie's not a killer."

"Only of husbands, it seems. Didn't she shoot hubby number one? I *do* believe I read that in the funny pages."

"That's never been proved. She was never tried for it. She was originally charged with second-degree murder, but it didn't stick."

"And her live-in? Patrick O'Malley?"

"An accident. O'Malley had a heart attack."

"I thought she confessed to the murder."

"The police claim what they have is a confession. Maggie was confused and disoriented when they brought her in. You can understand that."

"The press are already trying her. She's sure losing in their court. The first one with a handgun, the next on a boat, this one with a rifle."

"Look. If you don't want to take this on —"

"Oh, I didn't say that."

"Then you'll join us?"

"For you, Barry Kahn —"

There was a pause. "God bless you, Ms. Breen," Barry said.

"Call me Norma."

She could hear his sigh of relief, imagined the strain he was under. And she admired his loyalty to his friend, even if she was the "black widow" of Bedford, and almost surely guilty as sin.

88

MOST PEOPLE still didn't know the issues separating the Serbs and the Croats, but the murder trial of Maggie Bradford was being watched everywhere around the world. Reporters and television crews arrived not only from across the United States, but also from Europe, South America, Asia, and probably from the moon. The crush of the press was as great, Norma Breen thought, as at a presidential inaugural — only the desperation for the "inside" story was far more lunatic.

Christ, it's a goddamn murder trial, she thought. *Whatever the outcome, it won't change the world. So what if she killed a husband or two? Most of them deserve it!*

She pointed her dusty yellow Camaro down Clarke Street in Bedford Village and slowly drove past the buzzing courthouse for the second time that morning.

A procession of black umbrellas, vinyl raincoats, Boston Chicken and Dunkin' Donuts take-out bags stretched along the main street, past Hamilton Drugs, Willie's Newspapers, and the new public library. The slow parade turned onto Charles Street and continued five more blocks.

What a mess! What a freaking disaster area! Tourist buses

were parked down Millar and Grant streets: bright yellow school buses and Greyhounds with names like PITTSFIELD and CATAWBA on their foreheads. It was early December, and snow already hung in the air.

"*Maggie and Will: Bittersweet Love Tragedy.*" That was *today's* headline; similar phrases floated out to Norma from her car radio, including "*Three Strikes. She's Out!*"

Cute! Norma liked that one. Finally, a little sense of humor about this fiasco, which happened to be her *job* for now.

The chief defense investigator hated publicity, didn't care about the fame, or even getting rich. It interfered with her work, all those reporters scurrying after her. Still, she knew what she was in for. Maggie Bradford was a star. One segment of the public had decided she was guilty; the other, innocent as a lamb. And Norma?

Dammit, I still don't know what to think. Maggie isn't sure herself. What she told the police was damn close to a confession. The evidence is impressive.

Her yellow pass, pasted conspicuously on her windshield, enabled her to spin the Chevrolet into the blacktopped court-house parking area. The lot was already packed with similarly stickered state and local police cars, and private cars belonging to the attorneys and their aides from both sides.

Judge Andrew Sussman's blue Mercedes was in his private stall beside the courthouse back door. Nearby stood Nathan Bailford's silver Porsche, looking like a car a college boy might drive to pick up pretty girls on weekends.

And it was Bailford who came up to her as she hefted her slightly overweight body out of her car.

Bailford gestured toward the crowd outside the lot. "And today's only for jury selection. Imagine the scene when the real trial starts."

"How's your client holding up?" Norma asked. She had vis-ited the accused woman several times in the past weeks, find-ing her surprisingly down-to-earth, although remote, neither helpful nor hindering. *"Confused,"* she was told. *Clinically depressed,* Norma described her.

"The same. Hasn't really changed since the night of the killing. All lows, no highs." He looked at her anxiously. "Anything new on your end?"

"Nothing yet. Lot of balls in the air though. Sometimes I feel like the *court* juggler. Ha, ha."

Norma didn't tell the lawyer that there were aspects to the killing that troubled her a great deal. There was nothing really specific yet, just things that didn't hang together, or hold up to close scrutiny.

What did seem clear was this: If Maggie shot her first husband, she was forced to do it. If she shot Will Shepherd, she was also forced to. By what or by whom was unclear.

The real trouble was that there *were* two killings. One might be explained — temporary insanity, self-defense, long-term abuse. But *two?*

She would go back to the murder site that afternoon, looking for more information, looking for some trail to follow.

There was something she hadn't found, something crucial. There had to be.

Dammit. Something was definitely wrong.

In Palm Springs, a California hazy, grapefruit-pink desert sun slid over the rocky stubble topping the mountains. The early rays came shimmering down onto the swimming pool and the surrounding red tile terrace.

Peter O'Malley laid aside his copy of yesterday's *New York Times.* He removed his new mirrored Ray-Ban sunglasses, put them on a wrought-iron drink stand, and stared at the sparkling blue sheet of pool water.

His mind was sparkling too. On the surface itself, superimposed over the reflection of the stucco pool house, he could almost *see* the face of Maggie Bradford. Just as he had seen it on television last night. Pale, shadows under the eyes. She looked like a damn zombie, out of it, and his heart leapt at her plight.

Serves her fucking well right!

Later that night he'd heard her singing voice, the sound that literally *destroyed* him, blaring from his car radio. Her songs were all over the radio, of course. *The caged songbird*, the deejay called her.

Well, that voice wouldn't be around much longer. Not on the radio (who would play the songs of a convicted murderess?), not in the boardroom of his father's company either.

He put his dark glasses back on, picked up the pen and legal pad he had brought with him to the pool, and began the letter that he believed would guarantee the process of sending Maggie Bradford to her doom.

What goes around, comes around, sweetheart. Now you get yours. Trust me on that. Your "affair" with the O'Malleys isn't quite over with yet.

89

EVERYBODY who came into close contact with Dan Nizhinski, the Westchester County district attorney, had the same reaction: he was too good to be true, he was perfect for his part.

First, there were his looks. He was six foot one, with corn-blond hair prematurely thinning on top but long on the sides. His face was somewhat weatherbeaten, making it look older than its thirty-six years, but the lines around his light blue, sparkling eyes gave them a mischievousness that made women jurors light up and men jurors consider him their friend.

Second was his courtroom manner. Standing ruler-straight, he seemed to take the jurors into his confidence, yet distanced himself enough so that they regarded him with awe. "I'm telling you the truth," he seemed to be saying. "Trust me. Astonishing as the revelations are, the facts support them."

Right now, though, at ease, cordovaned feet resting on top of his desk, he was addressing his assistants about the upcoming trial.

"The facts aren't in doubt," he said for what must have been the tenth time. "She just about admitted she shot him, handed over the murder weapon to the police, has cooperated more with them, I gather, than with her own attorneys. Such behavior is not uncommon in murder cases.

"But" — and here he paused for dramatic effect — "but this woman has enough money to buy the best legal and investigative resources available. Nathan Bailford himself will do the actual cross-examination; he's had more experience in murder trials than he has in corporate ones. It's how he made his reputation. And they've hired Norma Breen as their investigator. If there's something exculpatory to find, she'll find it — only there's nothing, damn it. *Nothing!*"

Another pause, this one to control his emotions. "The defense they'll offer, the only possible defense, is self-defense. That Maggie Bradford was defending herself against Will Shepherd, that if she hadn't killed him, he'd have killed her.

"Well, I say that's bullshit, and when we're finished with her, so will the jury. It's a defense that makes me sick. We're talking about *Maggie Bradford!* She couldn't have gone to the police? She was *afraid* of him? Well, it might have worked in the shooting of her first husband, but it sure as hell *ain't* gonna work here. She's a superstar. Any court in the world would have *guaranteed* her protection if she'd asked for it. A battered wife? My ass."

A third pause, a sip of coffee. The three others in his office knew his judicial beliefs, were inured to his melodramas. They also understood just how good he was at his job — and just how much this particular trial meant to his career.

"Two husbands, two deaths. That's putting a charley horse in the long arm of coincidence, as S. J. Perelman once said. But then, *then,* there's the death of a *third* man in the life of Maggie Bradford. A man she supposedly loved most of all.

"Patrick O'Malley, her live-in lover, died of a heart attack on his boat. Well, *was* it a heart attack? So the autopsy said. *But,* we don't know what brought it on."

Nizhinski continued speaking in his very controlled voice.

"Maggie Bradford is a killer. Cold-blooded, basically heartless, and until this last time, clever as the devil himself.

"But we've got her now. Guilty as charged? I've never been so convinced of anything in my life!"

Nizhinski finished, and he looked around at his assistants. "Any questions, cubs, or are you too dazzled to speak? Anyone see any way we can lose this one? I sure can't."

90

I'M NO EXPERT on prisons, and don't want to be, but if the Bedford Hills Correctional Facility for Women is "one of the most luxurious," then I pity the women incarcerated elsewhere. This stinks big time, especially when you're innocent; but even if you're not, this can't be the way to proper rehabilitation. I am absolutely certain that it isn't.

I have no cellmate — because I'm a "star." I exercise, and eat the bad food, alone. I've made a friend, another woman accused of killing her husband. The grim irony isn't lost on either of us.

I'm surrounded by drug addicts, small-time thieves, gang members, arsonists, a few murderers. Jennie visits a few times each week, and I can't wait to see her. Allie's been told I'm away, and to mind Mrs. Leigh. I miss them so much I can't write about it.

When I think about my sweet girl, my darling boy, I can *feel* my heart ripping — I'm forced to double over with pain. I don't feel sorry for myself; I just can't live without the two of them. I can't let myself go to pieces, for their sake.

*　　　*　　　*

I finished the last entry before the lights went out. It sounds like a long whine, and I'm not like that. Not even locked up in this prison. It is now six hours before the trial begins.

What will ultimately happen? What will the verdict be? I have no idea. None, zero, not a clue. When I hear the evidence, will I be any closer to the truth? Finally know how it all happened? Who will tell me what lies hidden in my heart?

Will *you* be closer to the truth? I've told you everything so far. What do you feel? *Are you sure?* Am I telling the truth — or am I just another celebrity liar?

Are you really sure about me?

When really bad trouble comes, do I simply shoot my way out? Is killing my only weapon? Do I have a tendency to get myself involved with monsters?

Am I a monster myself?

91

HERE WE GO!

"You ready, Mrs. Bradford? Everything's going to be fine. Let's go now. We're going to get you inside the courtroom as fast as humanly possible. We need your help with that. Keep your head down. Keep walking."

"I'll do my best, Bill."

"I know you will."

More perks. They sent a specially trained guard up from New York City for me. A pro at this. His job is to oversee the *other* guards who'll protect me from the press.

He'll lead me inside, sit near me while the trial's going on, then get me back to prison as quickly and easily as he can. Bill Seibert's his name. A nice man, actually. Nice manners and an even disposition.

I felt him push me gently from behind, and I tripped slightly as I got out of the van. *A great start, huh?* I could already see the headlines: *MAGGIE TRIPPED UP ON FIRST DAY!*

I walked into the blinding TV lights, closely packed human bodies, and a barrage of embarrassing questions: Did I do it? How did I feel? Was I able to write in prison? What were the inmates like? Did I sing any of my songs for them? *Give me a break!*

The level of stupidity and "high sleaze" was beyond anything I could imagine. I felt as though I might be sick. My legs were unsteady as I tried to walk. The handcuffs I wore made me feel guilty.

"Just follow me," Seibert said. "Don't stop for anything. Don't say anything to anybody, Mrs. Bradford."

I did just what he said.

He was the pro.

State troopers in cowboy hats could barely hold back the crowd. There were a few boos, but cheers too. The scene made me absolutely dizzy. The last time I had been in such a crush was in San Francisco — not exactly something I wanted to remember now.

Hands grabbed at me from across the police barricades. *Don't touch me. Please leave me alone! I don't belong to any of you.* The thought of a stranger's hand on me made me want to scream out loud. I held it in, held everything inside.

Blessedly, most of the loud, unruly crowd was shut out by a great oak door.

Suddenly, I was inside the high-ceilinged courthouse foyer. Court clerks, extra — mostly elderly — policemen, and minor village dignitaries stared at me now as though I were an alien from outer space. There were the usual black-and-white photos on the white plaster walls leading up a marble staircase; state, local, and American flags hung limply on gilded poles. It was so unbelievably weird.

Barry and Nathan hurried to me, Nathan shaking my hand, Barry kissing me on the cheek. They followed me inside the crowded courtroom. Everything seemed so unreal. Barry and Nathan seemed unreal to me too.

I actually felt physically sick. I thought I was going to throw up. The terrifying excitement seemed to have entered the room like deadly gas. Every face turned toward me as if on cue. Ordinary people. Famous writers in the gallery.

This was so horrible, so bad.

I struggled to keep my head up, *to look innocent.* I sat beside Nathan at the defendant's table; Barry took a seat reserved for him in the front row of spectators.

I held on to the defense table with both hands for support. I was trembling. I felt cold and so very alone.

I looked around for Jennie and Allie. Only Jennie was there, of course. I knew that. We waved at each other, and Jennie started to cry. *So strange and weird and wrong.*

"Hear ye! Hear ye! All people having business with Part Forty-four in this court, give attention and ye shall be heard. The Honorable Judge Andrew Sussman presiding."

It was the court clerk's big moment onstage. Every eye in the crowded room was on him. *Good. That meant they were finally off me.*

The trial was beginning.

My murder trial.

92

STRANGE *as a five-legged station wagon!* Norma Breen said to herself. *Nuts! Crazy! It doesn't add up. There's a piece missing here somewhere.*

Why had one gunshot, fired as Maggie Bradford was falling, been enough to kill that sorry bastard husband of hers? But it had, hadn't it. Not much question about that.

She was looking for the hundredth, or maybe the thousandth time at the police photographs of the murder site, taken just after Will's body had been discovered.

The body was lying facedown.

Bad luck, Will . . .

Or did you plan to have some bad luck? Did you shoot yourself, you sorry fuck? Is that your game?

He had been running away; that much was obvious from the footprints. Maggie had chased him and they had struggled. She had shot him in the head. He had fallen.

End of story, end of Will Shepherd.

Beginning of this current knotty mystery.

Norma felt a tingle travel up her spine. *Something didn't mesh. Something just wasn't tracking for her. What the hell was it?*

What was the missing piece of this goddamned five-and-dime jigsaw puzzle?

She would have to run some more experiments. Call in some favors too. Keep all those balls in the air. She would find something to set Maggie Bradford free.

To kill again?

93

IRONY OF IRONIES. I thought so anyway. *The prosecutor loved my music* — at least he used to.

I had met Dan Nizhinski once at a party at Nathan Bailford's house. He was there with his wife, an ordinary-looking woman who wore huge, oval-rimmed glasses and no makeup. I remember wondering why so attractive a man would marry this woman, but when we got a chance to talk, I liked her a lot. The Nizhinskis told me they were both fans. Hoopty-doo!

Well, I didn't like Dan Nizhinski now. He was tall and looked very scary, and the way he addressed the jury was like a beloved teacher speaking before a class of his best students.

"He's good," I whispered to Nathan.

"So are we," he answered, but his confidence did not spill over onto me.

The jury was made up of a corporate secretary in her early twenties; a high school principal; two housewives; three retirees, one of whom was an ex-army colonel; a freelance writer; two self-employed businessmen; a clerk in a Ford dealership; and an actor, "currently unemployed."

Six men, six women. Different backgrounds. With the power of God, they would somehow set me free. Or so I hoped.

My biggest fan, Dan Nizhinski, was talking about me again. Not exactly singing my praises though.

"You will hear evidence that the defendant, Maggie Bradford, did plan, over a period of several weeks, the murder of her husband, Will Shepherd.

"You will hear that this calculated murder was accomplished in a particularly cold-blooded fashion, as Will Shepherd ran for his life, as he tried to escape.

"You will discover that Will Shepherd was no ideal husband, but whatever his sins were, they were not enough to justify murder.

"And you will be presented with such a body of overwhelming evidence that there will be no doubt in *any* of your minds, as there is none in mine, that Maggie Bradford is guilty of murder in the first degree and should be punished to the full extent of the law."

Dan Nizhinski headed for his chair at the prosecutor's table, then stopped and returned to the jury, as though what he were about to say had just occurred to him, though I'd bet he had rehearsed the movement, and the speech, many times.

"One further thing. I forgot one thing. The murderess we are dealing with here is not an ordinary woman —"

"Objection! Your Honor," Nathan Bailford stood up and bellowed. "The district attorney has put a label on my client. She's not a 'murderess.' "

"Sustained."

"— Her name is Maggie Bradford, and it is a household name. She is not the woman you see on television; television presents *images,* not truth. She is not as sweet as her voice, as alluring as her melodies, as compassionate as her lyrics.

"You must divorce the public Maggie Bradford, the singer

and the songwriter, the star, from the real Maggie Bradford, the woman who sits before you charged with a hideous crime.

"Don't be fooled by images, taken in by fame, deluded because this woman writes so convincingly of good. The real Maggie Bradford had access to a gun. The real Maggie Bradford knew well how to pull the trigger. The real Maggie Bradford thought nothing of taking another's life. Why? Because she could *do anything*. She was a *star*.

"Well, when a star falls it blazes as it hits the atmosphere and is then extinguished. To Maggie Bradford, you, ladies and gentlemen of the jury, are her atmosphere, and because you stand for justice, *embody* justice, she will never shine again . . . she *must* never shine again."

94

NATHAN BAILFORD rose and, with passion to match the prosecutor's, outlined the defense. Throughout both speeches, I imagined that the lawyers were talking about somebody else — the disconnectedness I'd felt ever since I'd been accused of shooting Will had returned.

"The district attorney has painted a picture of a cold-blooded killer," Nathan said in a gruff, dusty whisper. "It's a scary picture, and perhaps, when it comes to killers, an accurate one. But it's not a true picture of Maggie Bradford, as you'll see when you hear from her friends, from her close colleagues, and from her."

I sat up in my seat. Quickly, I scribbled a note to Barry: *We agreed that I wouldn't testify. I will not!*

He wrote back: *Fine. Then tell us why you shot Will!!!*

And I: *No. I can't do that either.*

I had told them again and again — I wouldn't testify. I couldn't. I had my reasons for remaining silent, even if it kept me in prison for the rest of my life.

95

"MR. SHEPHERD?"

"Speaking."

"Mr. Shepherd, my name is Norma Breen, and I'm calling you from New York. You probably don't know who I am —"

"Oh, but I do. You're investigating my brother's murder. The lurid tales make the front pages here too. How can I help you?"

"I found a note from you in his possession. A simple note, actually. An odd one to keep. It said, 'Fuck you, Will.' Can you tell me what that was in reference to? And why your brother might have chosen to keep it?"

There was a brief silence. "Yes, I believe I can. He wanted me to join him in a business venture. I was in the States at the time, and he asked me over to his house. I said no."

"And that's the language you used? With your brother?"

"It was the only language he understood. We weren't very close. My brother was a crazy bastard, I'm afraid. My brother wasn't my favorite person, I might add."

Norma had known the brothers weren't close. Still — "Please tell me why. I imagine this must be difficult for you."

Palmer Shepherd laughed over the telephone. "How much time do you have? It's a long story."

"Lots of time, if you think it'd help."

"I don't see how it bears on the murder trial. By now, you must know what kind of man he was. But I could fly over to see you. Actually, I have a lot of sympathy for Maggie Bradford. You can't begin to imagine how much."

"That's kind of you. I'll certainly ask you to if I think it's necessary."

"Good. My offer is genuine. Maggie might have killed him. I'm surprised no one else did first though."

"Can you imagine why she might have done it?"

"I didn't know anything about their marriage. I stayed away on purpose. But Will was the Devil, Miss Breen. Will was *a bad man*. Frankly, whoever did it, did the world a service. I believe that with all my heart."

96

THE TRIAL moved ahead — *very slowly*. Day after exhausting day, week by week.

After testimony was finished on the exhausting twentieth day, Barry and Nathan came to visit me in prison. I almost didn't agree to see them.

I knew they wanted to press me again for an explanation, an alibi — something that I couldn't give them. I knew they were worried that the trial wasn't going our way.

"Tell me what you know about Palmer," Barry said once we were together in a small conference room used for just such meetings.

I was somewhat puzzled. It seemed a strange way to begin our conversation. Palmer Shepherd?

"What about him? He's Will's brother, of course. They weren't close. I only met him twice. He offered his condolences — *at the wedding*."

"Was he close to his aunts, do you know?"

"Not as close as Will was."

The words came out fast and must have had a ring to them. Barry looked at me sharply, then his eyes became sad and distant.

"You *know* about Vannie and Will?" he said. "So why didn't you tell us? Why did we have to find out from Will's brother?"

Long-suppressed anger rose. I had to let some of it out. "I don't know anything. I might have suspected something. Barry, what are you trying to do to me?"

He looked at me unwaveringly. "Tell me the truth, Maggie. Was she ever in your house? Was Vannie ever there?"

"Only at our wedding." I remembered the image vividly. "She was very attractive — his mother's younger sister. You were there, Barry. You saw her. Will never got over his mother."

"I guess not! Did he ever bring any other strange women home?" Nathan asked.

"Never. Why would I allow that? That doesn't make any sense, Nathan."

"Let me ask again," Nathan said at last. "Will didn't try anything *funny* in the house? You have to trust us, Maggie. You mustn't keep secrets from us. Not at this point in the trial. We have to know what the prosecution does."

I hesitated, just for an instant. I tensed. I didn't like where this was going.

"No," I said. "I don't have anything to tell you. Why would I hold something back?"

Barry pounced. "You're lying right now. Dammit, Maggie. You're breaking my heart."

"I swear to you —" I whispered. I *was* lying, of course. I *never* lie — but I had to now.

"Who was it?" Barry nearly shouted at me. I'd never seen him this angry before. Veins pulsed all over his forehead and neck.

"Please! . . . Barry, no!"

His face suddenly went pale. His eyes closed, then slowly opened again. "Of course," he said and I could see tears in his eyes.

He looked toward me with such tenderness and pity that I was sure *both* our hearts would break.

"Oh my God, of course," he said. "Will was after Jennie, wasn't he?"

I stood and called for the guard. "Take me back to my cell. Take me back right now!"

I went away with the guard. I wouldn't say another word to either Barry or my lawyer. I couldn't, I wouldn't, drag Jennie into this.

97

"THE PROSECUTION calls Peter O'Malley."

I blanched as I heard the words spoken in open court. Actually, I was getting used to the feeling of constant anxiety and fear. We were twenty-nine days into testimony, most of it very bad for me.

Over strenuous defense objections, Judge Sussman had allowed Nizhinski to introduce evidence about the death of Phillip Bradford. Now the district attorney planned to get in as much as he could *about Patrick's death.*

It would be difficult. He could do no more than *imply* that I had been responsible. But that's what Peter wanted, I knew. To imply, to insinuate, to hurt me in any way that he could.

In a very strange move, the court had been cleared of spectators for the testimony. Peter had agreed to talk, but his lawyer had convinced the judge to allow Peter privacy.

I didn't understand. Why should Peter be protected? But very soon, I understood everything. Peter's testimony took forever in real time — there must have been a hundred objections from my lawyers — but the bottom line *would have sounded something like this.*

"Mr. O'Malley, are you a member of an establishment called the Lake Club?"

"I am."

"The club is located in Bedford Hills? Just off Greenbriar Road?"

"It is."

"What is its membership?"

"About five hundred people."

"And the activities are those of most country clubs — golf, tennis, swimming, dinners, and dancing in the evening?"

"That's right."

"Yet the Lake Club provides something more, does it not?"

"For some members, yes."

"Something not available to the full membership, but only to a special few."

"Correct."

"Are you one of those few?"

"I was."

"Who else is among the group?"

"Prominent people, on the whole."

"What does the club provide for them?"

"A meeting place, mostly. There are discussions of financial issues, matters of government."

"And after the discussions are over?"

"There's — entertainment. Not always, but on occasion."

"I see. Can you describe this entertainment?"

"Sexual entertainment for the most part."

"Can you be more specific?"

"Girls, and sometimes young men, are provided."

"Prostitutes?"

"I wouldn't exactly call them prostitutes."

"They're there for the members' 'entertainment,' and they get paid for their services?"

"Yes."

"A rose by any other name . . . tell me, Mr. O'Malley. Do you reside in Bedford Hills?"

"No. Manhattan and the West Coast."

"Yet you are a member of the Lake Club?"

"Yes."

"You've also participated in these late-night parties?"

"Yes."

"Why is that, Mr. O'Malley?"

"My father, Patrick O'Malley, was a big deal at the club. I was granted membership when he died."

"Did he participate in the after-hours entertainments?"

"Yes."

"That is, he slept with young girls."

"Yes."

"Did Patrick O'Malley have a relationship with Maggie Bradford?"

"For many months. Maybe it was a couple of years."

"And do you have a half-brother?"

"Yes. They all lived together."

"Would you say that Patrick O'Malley and Maggie Bradford were in love?"

"So my father told me."

"Yet he did not drop his membership in the club?"

"No."

"Nor stop sleeping with young girls?"

"I don't know about that."

"Was Mrs. Bradford aware of these 'entertainments' and your father's part in them?"

"Yes."

"How do you know?"

"She had pictures of my father and at least two of the girls."

"She had *pictures*?"

"I found them in her bedroom. Their bedroom. After my father died. I helped collect his papers."

"They were graphic pictures?"

"Very. My father and two girls."

"We don't need the details. Not at this time. Mrs. Bradford had possession of the pictures?"

"Yes."

"What did she think of them?"

"I don't know. She never told me."

"What did *you* think of them?"

"It's always a shock when a son sees his father *in flagrante*."

"Of course. But you weren't *surprised*."

"No."

"Now tell me, Mr. O'Malley, how did your father die?"

"I don't know."

"You don't know? How is that possible."

"He died on a boat. The cause was supposedly a heart attack."

" 'Supposedly'? He was alone on the boat?"

"No. Mrs. Bradford was with him."

"And they were alone together."

"Yes. The Coast Guard found the boat. Mrs. Bradford told them how he died."

"Did they believe her?"

"Evidently."

"Tell me, Mr. O'Malley, did you know Will Shepherd?"

"Yes."

"Would you say you were friends?"

"Social friends."

"You had business dealings with him?"

"Yes. Business and social."

"Ah. Social. Was Will Shepherd a member of the Lake Club?"

"Yes."

"Of the club within the club?"

"Yes."

"Then he partook of the 'entertainment'?"

"Definitely."

"Did Maggie Bradford know?"

Peter O'Malley paused, twisted in his seat, then he looked straight at me. "Yes, she did. That's probably why she murdered him."

As I said, there were a hundred objections during the testimony, but that was how I remembered it, and I'm sure how the jury did as well. I was losing . . . everything that I had ever loved or cared about.

98

NORMA BREEN came to visit me that night just after the dinner hour. She had become one of my favorite people to see. We were both around the same age, both from blue-collar backgrounds, and we understood each other.

"Maggie, I hate to tell you this. I don't like your songs," she started in that night. It was Norma's quaint way of saying "hi."

"Bitch," I said, but I smiled at her. She made me laugh when nobody else could; she was my buddy.

"No, you're the bitch. You won't help me do my job — which is, ironically, to help you get out of this zoo."

I was still smiling. We both were, though the subject was deadly serious. You can only be deadly serious for so long, for so many hours, days, months in a row.

"I hate to tell you," I told her, "I don't like the way you do *your* job."

"Too tough for you, huh? Too edgy?"

I put my hand across the table on top of hers. She was single, available, but probably because of the extra twenty pounds she carried, a lot of men were overlooking her. Their mistake. *Big* mistake.

"What's on your mind today, sweetie?" I asked her. There was always something with her.

"I want to try to talk you out of your martyr thing. I hate Mother Teresa anyway. Stop being a martyr, Maggie."

"I *am* a martyr. That's what I had to do to be loved in our family, when I was a kid. I can't help myself."

Norma flipped over my hand, and she clasped it hard. "I love you, Maggie. I've learned to, in a very short time for me. A lot of people love you. You're unfuckingbelievably lovable."

I snorted out a laugh — my darkest humor was bubbling up. "Yes, everybody loves me but my husbands."

"Maybe you picked a couple of losers, so you could play martyr? Like you said, maybe you can't help yourself, Maggie. Only *you can, you can help yourself.*"

I sighed deeply. I thought that I knew where Norma was going. I was tired of hearing it from Barry and Nathan, but suddenly hearing it from Norma, from another woman, it sounded a little different.

"I can't though," I finally said. "Nice try, but I just can't do it. I can't put Jennie up there."

"You can," Norma insisted, and suddenly she began to gush tears. She'd never done that before; never completely let down her guard. Then we were both sobbing, holding hands, and crying our eyes out like a couple of old ninnies.

"I talked to Jennie, Maggie. She says the two of you have to talk. She said to tell you this was a 'continuation' of Pound Ridge, and that *you owed her.*"

289

99

FOR THE LAST TIME, Norma Breen went to Maggie's house in Bedford Hills. She was convinced she'd missed something; that everybody had. What in God's name was it though?

Mildred Leigh met her at the door and offered her a cup of coffee. Allie was playing in the living room, and Norma was grateful for the chance to talk. She hadn't interviewed Mrs. Leigh at any length; maybe this time she could get some useful information.

"I know you've been over and over this, but tell me about the day of the murder," Norma said. "Were you in the house?"

"Until about six-thirty, then I left. It was my night off." She blushed. "And I had a date with Mr. Frazier. Didn't come back till the next morning, and then only to find the police and the press and Maggie accused of something she would never do."

She seems pleased with herself, Norma thought. *Makes sense. Her fifteen minutes of fame.* "Did anything unusual happen before you left?" she asked. "Anything you can think of might help Maggie. Say whatever comes into your head."

"It was a day like any other. No, nothing was very different. Nothing I can remember. Just like I told the police."

"The two of them didn't argue? Nothing like that?"

"They barely saw each other. Mr. Shepherd was in town, in New York for most of the day. I didn't hear any fighting."

"Describe what they did. Anything that you think of, Mrs. Leigh."

"Well, Maggie, she was in her study. Writing her songs, I guess. She would come out to talk with the children during her breaks. She and Allie love to play."

"And Mr. Shepherd?"

"He got back from the city at some time. Don't know when. Later that night, I saw him by the club. He was heading on back to the house."

Norma was momentarily confused. "You were at the club, Mrs. Leigh? Why were you there?"

"J.C., he has a house there, on the grounds. Opposite side of the main building from the parking lot."

"Do you know what Mr. Shepherd was doing there that night?"

"No, ma'am. Just saw him walk past J.C.'s."

"What time was this?"

"Around ten, ten-thirty. Something like that."

"You only saw him briefly?"

"Yes, ma'am. J.C. and I, we had better things to do than watch Mr. Will Shepherd."

"I'm sure."

What was Will doing by the club that night? It didn't track with what Maggie had told her.

"But he wasn't there for one of the parties? The ones that took place late?" Norma asked.

Mrs. Leigh glanced at her conspiratorially. "J.C. tell you? You know about those carryings-on?"

"Sure do. Did you happen to notice how Mr. Shepherd was dressed that night?"

"It was dark, ma'am. Only thing I know for sure, he was carrying his rifle back from the club."

Norma could feel the small hairs rise on the back of her arms. "His rifle? Are you sure?"

"They shoot skeet there. At the shooting range down past the golf course. He often did that."

"But not on the day he was killed."

Mrs. Leigh sighed. "I told you. He was in New York most of the day. Left real early for him."

"You told the police all of this?" Norma asked.

Mrs. Leigh nodded. "Everything that I'm telling you now."

"About Mr. Shepherd and the rifle?"

"Of course."

They finished their coffee. "Thank you, Mrs. Leigh," Norma said. "You've been very helpful."

"Happy to oblige. You see that little boy in there? He's a sweetheart, and he loves his mommy. We all want her to come home. We miss Maggie so bad."

"So do I. Is there a phone I can use?"

"In the den. I'll show you."

"I can find it," Norma said. She had to stop herself from running.

100

"BARRY, I'm up at Maggie's house. I'm onto something. At least I hope so. *No*, I actually think I have something real going."

Norma had closed the den door behind her, but she nevertheless whispered into the phone.

"I'm listening," Barry said.

"You know that celebrated rifle in question?" Norma said. "Mrs. Leigh saw Will carrying it the night of the shooting. He was out by the country club, which more and more seems to be figuring into this brutal mess."

"Why would he have had the rifle at the Lake Club?"

"First question I asked myself." Norma's voice rose in her excitement. "That's why he *went* to the club. *To fetch it*. It's where he must have kept it when Maggie told him to get rid of it. She said she looked everywhere around the house, but she could never find it. *It was at the club*."

There was a long pause. Finally Barry said, "Now why would he want to do that? Did he stage his own suicide, Norma? Is that it? Did he frame Maggie?"

Norma felt a sudden surge of frustration and bewilderment.

"Goddamnit, I don't know yet," she said. "Not a clue. That part doesn't make any sense to me.

"But I'll tell you what I *do* know," Norma spoke again. "The Bedford police knew Will went to fetch the rifle, and they kept it to themselves. Something's rotten in the state of Bedford, and I'm going to find out what, and who, and why."

"Sic 'em, Norma."

"*Grrrr.*"

101

I LOOKED at Jennie as she entered the visiting room and I wanted to cry. I wouldn't let myself. I needed to be strong now, for both of us. I needed to listen to Jennie.

I couldn't take my eyes off her though. I'd always loved her, much more than I cared about myself. People said we were a lot alike, only I saw Jennie as having few, if any, of my faults and weaknesses. We did look like each other. Jennie was tall now, almost five nine. Her blond hair was as long as mine. We had the same eyes.

I love you, I thought as she sat across the table from me. I hated the table being there, separating us now. I needed to hug Jennie, and to be hugged back. Never more than right at that moment, right now.

Suddenly, she cracked a smile. It was pure Jennie. "I have a message from Norma. She says she has proof that Mother Teresa is total bullshit. That she's actually a Vegas act, in it for the money."

I laughed out loud at the joke.

"Norma's trying to help you, Mom," Jennie leaned across the table and said in her most mature voice.

"I think I know that, Jen. How are you?"

Jennie rolled her eyes. "Believe it or not, I'm good. I'm not great, but I'm okay." She blew me two kisses. "Those are from Allie. Actually, he sent you a hundred kisses."

"Does he still remember who I am?"

She rolled her eyes again. "We make him watch videos of your concerts so that he doesn't forget. We read him your letters, show him your pictures. I'm here to talk about something else. We're going to talk, Mom dear."

"I understand," I said to Jennie. "I respect your wishes."

"Good, that's a neat start. Now, I think you have to ask me questions, *because* you have certain ideas in your head, but I'm not sure what they are. So we'll employ the Socratic method."

I smiled. "I'm not even going to ask you about your grades."

"Tops in my class. Stay on track. Stay with me here."

This was the hardest yet, the worst thing I'd been through. *Yes, I had certain ideas in my head. No, I wasn't ready to talk about them. Maybe I would never be ready.*

"I guess we could start with the night of the . . . of Will's death," I said.

"That's a very good place to begin — *at the end.*"

"I saw Will up in your room. What was he doing there, Jennie?"

"He came to say good night."

There was an innocence in Jennie's words that made me stare. "That's all? Jennie, you can't lie, either to protect Will, or even my feelings. Are we agreed about that?"

"Sure. Those are the game rules. We're agreed. Now, let's play."

"You tell me the truth, and I'll do the same. Anything you want to know. About Will's death."

Jennie's eyes stayed on mine. "I do have questions."

"First me, then you, okay?"

She nodded. "Yep. That's fine with me."

I didn't know exactly where to go next with my questions. I picked an obvious place.

"Did Will come to your room to say good night often?"

"He did sometimes. He'd bring me warm milk. He said that his aunt used to bring him tea, when he was a boy in England."

The mention of Will's aunt startled me, though Jennie couldn't have known why. I took a deep breath. I didn't know if I could go on with this. Prison wasn't the place I wanted to have this kind of talk with Jennie.

She reached for my hand. "Can I try to make this easier . . . for both of us?"

"If you think you can," I whispered. I didn't have much of a voice left. I felt hollowed out, empty. Out of it. Unreal.

"Will was very complicated. You already know that. I think he, I think part of him, actually wanted to be a good father. He would come up to my room and talk sometimes, just talk. I think he wanted to prove he could be there *and just talk*. He told me a lot about when he was growing up. He was a good listener. Sometimes."

"Yes, he could be," I remembered.

"I had a wicked crush on him, Mom. I thought he was so beautiful, like a god, like Ralph Fiennes or Mel Gibson on steroids. I used to think about him *all the time*."

"But nothing ever happened?"

"I know he told you that he did, *that we did* — I was there, I heard it — but nothing ever happened, Mom. You don't have to protect me. Please believe me, *nothing happened*."

I put both my hands up to Jennie's face. I wanted to be even closer, but that was the best we could do in this horrifying place.

"Let me be your witness, Mom. Please, please, let me do that for you? I *need* to help you, just this once. I think I can. Nothing happened between Will and me. You don't have to protect me."

102

NORMA BREEN was in one of her usual bitching, grousing moods when she arrived at the Lake Club. *The missing goddamn pieces to the puzzle! They're around here somewhere,* she kept telling herself, hoping that it might come true if she said it enough.

She had come to the club, specifically, to see J. C. Frazier. J.C. was in his late forties, his face weathered by the outdoors, his body trim and well muscled.

Well, he's a looker, Norma Breen thought as she sat with him on the porch of the main building at the Lake Club. *Now, let's hope he's a goddamn talker.*

Norma eased into things, convincing J.C. to verify what she already knew: that there were late-night "parties" at the club; and that Will Shepherd had been an invited guest on several occasions.

"Would there be a list of names anywhere?" she asked. "Of the party boys?"

The groundskeeper shrugged his broad shoulders. "If there is, I've never seen one. I sure doubt it."

"Then tell me some of the names. People you've seen here after hours. C'mon, J.C."

J.C. shook his head. "Couldn't do that. If anyone found out I had told, I'd lose my job. I'm not even supposed to *know* about it."

"But you told me about Mr. Shepherd."

"I'm trying to help you. I just can't help as much as you might like."

"Dammit, this is a *murder* investigation. What you know might save Mrs. Bradford's life!"

J.C. shifted uneasily in his chair. "I realize that. That's why I'm talking to you. Only don't make me tell you the names. That, I can't do."

Norma glared at him. It didn't seem to make any difference though. "Then at least show me where. Let me take a peek for myself."

"Oh, Ms. Breen, if I did that —"

"If you don't I'll have you subpoenaed and you can testify about it in open court." *Grrrr, take that!*

He winced. "The entrance, then. Only if anybody asks me, I'll say you found it yourself."

"It's a deal." Norma smiled. "Now show me."

103

THE TWO OF THEM followed a winding path all the way around to the far side of the clubhouse. There was a heavy wooden door there that looked like it would only be used by the maintenance staff. J. C. Frazier had a key.

"This is it, huh?" Norma asked. It was cold and dark on that side of the building. *Like the black hearts of the lousy bastards who come here to get their kicks.*

Inside, Norma found it was comparable to the rest of the exclusive club. She and J.C. walked back through a deserted billiard room. There seemed to be a gauzy haze hanging in the air.

They entered a surprisingly elegant barroom with mahoghany paneling everywhere. Norma knew that this was the place. The club within a club. *The rich boy's playroom.*

"This is where they met, right? It's where they had their sex parties?"

"Yes ma'am," J.C. muttered. He seemed serious and withdrawn.

Norma could almost picture "the boys club." Their expensive clothes, the best whiskeys, their high-and-mighty demeanor, their prostitutes. She wasn't sure about it, but she sensed that *this room* might be central to Maggie's defense. She believed there was even the possibility that one of the club members had killed Will Shepherd.

Had Will finally fucked the wrong wife? Or screwed one of these powerful men in a business deal? Done something else to get himself murdered? Norma thought it was very possible that he had.

"Pour yourself a drink, J.C.," she said to the groundskeeper of the Lake Club, "then plop your butt down. We have to talk. We're *going* to talk."

He shook his head. "I can't do that."

Norma pointed her hand at the much taller and larger man. "Listen, you, and listen good. Maggie Bradford might yet be convicted of murder, but not because you held the truth back. You talk to me, now, or you'll lose your job for sure, and you'll lose a whole lot more than that. That's a promise I'll keep."

J. C. Frazier walked to the bar and he poured himself a shot of Maker's Mark.

"Good choice," Norma said. "Make that *two* shots, one for me. Then you can tell me exactly who was part of this club within a club. I want *the names*. I want every name that you know."

J. C. Frazier poured Norma Breen a drink, then they both sat at the wood-paneled bar. Finally, J.C. began to talk. He even cried.

When he was through, Norma couldn't believe what she had heard. *She could not believe it. Jesus, capital H, Christmas!*

Everything just changed, Norma thought. *My God, the whole world just moved. The enemy blinked. Gotcha, you lousy bastards. Gotcha.*

104

HOW GROWN UP *she is, how composed, and close to being a woman,* I thought as Jennie walked to the stand to begin her testimony in court. Her face seemed to glow; her long blond hair was shining. Jennie looked so confident and serene. I wished I could say the same for myself.

Nathan led her through her story with extreme care. How Will came to see her on that fatal night. How he was standing at the foot of the bed, "leering" at her, when I came in.

" 'Jennie and I were just about to have some fun. Care to join us in bed? Ménage à trois!' That's what he told my mother. I don't know why he said it, *but he did,*" she told the jury. There was no way they couldn't believe her.

And as Jennie repeated Will's words, I felt the same paralyzing rage that had overcome me then. *I'm glad he's dead,* I thought. *It's horrifying, but I am glad.*

Nathan took less than forty minutes with her. That was our agreement, and he had practically signed it in blood. He finished, and then he sat down next to me. He took my hand and I squeezed his. "Thank you, Nathan," I whispered to him, "for being so patient with me."

"Thank you for trusting me," Nathan whispered back.

The jury's faces remained impassive, but I could see that the women at least were touched by Jennie.

I had not killed in self-defense, I had killed defending my daughter. Now they knew. Jennie had done what she'd meant to do.

Unfortunately, now came the bad part. Dan Nizhinski slowly approached the witness stand. *A killer whale,* I thought, *about to eat a minnow. He's doing this to get famous. That's all this is to him: instant fame and celebrity status.*

"Miss Bradford — Jennie," he began softly, almost apologetically.

"Please don't call me by my first name." Jennie met his stare and did not waver. "You don't know me, Mr. Nizhinski."

The prosecutor sighed. Score one for Jennie.

"You have a good friend by the name of Millie Steele?" he asked after the briefest pause. It was hard to knock Nizhinski off his game.

Jennie seemed surprised by the question. "Yes, I do," she said.

"She's your *best* friend, isn't she?" the prosecutor continued. He was being unusually nice.

Jennie hesitated, then she finally nodded. I could see her mind working, trying to figure out where he was heading with the questions.

"You'll have to answer the question verbally, Miss Bradford," Judge Sussman spoke from the bench. "Is Millie Steele your best friend?"

Nathan Bailford slowly rose from the defense table. "Objection, Your Honor. I don't see what Miss Bradford's relationship to Miss Steele has to do with this case. Need I remind everyone, Miss Bradford is only fifteen years old. This trial, especially this testimony, is an unbelievably painful experience for her, and it should be kept as brief as possible."

"Your Honor," Nizhinski responded, "the jury will soon see

exactly where this line of questioning is leading. It's an important point, I promise you."

"Proceed," Sussman said. "I'll hold you to your promise though. Tread very lightly."

Nizhinski moved closer to Jennie, and I flinched. I didn't like that one bit. I could tell Jennie didn't either.

"You talk to Millie Steele a lot? At school? Sometimes after school?"

"Yes, sir. *Before* school too," Jennie said and she smiled. So did everyone on the jury.

I could see she was still puzzled though. *Where was he leading her? Watch out!* I wanted to call to her.

"Would you ever lie to your friend? *Have* you ever lied to her, that you can remember?"

"No. Millie and I don't lie to each other."

"Then listen to this, Jennie. On the thirteenth of October, your best friend Millie Steele made the following statement at the Bedford Hills police station —" He paused, and opened the thick binder he had carried with him to the witness stand. The binder was intimidating in itself, thick, with a black leather cover.

" 'Jennie was in love with her stepfather. She told me time and time again she wanted — she wanted — well, she wanted to go to bed with him, and would try anything to seduce him.' "

Nizhinski closed the folder gently. "Did you tell Millie Steele that you were in love with Will Shepherd?"

What's he doing to her? I thought as my stomach clenched. *Yes, she had a crush on Will.*

"Yes, but —" Jennie tried to answer the question he'd asked.

"Just answer yes or no, please. *Were* you in love with your stepfather?"

He's torturing her! He should be stopped right now. "Nathan?" I whispered.

"Wait, Maggie. Listen."

"I had a crush on Will. Yes, sir."

"Did you ever try to seduce him?"

"Not really."

"That's not answering my question, Miss Bradford. Yes or no: Did you try to seduce him?"

"Yes. In a way I guess."

"Did you go to bed with him?"

"No! You're such a *bad person!* No!" Jennie told the prosecutor. "No!"

No! Thank God! Now let her go.

"Then *where* did you make love with him? Millie Steele says that you did!"

"We never made love!"

"Forgive me, but that's difficult to believe. You're an attractive young woman, Jennie. Will Shepherd was susceptible to attractive young women. We've heard that again and again in this courtroom. Are you telling me that even though you threw yourself at him, he refused? His reputation says otherwise!"

Jennie finally began to cry. Her sobs were the only sounds in the courtroom. She was a young girl again.

"Nathan, please," I whispered again.

Nizhinski, relentless, moved even closer to Jennie.

"In fact, isn't it true that you and he had been lovers for months? That the defense contention your mother killed him to protect you is therefore nonsense. That your mother killed him for *revenge?*"

"I *didn't* throw myself at him! He *never* touched me! He never did anything *indecent*, like you're doing now."

Nizhinski took a step back and stared at her. "Do you know what perjury is?"

She nodded.

"Answer yes or no, please. The court stenographer can't record a nod."

"Yes." Her voice was faint.

"Do you know what the penalty is for perjury?"

"Not exactly. Will you unjustly put me in prison — like you did to my mother?"

"The penalty for perjury *can* mean jail, but there's no injustice here, Miss Bradford. Your mother killed Will Shepherd because she *thought* the two of you were having an affair."

Nathan was on his feet beside me. "Objection! *Objection!*"

"No further questions," Dan Nizhinski said and walked away from Jennie.

The courtroom erupted all around us. It took minutes before the banging of Judge Sussman's gavel caught anyone's attention.

Jennie was led from the witness box. She was crying. I reached my arms out to her, but I couldn't touch her.

"It's all right, Mom," she said. "Nobody can hurt us. Nobody can hurt us anymore."

I only wished that were true.

105

NORMA BREEN chewed on Rolaids, tasty, orange-flavored ones, as she sat in court and listened to the closing arguments. She had a secret, an absolute mindblower, and she had to bite her tongue to keep from blurting it out.

Maybe we can throw out this bullshit trial, Norma thought as she sat in the back row of spectators. *Or maybe, despite all the evidence, Maggie will be acquitted. Maybe the jury will see that she had to kill — and let her off on a technicality. Or at least give her the lightest sentence permissible under the law, the least punitive verdict. And maybe Mel Gibson will call me for a date while I'm sitting here on my oversized rump. You never know, right?*

Norma had decided that her best strategy was to wait for the verdict. And now, as she listened to Nathan Bailford's rebuttal, a spark of hope glimmered in her heart. *This is a good woman. Spare her. It's only right. Do the right thing, huh.*

In his redirect, Nathan had interpreted the facts so succinctly that Norma was left feeling that Maggie was the victim, Will the killer.

Still, the defense lawyer couldn't *change* the fact that Will was dead, Maggie alive. And he couldn't solve the other important question — if Maggie hadn't, then who *had* killed Will?

The prosecutor got up and immediately dismissed Nathan's case as a smokescreen. Murder was murder. That's what it was; there was no other name for it. Murder with a single motive: revenge. And because Maggie had picked up the gun, brought it knowingly into her daughter's room, it was *premeditated* murder, and deserved the maximum penalty: a life sentence.

Yet with it all, Norma considered, *something is terribly wrong about this trial.*

She was still uncomfortable. It was the gut feeling she'd had from the very start. *Maggie did not kill Will Shepherd.* She was convinced of that. *Will had committed suicide, hadn't he? According to Maggie, and even Palmer, he'd been threatening to do it for years. This was his final, terrible revenge against Maggie.*

Maybe if they had put Maggie on the stand, a reason would have emerged. Norma had reluctantly agreed with Barry and Nathan that such a strategy was a mistake. Maggie could only verify her statement to the police — that she didn't know for sure what happened, that she *might* have killed him — but it was a close call, and now Norma was second-guessing everything about the defense effort. *Everything.*

Ah well, it was too late for second guessing. Nathan Bailford finished his closing statement and wearily sat down.

The forty-six-day drama was finally over.

It was next to impossible to read the jurors' faces.

Yet Norma could guess: Maggie Bradford was going to be convicted of murder.

And then, she thought to herself, *the real fireworks can begin.*

106

"NEVER IN DOUBT. It wasn't even close, sports fans. To the victors! To us!"

Dan Nizhinski sat back in his chair, took a big sip of pilsner, and beamed at his three associates.

"To the victors!" the group chanted.

"What was it?" he asked, as if he didn't know the answer, "the all-time record for fastest verdict in a major murder case?"

"Not to suck-ass too much, but you did a great job, Dan," Moira Lowenstein, his youngest associate, said. "You got the jury to waive their emotions and look hard at what actually happened. No mean feat. You got them to realize that if they let her go, they subverted the whole system of justice."

"I couldn't have done it without you all," Nizhinski said, insincerely, leaving them with the impression he could have succeeded just as well with anyone else.

"What's next for you, boss?" Bob Stevens, Nizhinski's closest associate, helped himself to his fourth beer in less than an hour.

Nizhinski grinned. He was still performing, couldn't turn it off. "To tell you the truth, I haven't made up my mind. The exposure during the trial won't hurt. I have to admit that, I guess."

"And the state could use some cleaning up," Moira added. Peter Eisenstadt, the third associate — the quiet one — glared at her. *Yeah, and guess who wants to go to Albany on your shirttails, boss?*

"I'll decide in due course," Nizhinski said. They all knew he would run for something big. "For now, let's enjoy the moment." He raised his beer can. "To a great victory."

"To victory," his colleagues echoed, and they all drank, laughed, congratulated one another.

Then the phone rang.

Dan Nizhinski picked it up himself. "Nizhinski."

"Kahn," the caller said. "Barry Kahn." Something in his voice chilled the prosecutor. "Norma Breen and I are coming right over to your office. She's discovered something that might interest you."

107

GUILTY.
Guilty.

The word rang in my head like a religious chant. No, it was more like a dirge. *Guilty. I'll go mad in prison. I'm already half-mad.*

Norma and Barry came to see me as soon as I was transported back here from court today. They were full of smiles and secrets. Don't worry, they told me. They would start appeal proceedings immediately in a higher court. Everything was going to be all right.

How could it be? A life in jail isn't "all right." Trust me on that.

I know there are appeals, and that my fate won't be decided for months, probably years. Still, the chances for reversal are small, no matter what anybody says. My chances are terrifyingly bad.

So why was Norma hopeful and cheerful? Why did Barry press me so hard to remember exactly what happened the night I shot Will when I've gone over it, and gone over it? Simple answer: They wanted to try and take my mind off what had just happened.

Guilty.

The Scarlet *M* still emblazoned on my chest.

I guess I never really expected this. I'd hoped that in the end I would go free. It just didn't happen that way.

Guilty.

108

THAT NIGHT in my cell, I stayed up until two, maybe three in the morning. I lay with my eyes closed, trying futilely to recapture lost images of my life on the outside. Allie. Jennie. Concerts I'd had. Finally, exhaustion overcame frustration. I fell asleep.

I didn't dream. It was as though I had fallen away into nothingness. The long, long fall from grace continues. A bottomless pit.

I awakened to a shock.

A gray parade of police officials was standing outside the cell, led by Warden Serra herself.

I glanced at my clock.

It was quarter past six in the morning.

I didn't get it, didn't understand.

I blinked, blinked, blinked.

Warden Serra and the others were still there.

Why were they here? What had happened?

Was I going to be moved to another prison?

Was I actually awake, seeing what I thought I saw?

I doubted it. This wouldn't be the first time I'd confused a dream and reality in here.

Warden Serra?

All these other people?

"Aren't you a little early?" I finally asked. My eyes were slowly adjusting to the harsh light of the corridor.

"Please get dressed, Mrs. Bradford," Maureen Serra said. "We've received a call from the courthouse. Something's come up. You're wanted in Judge Sussman's chambers immediately."

109

I FELT COLD and was shaking all over as three guards led me through the empty courthouse. I didn't understand what could be happening. Neither did anyone from the prison.

What was going on now? What could this be?

There were four people in the judge's chambers when I arrived. Judge Sussman sat behind a large mahogany desk. To his right sat Nathan Bailford, looking somber, but successful, as always.

Barry, sitting forward on a leather couch on the left side of the room, winked at me, but he didn't smile.

Only Norma Breen, dressed in a green tweed skirt and bulky brown sweater and sitting next to Barry on the couch, seemed relaxed. "Hi, Maggie," she said; she was the only one to actually speak to me.

"Hello, Norma. Everybody," I whispered. It all seemed surreal, as though I were dreaming. What in God's name was happening now?

There was an empty chair next to Sussman's, and he motioned toward it. In a daze, I did as I was told.

Sitting, I could look at the faces of the others — the same

view that Judge Sussman had, as though I had gone from defendant to part of the judicial team. I liked that a lot.

Papers were shuffled. Briefcases snapped open. Coffee container lids removed.

The briefcases, the papers, the store-bought coffee reminded me that these people were different from me, that they led different lives from outside a prison.

Still, no one spoke to me, not even Nathan Bailford.

They were waiting for someone to arrive. Dan Nizhinski? Somebody else? Who?

I wished that someone would tell me why I was here, then maybe I could stop quivering. My mind was racing badly.

"Mrs. Bradford," Judge Sussman finally spoke to me. "Ms. Breen has discovered some remarkable information," he announced. "We're only waiting for the district attorney — ah, here he is. Dan, welcome."

Nizhinski strode into the room like a matador into a bullring, stance erect, expression fierce, afraid of no one. I thought of Norma's line on Nizhinski: *a putz of the first order,* she called him.

He looked straight at Nathan Bailford. "What's this meeting about? If you think you can get the verdict overturned because of some technicality —"

"It's hardly a technicality," Judge Sussman interrupted the prosecutor. "Tell him your story, Ms. Breen. Please, have a seat, Dan. I think you'll need one in a minute."

Norma rose slowly. She glanced at me, then directly at Dan Nizhinski, who had stopped pacing and was watching her warily, not quite the same confident matador he had been a moment ago.

When Norma spoke, it was in an assured and commanding voice. This was her time in the spotlight.

"During the trial, Maggie, you may remember Mr. Nizhinski took testimony from Peter O'Malley. He spoke about 'private parties' late in the night at the Lake Club, where, I believe, you have been a dinner guest from time to time. You had dinner at the club proper, of course."

I nodded, still having no idea where Norma was heading. "It's kind of where I met Will, actually. I couldn't join if I wanted to. There are no women members."

"I'm sorry," Nizhinski spoke up impatiently. "What does any of this have to do with Mrs. Bradford's trial? She shot her husband. The jury's said so. It's over, Ms. Breen."

"It has everything to do with it," Norma said. "The new evidence — *who* attended private stag parties at the club, and who their guests were — suggests that *lots* of people might have had a motive to harm Will Shepherd. We have evidence that Mr. Shepherd was very *indiscreet* about the existence of these parties, as he was indiscreet about much of his life. There could even have been a nasty cover-up during the trial, shielding members, hiding a motive any of them could have for killing Will Shepherd."

"Then that evidence should have been presented at the trial. It's too late now. The verdict's been rendered." Nizhinski was as cocksure as ever.

I could see the tension in everyone. My own throat was dry. My stomach was a clenched fist. Only Norma seemed calm. Now turned prosecutor herself, she was relentless.

"It's my opinion — and I should add that it's also the opinion of the attorney general of the state of New York — that Maggie Bradford may have been the victim of an elaborate and very vicious cover-up. A cover-up known to, indeed perhaps instigated by, the Bedford chief of police."

"I *object* to this!" Dan Nizhinski shouted.

"Let her finish," Judge Sussman said. He seemed to be enjoying this almost as much as Norma was.

"Important people, leaders of industry, banking, and the media have been protected from police investigation — possibly from prosecution on criminal charges here in Bedford," Norma went on.

317

She exchanged a glance with the district attorney. "Please don't look quite so ill yet, Mr. Nizhinski. *It gets much worse.*"

She was a performer now, a star. No audience has ever listened more intently.

"You're right, Mr. Nizhinski. All this would have nothing to do with the trial of Maggie Bradford except for one important thing: *Maggie's defense counsel,* the man who knew what I'm telling you, and should have acted upon it in Mrs. Bradford's defense, couldn't possibly have done so.

"Because the defense counsel himself is a member of the secret club. *Nathan Bailford is a member!*"

110

ONE LOOK at Nathan's twisted, ashen face and I understood that Norma was right. The look alone was proof of his guilt. My attorney — my *friend* — was up on his feet. He was spluttering with outrage, but I saw the lies behind his words; I saw the humiliation in his eyes, the betrayal, the selfishness and evil of what he had done.

"Judge Sussman," Nathan said. "These are the most salacious lies, drug-induced dreams or fantasies I've ever heard. I can't believe we're here listening to this."

"No, they're *not lies*," Norma shot back at him. "I have witnesses. The groundskeeper at the Lake Club, and two of the porters. I also have a sworn statement from *a member of the club within a club*. One of your pals."

She pointed at him, and he staggered back, as though there were bullets in Norma's fingers. "May God, no, may Maggie Bradford and her poor children forgive you. I sure as hell can't. You've disgraced yourself, and your already disgraceful profession. You've nearly helped convict an innocent woman. My God, Nathan. I hope they put you in jail for a hundred years. Will you do that, Judge Sussman?"

I sat very still, tightly gripping the armrest of my chair. My cheeks were hot, and waves of light-headedness came and went.

Hold on, I kept saying to myself. *Be calm now. This is really happening. This isn't a dream. You aren't back in your prison cell. You're right here. This is real.*

Then suddenly I was in Norma's and Barry's arms. I was shaking like crazy. We were all crying. Norma must have read my mind. "It's *really* happening, Maggie," she said. "We were still talking with the attorney general late last night, or we could have let you know."

We embraced for a long time. I can't begin to describe how it was with me, but I've never experienced anything close to the relief I felt that day. I was completely out of it, euphoric, but I knew what had just happened. I knew. I knew.

"Obviously I'll have to declare a mistrial," Sussman said to Nizhinski, his voice cutting into my consciousness, "but you may want to retry. Nothing here obviates the fact that Will Shepherd was killed and the detectives say Mrs. Bradford has admitted shooting him. We'll have to give her time to hire a new lawyer and prepare her defense. She might even want to change her strategy. Can you tell me what you plan to do?"

Nizhinski was actually speechless for several seconds. "This is all — well, it's a shock," he finally managed to say. "I don't know what I'll decide. I need some time to regroup, Your Honor."

"When you do, call me," Sussman said.

Barry spoke to the judge. "I'm not a lawyer, so I don't know the right legal words, but do you think Mrs. Bradford could be allowed to go home?"

Sussman turned and looked at me. "*She is released on her own recognizance,*" he said.

111

LIKE THE YOGI BERRA SAYING — it was déja vù all over again. But it had to be done this way. This was our justice system, in all its glory.

Months had passed. The *second* trial was about to begin, and if anything, it would probably be more disheartening than the first. The State still believed that I was guilty of murder, and because they insisted on trying me again, so did a lot of people.

I continued to wear the scarlet M. I felt as though great chunks of my life were being chiseled out of me. *Probably, because they were.* And I was hurt.

I arrived at the courtroom with Jennie, Barry, and Norma. Barry and Norma were an odd couple now, but sweet and wonderful to watch. Amazingly, they weren't too grumpy around each other.

Once we were inside the courtroom, I walked on steady legs to a familiar seat at the defense table. My new lawyer was Jason Wade, from Boston. He was an expert in murder defenses, very no-nonsense, and I liked him. Most important of all, he wasn't Nathan Bailford, who was now a permanent fixture in my bad dreams.

Weird, weird, so very weird.

"Maggie looks so great!" I heard one of the spectators say. *Maggie!* As if we were old best friends.

"You do. You look fantastic," Jennie whispered against my ear. It was like old times between us, only better. Jennie was one of those rare people you could stay up with all night, just talking. *I had* — only the night before. Even Allie had stayed up with us past ten. JAM was back together again.

The trial took eleven weeks. *Our tax money at work!* The same people gave much of the same testimony, though the cross-examination had a different slant, headed in a different direction.

The courtroom became increasingly hot as the summer wore on, but I didn't mind the heat, didn't mind the repetitiousness of the questioning, didn't even mind the notoriety and the consant sleaze of the press.

I wanted to be found innocent. But more than anything, I wanted to be freed from the purgatory I had lived in for so long.

I *wasn't* guilty. I was sure of that.

I *was* innocent.

I would have given everything I had just to hear those words uttered *once.*

112

I LEANED FORWARD to hear each and every word inside the jam-packed courtroom. Suddenly, I couldn't force enough air into my lungs. I felt as though a dry cloth were blocking my throat. Claustrophobia was striking again.

The faces in the courtroom were becoming blurry and ill-defined. Blood pounded in my brain like small hammers. The back of my neck was sopping wet.

The twelve jury members were slowly filing into the right side of the room.

Again.

They had reached a verdict.

Again.

I could not get my breath as the folded piece of paper was handed to Judge Sussman. He read the verdict to himself, then passed it back to the jury foreman. The procedure was necessary, I suppose, but cruel.

"Publish the verdict," Judge Sussman instructed.

"We love you, Mom," Jennie, sitting behind me, whispered. Norma slid her arm around my shoulder. Barry stroked my hair from the row of seats behind. My family, my friends, I couldn't leave them again, but that was a distinct possibility now. That morning, *USA Today* had the odds of acquittal at *even*. People were actually betting on the outcome in Vegas and London.

My mouth seemed to be filled with cotton. I was numb all over. I was sitting in that courtroom, and yet somehow I wasn't there at all.

The foreman began to speak. His voice was high-pitched, and yet surprisingly distant, as though there were a screen between him and the rest of the courtroom. There wasn't another sound.

"We find the defendant, Maggie Bradford, *not guilty.*"

Not guilty.

Not guilty.

I had to close my eyes. I felt so tired and weak, and strangely, not completely relieved for some reason. I was only vaguely aware of cheers in the courtroom. People were congratulating me — Jason Wade and Norma, Jennie and Barry. Faces loomed before me like enormous balloons. The sound was as blurred as the images. Everything seemed incredibly odd and queer.

"Oh, Maggie, you did it! You won!"

How could this simple moment be so confusing to me? I was rushed from the tumultuous courtroom, enfolded in a safe cocoon of lawyers and friends and my precious family. Surrounding us were the press and fans. *Faces* were pushing microphones at me, screaming questions, begging for an autograph, even now.

Jason Wade would have to deal with them. My lawyer could answer their questions. Sign their autographs too.

I was actually *pushed,* like someone on wheels, through the cavernous foyer, then much too fast down the steps of the courthouse, and into a waiting car. Not a limo, just a regular car. I had insisted on that.

I jumped at what sounded like a gunshot. Pain pierced my heart. *The automobile door had slammed shut!*

Then the "regular" car started to slowly move through the press of people who had been waiting outside for a glimpse of me, win or lose. The car floated behind an escort of police cruisers, sirens crying, revolving red roof lights casting shadows on the faces of the onlookers.

I remembered the MP car in West Point. Its light was revolving too, only there were no onlookers, and it was so cold. I remembered so many scenes leading up to this moment.

I watched out the car window. People forming the tremendous crowd clogging Broadway and Clarke Street seemed to be clapping and cheering, shouting out my name. I couldn't relate to any of it.

I held Jennie and Allie tightly, never wanting to let go of them. *They held me back.* We were JAM again: Jennie, Allie, Maggie.

"I love you so much, Mom," Jennie whispered and kissed me on the cheek. "You're my heroine in shining armor."

"And you're mine," I told her.

"Mommy," Allie said, and hugged my side. "My mommy."

"Allie." I kissed the top of his head. "My Allie and my Jennie."

113

"MAGGIE! Maggie Bradford!" the crowd of idiots shouted *at her car.*

The murderer clapped and cheered too, pretending delight at the scene. He was concealed in the crowd choking the Bedford Village crossroads. Well concealed.

The murderer watched as Maggie's car passed by, then finally disappeared around a street corner.

Then the murderer disappeared as well.

BOOK SIX

HIDE AND SEEK –
AGAIN

114

FIFTH AVENUE. Eastertime. New York City. Delightful! Absolutely the place to be, no?

The world's most beautiful women were on parade. Primping, prancing, shopping their little hearts out.

And every one of them eminently fuckable, Will thought. *Every one could be mine for the wooing. Some things never change. They just get better and better.*

He strolled among them, in no particular hurry, early for his appointment. He was dressed in khaki slacks and blue blazer. His dyed-black hair was cut short and meticulously combed.

The Black Arrow, he thought and smiled thinly.

Some of the women definitely looked at him — *as well they might,* he thought. He hadn't lost much as far as appearances went. If anything, he looked even better nowadays. Dark and mysterious, right? Just the way so many women liked their fantasy lovers.

At Fifty-ninth Street, he turned east toward Park, then north to Sixty-second Street, where he disappeared into a yellowish-brown Deco building on the corner. He bought mints at the lobby's newspaper store, and checked his appearance in the mirror.

Carefully cut dyed-black beard, blue eyes (the contact lenses were a good touch; an excellent touch), perfect tie from Liberty of London, the natty blazer. Just the right look for today's important meeting.

Then Will took the elevator to the twelfth floor and found the office he was looking for: *Marshall and Marshall, Attorneys.*

He pushed open the dark oak door. Immediately, he was treated to a wall of windows and a view of the teeming avenue below. Impressive and overstated, in the American way.

The company's receptionist was Irish-American from her look, a smiling, auburn-haired, alabaster girl, blooming nicely in her mid-twenties. She was first class, expensive. Like the firm that employed her. *Nice decorative touch,* Will thought.

He casually rested the Mark Cross folio on her desk.

"Good afternoon, sir. May I help you?" she asked. She was more than pleasant, he noticed. Not offended by his folio invading her space. Or maybe, like a good Irish person, she just didn't show it.

Will smiled, low-key but seductive, his charm intact. "I'm here to see Mr. Arthur Marshall. It's about an inheritance. He's expecting me, I believe."

"Yes, sir." The girl tried not to stare at the very good-looking Englishman standing before her. "Whom should I say is calling?"

"Palmer Shepherd," said Will.

115

I LOOKED AROUND the warm, familiar living room of our house and I couldn't help beaming, almost giggling out loud. *Hooo boy!*

This was the best. This was the most important thing now. The party!

A dozen of Allie's boy and girl friends from kindergarten had come to the house for his fifth birthday. No one had declined, and that meant a lot to me, and more important, of course, to Allie.

It was a strictly old-fashioned party, which Jennie and I had meticulously planned. Games and silly hats, a birthday cake for the birthday boy, a present for every child, and lots of presents for Allie the Wonder Boy.

It was going perfectly. Barry and Norma had stopped by to help. So far, we'd had tons of laughter and fun, one minor collision, not a single tear had been shed.

Allie finally came up to me. He beckoned for me to come down to his level, his size, his turf.

I knelt so that we were face to face. As he almost always did, Allie twirled my hair around his fingers.

"Know what?" he said, and his eyes had the most wonderful twinkle. "Well, do you?"

"What? You tell me. The cake is too big for you to eat all by yourself? Okay then, share it with your friends."

Allie laughed. He got all my jokes. I got his too.

"No, I just want to tell you the *very* best thing, Mommy. The *very* best thing is that you're here."

It was the happiest party, the best moment, and suddenly I was crying, and I was feeling so good that I could be there at my son's party.

"I knew somebody was going to cry soon," I told Allie.

He hugged me, and gave me kisses to make it better. But I was already better.

116

HAVING WATCHED my good mood at the birthday party, Barry the Manipulator took the occasion to try and lure me into the city, and up to his studio. I surprised him: I told him I'd come. I was ready for a little manipulation.

When I got to New York, Barry was hyper and excited, the way he usually got when he'd just written a good song, or completed an especially good business deal.

"You're scaring me. You're *too* happy," I told him, but I was laughing. Everything seemed good to me now. I was so buoyant, and free. God, was I free!

"I have a scheme," he said to me as we sat down beside his piano. "I've been scheming on your behalf."

My good mood was a match for his. And more. "Thanks, but no thanks."

Barry completely ignored me. "There's a *great* concert happening up in Rhinebeck, New York, in July."

"Barry, I read the papers. I'm not a hermit. Bedford is less than thirty miles from Manhattan. The answer is, regretfully, no. But thank you just the same."

"It's two days of fun in the sun. I know the promoters and

they're first-class people. They've booked seventeen acts. *Eighteen* is their magic number."

"I'd love to, but I can't. Do you happen to remember what happened to me out in San Francisco?"

Barry went right on talking. "Tell you who they've got already. Bonnie Raitt, k.d. lang, Liz Phair, Emmylou Harris."

I nodded. Started to laugh. Bit my lip. "Gee, all women. Why did you happen to start with the women?"

"You know, I never even thought of that. You're right though, I did."

"I don't think I can, Barry. I appreciate the offer, if that's what this is."

Barry wasn't in the mood to show any mercy. That was good though. It meant I didn't look as though I needed any.

"Use it, or lose it," he said. "Unless, of course, you've already lost it."

"No, I sang in the shower today. I was pretty great. I've still got it. Better than ever, actually. Passion, edge, maturity, effervescence."

Barry played the lead-in to "Loss of Grace" on his piano. I had to admit, a shiver went up my spine.

"I'll *think* about it," I told him. "But I honestly don't believe that I c-cc-can ss-ss-sing in public."

I winked at him. It was good that I could laugh about the stutter, about San Francisco.

Barry nodded, and then he smiled. "I'll take that as a yes."

He continued to play "Loss of Grace," and, as he did, I started to sing again.

And I had to admit, like everything else in this second life of mine, it felt so good, so right.

I didn't stutter, or stammer. I sang. And if I do say so myself, sang kind of beautifully. With passion, and with a real edge.

"Your timing is off, your phrasing is a mess," Barry shook his head and said. "Welcome home, Maggie."

117

MAGGIE STILL LOVED to walk the streets of New York with the other commoners. She was such a woman of the people, wasn't she? Maybe that was why so many of them identified with her, loved her songs, loved her.

She wore a kerchief and dark glasses, but every so often someone recognized her anyway. She was always so goddamned gracious. Sign an autograph. Move on with that shy little smile of hers. *Ingratiating bitch.*

Will walked several blocks behind her. No one bothered him for autographs anymore. He didn't exist, did he? The Invisible Man. Deceased and buried, right?

He followed her out of New York and up the Saw Mill early that evening. This was all very familiar to him, the road to Bedford. And ruin.

What wasn't so familiar was the bizarre path his life had taken. How do you top off a life that's been incredibly full, and is suddenly falling apart badly? Where does one go from the top?

How clever he had been up until this point, Will thought. That fatal night, he'd shot Palmer and hadn't felt a thing, no remorse about Palmer. That was the only way to stop the extortion money his greedy brother had been grubbing since Rio.

He had dressed his brother in his clothes. Then he placed the body on the grounds of the estate. He had gone inside and caused a ruckus. He'd lured Maggie outside, jumped her, beat her up, and fired the shot that practically blew Palmer's face apart. Then he'd disappeared. And just *watched* the rest.

Unfortunately, his new life had turned out to be another kind of hell. Sometimes he believed that he might be a devil, and he was living in hell.

Rio was the turning point, he knew. Killing that first girl. Crime and punishment had followed him after that night.

Up the road, he saw Maggie turn into her driveway. He hated that she could be happy without him. Strange as it seemed, he had tried to love her. He'd wanted her to save him from himself.

He knew the turning point with Maggie too. He was sure about that. It was the first time he'd failed with her in bed. It was while he was *Mr. Maggie Bradford*. He had thought about killing her nearly every day since then.

She'd failed him, and now she and her little family had to pay the awful price. *Crime and punishment.*

Will went for dinner at a little bar and grill in town. An old fave for the locals.

He thought it was quite something that he could sit there eating a greasy burger and fries, and that no one recognized him anymore.

Well, why the hell should they? He was ancient history, if he'd ever been history at all.

The Black Arrow. That's what he was now.

He wore a navy blue ballcap without an insignia, a gray sweatshirt, and khakis. He fit in okay with the bar crowd watching the Knicks lose badly to Indiana.

Nothing special about him, really. Other than that he was

stark raving mad, of course. Probably not the only madman sitting at the crowded horseshoe bar either. Not the only guy here who was a little homicidal toward his wife.

"The Knicks suck," the young brick seated next to him passed along the sum total of his acquired wisdom.

"Burgers here suck too," Will said, and the other man laughed.

Soul brothers, are we? Will wanted to continue the conversation in earnest. *Think so? Want to come with me to my ex-wife's house? I'm going to kill the bitch and her two kids. You in? You with me on this?*

"Patrick Ewing *really* sucks," the other man contributed another choice nugget.

Will nodded sympathetically, and figured it was time to get out of the bar. Truth be known, he didn't know the Knicks from the Yankees from the New York Jets.

It was dark outside. He could see that through the bar's front window.

"Well, time to head on home to the missus," he told his new mate, then stood up at the bar.

Sure you don't want to tag along, pal? This is going to be a big night in Bedford. I can promise you that.

118

IT WASN'T MUCH of a problem for him to get onto the estate grounds undetected. Will parked in one of the Lake Club lots, then crossed over through pine woods and a narrow meadow.

No sweat so far. Just the way he'd figured it.

Walking in the field of high grass made him remember something. He'd ridden on horseback there with Allie, when he was only a baby. He'd done it to impress Maggie. He *knew* it would touch her down below her belt. He knew a woman's soft spots, knew the buttons to hit. He had carefully pushed all of Maggie's, every single one, one by one.

He had been inside the house on a trial run the week before, so he'd already figured how this would go. The cellar door under the original wing was open, as it always was.

He didn't use his flashlight until he was safely inside. The cellar was a creepy place. The house had been built on bare ground, and the original boulders were still down there. There was a wooden stairway up from where the freezer was to the kitchen.

Will used the stairs and was in the house by a little past

11:40. It was a school night and everyone had gone to bed. *JAM! Jennie, Allie, and Maggie . . . Notice, no Will.*

Maggie was still a country girl at heart — early to bed, early to rise. The quiet house reminded him of a damn morgue, which seemed appropriate enough.

In a way, Maggie had given him the idea for tonight. Probably for good reasons, she noticed every news story about a husband who ran amok and killed one or more family members.

That was pretty much what Will planned to do tonight. Kill all of them, right there in the house. Then disappear for good. The murders would never be solved, and that struck him as just the right touch.

He had a Smith and Wesson, sixteen shots, plus a nasty hunting knife. That was more than enough firepower. If need be, he could do the job with his bare hands. There was merit to that approach too, the personal touch.

"Families really suck," Will mumbled as he walked up the thickly carpeted stairs to the second floor.

There wasn't a sound to be heard up there. *Maybe this is a trap,* he thought, *but he knew it couldn't be.*

This train was leaving the station. There was no way to stop it now. No way on heaven or earth to stop this from happening.

He was breathing real quietly, every breath even, and exactly the same.

He was feeling confident, real good about this. No guilt. No feelings at all.

It was the right thing to do.

Ever so slowly, he opened the bedroom door.

He could see everything in soft, yellow moonlight streaming from the window.

No surprises here. No surprises anywhere tonight.

"Hello, little buddy," Will said to Allie.

119

WHAT THE HELL *was that? What was that?*

We had all gone to bed early, and I'd fallen asleep almost immediately.

I had been dreaming about singing at a huge outdoor concert — and then completely losing it onstage. No need to call Dr. Freud in to explain that one.

I awoke and I thought I heard a noise upstairs.

Was Jennie just going to bed?

I sat up, looked at the luminous figures on the radio clock: 11:45. I didn't think Jennie would be up so late.

Then I heard another sound. Strange. *Well, one of the kids was definitely up.*

Then a louder noise, as though a bed were being moved around.

And finally, what sounded to me like a muffled scream or yell. Was I hearing things?

I got up quickly and hurried across the bedroom to the door.

I listened there for half a second.

Nothing more.

Then another muffled sound, this one farther away it seemed. I couldn't tell exactly where. Allie? Was Allie up for some reason?

I hurried outside into the upstairs hallway. The light was out, and I switched it back on.

No one was there. Not Jennie. Not Allie.

False alarm? Probably so. Things in the country always seemed to go bump in the night. Creaky floorboards, loose shutters, branches against a window.

I decided to check on the kids anyway. Maybe somebody was sick, or maybe one of them was having a nightmare. Goodness knows, they'd been through enough.

I gently opened Jennie's bedroom door, the first one, next to mine.

Jennie was gone!

I ran as fast as I could down the hallway to the front left bedroom, which had a choice view of our horse pastures.

I yanked open the bedroom door.

Allie was gone too!

120

THERE'S AN EXPLANATION for this. Has to be.

But I was frightened as could be.

I ran down the stairway loudly calling out their names, "Jennie! Allie! Where are you two? Where are you?"

There's a simple explanation.

No one was in the front hall, or the living room either.

But I could see a light coming from the den. Okay, the kids were in the den.

"Jennie? . . . Allie? . . . Is something the matter?"

I ran toward the den, clipping a pile of books on the edge of an old hallway table. The books fell loudly to the floor.

I turned the corner into the den, and I stopped. Everything stopped. All time, all forward progress, all sense of fairness and goodness in the universe.

Stopped.

Will was standing there with the kids.

I stared at the black hair and beard, but I knew it was definitely Will.

He had a gun, and he had Jennie and Allie, and the gun was loosely pointed at them.

"Hello, Maggie. Long time, huh?" Cool as could be. Psychopathic as they come. "Good to see ya."

"Are you two all right?" I asked the kids.

"We're okay, Mom," Jennie said. "We're okay. We're fine."

"They're okay," Will said. "What's the big problem? Haven't you heard of visitation rights?"

I walked further into the room. My heart wouldn't stop pounding.

Will was there. Will was alive.

"I hate you!" I said. I couldn't stop myself from saying it.

"Hate you too, darlin'. Hate you *more*. That's why I'm here," Will said and smiled. "Been hating you and hating you, for a long, long time."

I stopped myself and stared at him. I tried to be calm. "Why did you dare come here, Will? After all that's happened."

"Oh, lots of neat reasons. First of all, just to see the confusion in your eyes, the fear. I love that look. Makes me feel good all over."

"That's because you're a coward." I told him what I really thought.

"No doubt. I think you're right. *That's* exactly why I'm here. I'm afraid to go on living the way I am. That's it."

"You wouldn't hurt them. Why would you hurt them?" I asked him.

Will shrugged. "Because they're yours. Because you fucked me up even worse than I was. I could *function* before you. Now, Maggie — *shut up*. I mean it — *shut the hell up*." He pointed the gun at Allie. My little boy was trying not to cry but he was starting to shake. There was nothing I could do.

No one spoke, and Will smiled at the silence. He nodded his approval. Controlling son of a bitch.

"Okay now, here's what we're going to do," he finally said. "You all lie on the floor. Facedown. Keep very still. Everybody on the floor. Let's play a game, Allie."

"*Says who?*" Jennie suddenly turned and shouted at him.

"What, so you can kill us all a lot easier? That's what you're here for, isn't it? You punk! You piece of crap."

"Jennie," I tried to quiet her. Then I realized what she was doing, at least I thought I did, hoped I did, *prayed I did.*

"We're not doing anything you say!" I yelled at Will, just as Jennie had. "We all hate your guts!"

"We hate you!" Jennie screamed at him.

"We hate you!" yelled Allie in his tiny voice.

Jennie suddenly flew into Will's side, and I reached for the gun. I pulled on his wrist as hard as I could. *Both hands! The strength of a madwoman!*

At the same time, I brought up my knee — as hard as I could — into Will's groin.

Will *woofed* out air. He groaned. The gun actually came free, and I had it.

I had the gun in my hand. Now what? *Now what?*

I backed away from Will as quickly as I could. A lot of fast steps in a hurry.

So did Jennie and Allie.

"C'mon, c'mon. Get out of here now. Jennie, call the police. Call nine-one-one. Hurry. Please. Go!" I told the two of them.

Will looked at me and seemed confused, as if this wasn't in his playbook. Then he smiled again, the smile I remembered so well, the one that had always been so effective for him. Killer smile, right.

"Isn't this something," he said with a heavy sigh. "Not exactly the way I planned it. *But.* A good scorer, *a striker,* has to improvise. I know you never wanted to follow soccer, Maggie, but for a great striker, there's no team, there's no win or lose, there's nothing but the goal."

"Will," I said to him, "now *you shut up.*"

"Do you know what my goal was tonight, Maggie? Do you really get it?"

"Yes, I do. To kill us. *Jennie,* please go. Allie, go! I mean it. *Now!* Call the police, Jennie."

"Mom," Jennie said, and she was talking *very softly*, very slowly, "you come with us. Back out of the door with the gun. Come with us."

"Do you know the rest of my goal, Maggie?" Will continued to speak to me. "I think I have this figured out."

I thought I did too. I thought I understood him real well.

"To kill us, and then to kill yourself," I said.

Will slowly clapped his hands together. Applause from the great man.

"Mom, please come with us," Jennie begged. "Please."

Then Will started to walk right toward me.

"*Can you do it, Maggie?*" he said. His eyes were pinned onto mine now.

"I can do what I have to do," I said.

"Mom, please."

"Can you really do it, Maggie? Can you *start* this nightmare all over again? Or would you rather die? Can you pull the trigger?"

Will kept walking.

The *striker*.

Advancing on goal, just as he'd said. No team concept. Just Will — the loner. The ultimate loser.

There was no good answer to his question. There was no easy way out of this.

But maybe there was a way. *Maybe there was.*

Will kept walking toward me. He held eye contact. Then he smiled again.

I fired!

"Mom! Mom!"

He grabbed his leg, and *nearly* went over, *nearly* went down.

"Oooohh!" he moaned. "Jesus Christ, Maggie. You're quite the tiger, quite the defender."

Will started to move forward again. It was as though he hadn't even been hit.

The striker.

The attacker.

The best in the world at this.

Unstoppable once he started toward his goal.

To murder me and the kids, right here in our house.

Will took a knife from his shirt. Big knife, hunting knife. He raised it toward me. He *lunged*.

I fired a second time.

NIGHT SONGS

121

SOUTHERN CONNECTICUT in early November. Four and a half months after the shooting. Will and I were finally off the front pages of most newspapers and magazines.

There was just one more story to tell.

It was a bright and crisp fall afternoon — high school football weather. Only to me, peering out the tinted Plexiglas windows of my car, it seemed a gloomy day, a day meant for unfinished business.

Norma had come along with me, but I drove. I needed to be in control. I thought that I was. We'd see about that soon enough.

I was trying to be brave, to survive this final test.

I hadn't done anything wrong — *not ever.* I'd just protected what was important, my family. Sure, I had made mistakes, but who doesn't. With Will, I'd been a victim for his obsessions. He had lied so brilliantly, right from the start of our relationship.

Norma and I talked everything through again during the drive from Bedford. Finally, I pulled up at the Institute for Living, a Federal-style building in the outskirts of New Haven that looked like a cross between a college administration building and a prison. It was neither, nothing so benign. It was a mental hospital, supposedly one of the best.

Norma and I hurried across a poplar- and maple-lined parking area, then into the vestibule, where we approached a receptionist dressed in nurse's white.

"We're here to see Mr. Shepherd," I told her, and if she recognized me she didn't show it. I appreciated that.

"I'll have someone take you to his room," is all she said. An aide eventually materialized to escort us.

Outside Will's room, I stopped. "Can you wait here?" I said to Norma. "I think I want to see him alone."

"You're sure, Maggie? You don't have to punish yourself, honey."

"I'm sure. I'm not afraid of him anymore." *Not too much anyway.*

"Good for you then. I'll be the short, dumpy broad waiting outside. Maybe some guy in here is nuts enough to fall for me."

The aide unlocked the door and I entered. *I entered.* It was a plain enough room: clean, a made bed, desk, desk chair, easy chair, and standing lamp its only furniture. There was a bookcase built into the far wall holding a few new paperbacks, obviously unread, and a small sink for washing. It reminded me of prison, only it was nicer.

Will was standing by the window. There was no sign that he *ever* sat down. He was looking at me, looking *through* me, I guess I should say.

I'm not afraid anymore. I can do this. Whatever is necessary, I told myself.

If it was possible, Will was even more handsome than when I had first met him in London. His hair was its natural blond, long and full. It caught the afternoon sun through the heavily screened window.

"Hello, Will."

Nothing.

His face was clean shaven and pale pink; his body seemed to

have the same lithe grace, even standing still, that it always had.

"It's Maggie, Will."

He looks like a grown-up little boy, I thought, remembering Will at the very first Lake Club party, at our wedding, confessing his sorrow and pain, *and all his lies.*

I had loved him — because he could make himself seem so lovable. He was a very good actor after all. He had fooled so many people — half the world. He had worked hard to fool me.

He made a strange sound, a high-pitched wail that reverberated in the hospital room. The second shot I'd fired at the estate had struck his head, caromed off bone, but done severe damage anyway.

"Mmahhlah . . . mmahhlah," he said to me. He seemed *insistent*; but I didn't understand.

What was he trying to say?

Was it Maggie? Mother? Was it Mama? What was it?

I sat in a hard wooden chair directly across from him. I forced myself to look at his face.

I'm sorry I did this to you, Will. But I'm not guilty about it. I sleep at night — I sleep just fine. You did this to yourself.

I thought of the murder he'd committed in Bedford Hills; of his terrifying betrayal of me; of what he had done to Jennie and Allie, and what he'd planned to do to us all.

But I couldn't hate him. Not now. Not the way he was.

"Will, can you hear me? Do you understand what I'm saying?"

The dead stare didn't change. He couldn't understand, could he? He had gone to his own world forever.

It's so sad, I thought, as I watched him that afternoon at the hospital. *You're still young. You look so young, so full of promise. But you won't hurt me ever again. You won't hurt my children. I'm not scared of you, Will.*

A little past five o'clock, the aide returned. He was jangling his keys so I'd hear him come up on us. "Visiting hours are over."

"Thank you. I'll just be another minute. Please?"

I stood and walked to the window where Will was still standing. A cloak of solemn gray had already replaced the sunlight outside.

I turned to Will. "I feel so sorry for you," I said, "but I can't forgive you either."

I wanted him to say something. A final few words to remember him by. To explain why he had wanted to kill me. Why he had hurt us. Who was Will Shepherd, really? Did anyone know?

"Okay. Good-bye, Will. I'm sorry for you."

I gathered myself together, and started to leave the room. *I turned my back on Will. I wasn't afraid of him anymore.*

122

SUDDENLY, Will screamed with a tremendous force that echoed through the hospital. I whirled around toward him.

He shrieked again, his body rocking violently.

Aides came running down the hallway. A burly male nurse appeared with a plastic-sheathed needle clasped in his fist. I sensed that this had happened before.

"*Mmahhlah!*" Will screamed.

I thought that he might be having a stroke. Certainly this was some kind of fit.

"Mmahhlah. Mmahhlah," he continued to shout. His face and neck were bright red. His veins stood out against his skin.

I stared at Will in horror. *Maggie? Mother? What in God's name was he trying to tell me?*

In his eyes, there wasn't the slightest comprehension or recognition. He was pushed down firmly onto the bed, and I *felt* his legs shrivel.

The Blond Arrow, shriveling.

I had to get out of there. I nearly ran from the room. There was nothing I could do for him anymore. Norma was waiting for me at the end of the corridor.

"Maggie! My God! What was that? What the hell happened in there? You okay?"

I put my arms around her and held Norma tightly, as though to blot out those screams. Finally, the two of us walked out of the building and onto the black-topped parking area, the trees now ghostly silhouettes.

Halfway across the parking lot I turned. I felt as though someone had just stepped out of a grave.

I had the powerful intuition that something was chasing after me. *Mmahhlah* . . . *Mmahhlah* was coming fast, right behind me.

Those lifeless, haunting eyes . . .

But there was no one looking out from Will's hospital window. There was no one when I looked back.

123

IN HIS BARREN, insular hospital room Will screamed and screamed. Screamed and screamed. Until his throat was raw and felt as though it had splinters in it. *Still, he continued to scream.*

As the night-shift aides tried to feed him his dinner, changed him, and put him to bed, he continued to scream. His strength, his stamina, were amazing to all of them. He was still young, and very athletic, and so powerfully strong.

"Mmahhlah! Mmahhlah! Mmahhlah!" He cried over and over.

"Mmahhlah! Mmahhlah! Mmahhlah!

"MMAHHLAH!"

He had *seen* Maggie today. He'd been *aware* of everything. He'd wanted to speak to her, but he couldn't. He couldn't. *Mmahhlah* was all he could get out.

Why didn't she understand him? Why didn't anyone?

"Mmahhlah."

I'm alive!

I'm alive!

Please don't leave me like this!

I'm trapped inside this body. Can't you see that? Won't you help me?

"*Mmahhlah!*

"*Mmahhlah!*"

I'm alive!

I was halfway home to Bedford when it hit me, and I understood what Will had been trying to say to me at the hospital.

It took my breath away.

But I never went to see him again.

I never will.

The Midnight Club

James Patterson

Time after time, in an acclaimed series of runaway international No 1 bestsellers, James Patterson has delivered breathtaking rollercoaster thrills and incomparable page-turning readability. Now comes a mesmerising tale of non-stop action and suspense.

Nobody knows the underbelly of the city like New York cop John Stefanovitch. He's out to get Alexandre St-Germain, the most powerful member of the Midnight Club – a secret international society of ruthless crime czars, all of whom are 'respectable' businessmen. And Stef's the ideal man for the job – until he's levelled by a blast from St-Germain's shotgun and left for dead.

Now, Stef is back, wheelchair-bound, yet sworn to destroy St-Germain. With the help of a beautiful journalist and a Harlem cop, Stef is determined to crack the Midnight Club. And he's up against odds that are as unknown as they are deadly . . .

'It just might be his best ever.' *USA Today*

'Guaranteed: you'll devour this yarn-burner in one sitting.'
New York Daily News

'A fast-moving narrative that never lets up. The villain is one of the most awful monsters I've encountered in recent fiction.' CAMPBELL ARMSTRONG

'Sleek, fast, skilful and larger than life.' *Los Angeles Times*

ISBN 0 00 649313 0

Along Came a Spider

James Patterson

The phenomenal international No 1 bestseller.

He had always wanted to be famous. When he kidnapped two well-known rich kids, it was headline news. Then one of them was found – dead – and the whole nation was in uproar.

For such a high-profile case, they needed the top people – Alex Cross, a black detective with a PhD in psychology, and Jezzie Flanagan, an ambitious young Secret Service agent – yet even they were no match for the killer. He had the unnerving ability to switch from blood-crazed madness to clear-eyed sanity in an instant. But was he the helpless victim of a multiple-personality disorder – or a brilliant, cold-blooded manipulator?

As the whole country watched his pursuers falling into his every trap, he knew he had made it – he was controlling the deadly game, and he still hadn't made his most devastating move . . .

'Brilliantly terrifying . . . so exciting that I had to stay up all night to finish it . . . packed with white-knuckle twists.'
Daily Mail

'An incredibly suspenseful read with a one-of-a-kind villain who is as terrifying as he is intriguing. One of the best thrillers of the year.' CLIVE CUSSLER

'A first-rate thriller – fasten your seatbelts and keep the lights on!' SIDNEY SHELDON

'Terror and suspense that grab the reader and won't let go. Just try running away from this one.' ED McBAIN

ISBN 0 00 647615 5

Kiss the Girls

James Patterson

HIS NEW NO 1 BESTSELLER

Along Came a Spider was one of the most talked-about thrillers for years – a phenomenal international No 1 bestseller. Now its memorable hero detective Alex Cross is back – thrust into a case he will never forget.

This time there isn't just one killer, there are two. One collects beautiful, intelligent women on college campuses on the east coast of the USA. The other is terrorising Los Angeles with a series of unspeakable murders. But the truly chilling news is that the two brilliant and elusive killers are communicating, cooperating, *competing*.

'As good as a thriller can get. With *Kiss the Girls*, Patterson joins the elite company of Thomas Harris.'

San Francisco Examiner

'This novel is hard to set aside. Pattterson's complex tale chills, enthrals and entertains the reader in a dazzling and unforgettable reading experience.'   · *Toronto Star*

'James Patterson's *Kiss the Girls* is a ripsnorting, terrific read.'   *USA Today*

'Patterson hit the ball out of the park with his last go-round, the bestselling *Along Came a Spider, Kiss the Girls* is even better.'   *Dallas Morning News*

ISBN 0 00 649315 7

Jack and Jill

James Patterson

THE SPELLBINDING NEW
ALEX CROSS THRILLER

James Patterson burst onto the thriller scene with his No 1 bestseller *Along Came a Spider*, which first introduced Washington homicide detective Alex Cross. His memorable hero returned in spectacular fashion in another No 1 bestseller, *Kiss the Girls*, which is now a major film, starring Morgan Freeman.

Now – in James Patterson's most explosive and powerful novel yet – Alex Cross is back on home territory, tangling with a pair of killers who are picking off the rich and famous one by one with chilling professional efficiency.

As the whole country awaits the identity of the next celebrity victim, only Alex Cross, with his ability to get into the minds of deranged killers, has the skills and the courage to crack the case – but will he discover the truth before 'Jack and Jill' set their sights on Washington's ultimate celebrity target?

A relentless rollercoaster of heart-pounding suspense and jolting plot twists, *Jack and Jill* proves once again that no one can write a more compelling thriller than James Patterson – the master of the non-stop nightmare.

NOW AVAILABLE IN HARDBACK

ISBN 0 00 225231 7

Black Market

James Patterson

From the author who would go on to create the superbly chilling international bestsellers *Along Came a Spider, Kiss the Girls, Jack and Jill, Hide and Seek, The Midnight Club* and *Cat and Mouse* comes an early work of astonishing pace and tension – a breathtaking novel of high finance, international terrorism and irresistible page-turning suspense.

The threat was absolute. At 5.05 p.m. Wall Street would be destroyed. No demands, no ransom, no negotiations. A multiple firebombing – orchestrated by a secret militia group – would wipe out the financial heart of America. Stop the world's financial system dead.

Faced with catastrophe on an unimaginable scale, Federal agent Archer Carroll and Wall Street lawyer Caitlin Dillon are pitched into a heart-stopping race against time, tracking the unknown enemy through a maze of intrigue, rumour and betrayal towards a truly shocking climax.

'The action is fast and furious.'   *Wall Street Journal*

'A tough, twisting tale.'   *New York Daily News*

'Among the best writers of crime stories ever.' *USA Today*

ISBN 0 00 649314 9